WILHELM HAUFF'S NOVELLAS

WILHELM HAUFF

SANAGE
PUBLISHING HOUSE

Paperback: 978-936205109-7
eBook: 978-936205154-7

Printed by: Manipal Technologies Limited, Manipal

Sanage Publishing House LLP
Mumbai, India

sanagepublishing@gmail.com

Wilhelm Hauff (29 November 1802 – 18 November 1827) was a German poet and novelist.

Hauff's life.

(After *G. Schwab* .)

Wilhelm Hauff was born in Stuttgart, where his father lived as a government secretary, on November 29, 1802. He was only six years old when his father, who as a "supporter of the good old law" (1799) spent eight months innocently in prison at Hohenasperg, was transferred to the Higher Appeals Tribunal in Tübingen, was called back to Stuttgart as a ministerial secretary in 1808 and died there the following year. Hauff has portrayed his grandfather, who was a regional consultant, excellently in the old, honorable, law-abiding Lanbek in "Jud Süß." The widow Hauff, daughter of the Higher Tribunal Councilor *Elsäßer* in Tübingen, returned to her hometown with her children after the death of her husband. This excellent woman had a beneficial influence on the boy's soft, receptive mind through her moral, ennobling upbringing; His talent for storytelling developed early in the home circle under his mother, who was herself an excellent storyteller and his sister.

He attended the Schola Anatolica–named after the Mons Anatolicus, a foothill of the Oesterberg near Tübingen–with his older brother Hermann, who had a great talent for languages and a better memory than him.

A keen attention to everything and a good grasp of things led him to the independent development of his mind; his penchant for the creations of the imagination was already noticeable at the age of ten and eleven, and he was enthusiastic about light histories and novels; later, in his first volume of the "Memoirs of Satan," he portrayed this inclination with great humor and gave us a comical picture of his own poetic activities at school. Not particularly inclined to the noisy games of the boys outside, the brothers' favorite place was the old grandfather's large library, where the boys acted out in a variety of games what they had seen in the pictures in the folios; the Middle Ages and the period of transition to modern history in particular made a vivid impression on them; even modern history did not go unnoticed, and here it was the grandfather's conversations with his friends that the boys listened to unnoticed behind the stove; impressions from the Napoleonic era are often found in his novellas.

In this way the youthful mind created from the manifold images a picture of nature and man, the outlines of which became ever more definite and firmer; he soon became accustomed to handling these images with confidence in conversation and thereby laid the foundation for the gift of representation which later became his chief achievement.

His surprising talent for declamation led to him being chosen as a future preacher, and in 1817 he was admitted to the monastery school in Blaubeuren with fairly mediocre knowledge. A delicate constitution and periodic illness contributed greatly to his neglect of classical studies, and it was only in the splendid, healthy Alb valley near Blaubeuren that his health began to improve.

With a greater appreciation for literature and art than for theology and philology, he entered the University of Tübingen in 1820. Even though he showed little talent for the knightly skills of fraternal life, he nevertheless took a lively interest in everything that excited young minds at that time and he distinguished himself among the poets and speakers of the fraternities that were flourishing at that time, at least in Tübingen and other smaller universities. The mood of the time, the melancholy longing for freedom, the memory of the numerous victories and sacrifices, is expressed in many of his poems; some of his songs were also performed at the Wartburg Festival.

He delighted his inner circle of friends with his happy ideas, his talkativeness and cheerfulness, his extravagance. But even in a state of boyish and sociable exaltation, he never lacked prudence. Although youthfully vain, irritable and sensitive, he still listened to his He did not, like so many humorists, take his humor from himself, but was the first who had no qualms about mocking his own little weaknesses and persistently portraying them as a caricature of himself. At times he threw his ideas onto paper with rare ease and agility, not shying away from either his own or other people's weaknesses.

In 1824 he took his doctorate and looked for a suitable position as a candidate in theology. Through the mediation of an older friend, he found a position as a tutor in the house of the President of the War

Council, General Baron *von Hügel* , in Stuttgart, and held this position until the spring of 1826. In this amiable, well-educated family he became acquainted with the forms of higher social life; the cheerful, natural tone of the house enabled him to grasp many beautiful, fresh images from life, and such vivid impressions blossomed again as some charming description in his poetry immediately after he had received them. His position gave him time for study and work; he also passed the second theological examination in 1825.

The first small work he published in 1825 was the "*Fairy Tale Almanac* for the Year 1826 for Sons and Daughters of Educated Classes." Initially written for his pupils, this small collection demonstrates Hauff's true talent as a poet. These fairy tales, whose original material does not belong to him, but which are treated with free imagination and beautifully rounded off, are among the best of his works. A further series of splendid fairy tales followed in the almanac for 1827. The best of these, which not only captivate young minds but can also be read with ever-new joy by the mature man, do not belong purely to the realm of fairy tales-no! These legendary stories from the Spessart touch the heart and a lively, everlasting youthful freshness emerges from these works.

Immediately following this first fairy tale almanac is the first part of the "*Reports from the Memoirs of Satan*," which are rich in bright imagination and successful representation, and in which cheeky humor and apt satire prevail. The baroque student world, from which the young man had just come, gave him many opportunities to practice his talent; these Satan memoirs caused a stir and gave the author a wide reputation, but also caused much anger and sensitivity in his time through their satirical outbursts, and he was particularly resented for his attack on Goethe and his Faust. Some of these sketches, in which he drew characters from his circle of acquaintances, are full of compelling humor and rich satire, in which Hauff was a master. Hauff seems to have woven in the novella "The Curse" because he perhaps lost the desire to continue these communications.

Since Hauff noticed how easy it was for him to portray things and that his powers of observation also enabled him to deal with modern subjects, he decided to move from the ideal world of fairy tales and fantasy to the more realistic world of conversation. In the winter of 1825-1826, he wrote "*Man in the Moon*", a short novel set in modern life. According to hints from G. Schwab and the memories of *Wolfgang Menzel*, Hauff's initial intention seems to have been to interest the general public. Wolfgang Menzel, who had read the manuscript, reproached him for having written a fabrication à la Clauren (Councillor Heun in Berlin) and for not flying any higher than that of the Berlin Counsellor. He advised him to use even more colour and then to publish the book under Clauren's name. Hauff followed the advice. However, it is still questionable whether Menzel's portrayal is correct; it has recently been disputed by many. In any case, Hauff thus created a delicious satire on Clauren, combating a perverse and reprehensible manner more through exaggeration than through mockery and derision.

Wilhelm Hauff later felt, however, what he owed to those who demanded a more serious account of the writer; he attacked his opponent in a more thorough and decisive manner in his "controversial *sermon*," which was distinguished not less by his attitude and expression than by his biting wit and genuine humor. His controversial sermon is a devastating criticism of Clauren's style, borne of moral indignation.

The fame that Hauff found among the general public through his » *Man in the Moon* « and the desire to compete with modern writers led him more and more to the Representations of the modern world and the actual conversational tone in the *novella*. This gave rise to a series of stories that appeared in fiction magazines and paperbacks-he only wrote "*Jud Süß" later and the second part of the Satanic Memoirs*.

The success that Walter Scott had with his historical novels in Germany, too, prompted him to write a German historical novel, and he began his "*Lichtenstein*," which he finished in a very short time. This romantic legend was met with great acclaim throughout Germany. The charming material is not a legend, but a pure invention of the author, which climbs up like ivy to the old rocky castle of Lichtenstein. Despite some defects in the structure and characterization, there are great beauties in the details, and Hauff would certainly have achieved something perfect with a second novel of this kind. In his characterization of Duke Ulerich of Württemberg, Hauff deviated significantly from the historical truth and portrayed him far too ideally, and also allowed himself great historical license on the whole, but this novel is so noble and lofty in spirit, it is so borne by the author's loving immersion in the past of his homeland, so many shocking, poetic and also comic scenes adorn the work, that "Lichtenstein" will always remain a pearl of our treasury of legends and one of our people's favorite books.

After completing his Lichtenstein, Hauff left his previous circumstances. The income from his literary work enabled him to travel, first via Frankfurt and Mainz to Paris and then through Belgium and northern Germany. His kindness won him personal friends from all classes of society on these journeys, especially in Dresden, Berlin and the Hanseatic cities.

The young man from Württemberg's stay in the Prussian capital was made as pleasant as possible by the criminal director *Hitzig* in Berlin, whom he had met in Hamburg, especially by bringing him into contact with literary circles, especially with the famous Wednesday Society and distinguished men. In the late autumn of 1826 he returned to Stuttgart, strengthened by impressions and enriched by experiences. For poetry, Hauff's travels only contributed to *a* fully mature Fruit, the magnificent "*Fantasies in the Bremer Ratskeller*," which he presented to wine lovers in the autumn of 1827. This happy mixture of high-spirited humor and poetic seriousness, this lively characterization of the delightful characters, ensure the lasting value of the fantasies through their genuine, fiery poetry. Shortly before, he had written the story "*The Image of the Emperor*," which contains both historical and poetic truth; in it he created a monument to the above-mentioned Baron von *Hügel* , who was Napoleon's adjutant at the time.

Returning home, on January 1, 1827, Hauff took over the editorship of the "Morgenblatt für gebildete Stände" (Morgen Paper for the Educated Classes), published by Cotta Verlag, which he gave new impetus to; he published several essays and sketches in it. In February of the same year, he married a cousin of the same name, with whom he had long been linked by a tender affection. His friends tell cheerful stories of the young man's efforts to take this love, which should have taken the most straightforward course given the circumstances, into the realm of the fantastic and even of intrigue, so much did he need romantic involvement in his daily life. This union seemed to be the lasting foundation of his happiness in life and gave him a new desire to work. He entertained the idea of writing a historical novel based on the battles in Tyrol in 1809, and for this purpose he made a trip to Tyrol in July.

Unfortunately, in his new, young happiness, an early death approached.

The joy of the birth of a daughter was already dampened by the indisposition caused by the strenuous work he had done at the sickbed and deathbed of a dear friend who had died in a fall. At the funeral of another dear friend, he caught a severe cold, and a treacherous nervous fever overcame the reluctant man, who tried by force to return to the work he was used to and which he loved so much.

A few hours, his brother tells us, before the fever swept his mind into a wild frenzy, joy filled his features for the last time at the news of the naval battle of Navarin; the event that inspired so many poets to political and poetic works and brought joy to the entire educated world. He could no longer sing about the horror that had stirred the world, he could only rejoice over it; he carried his joy over into the madness of fever, and it was touching to hear how, believing himself to be the messenger of battle to the afterlife, he cried out more than once: "Let me go, I must go, I must tell Müller!" for barely two months previously he had personally met *Wilhelm Müller*, the singer of the Greek songs, in Stuttgart and had been mourning his sudden death for a few weeks.

Wilhelm Hauff passed away peacefully on November 18, 1827, after saying goodbye to his family and commending *his immortal spirit* to God. There was widespread sympathy for his early death, and it was expressed loudly and movingly in Stuttgart by a large number of people accompanying him to the grave. His spiritual colleagues vied with each other to celebrate him in obituaries.

Ludwig Uhland dedicated the most beautiful obituary to Wilhelm Hauff's early passing:

The young, fresh, colorful life,
The rich spring, which has not been given autumn,
Let us offer him a funeral sacrifice
The broken branch–the one full of flowers!
Only a moment ago, this spring's glow
The fatherland shines.– On rugged stones,
Whose castle was broken, rose again
A cloud castle, an enchanting building.
But in the cave, where the silent power
The earth spirit – creates mysterious forms:
Unfolded by the torchlight of imagination,
We saw them fashioned into heroic images;
And every echo, hidden in cracks and crevices,
Was awakened to become an animated human word.
With heroic journeys and festive dances,
With satirical masks and flower wreaths
Antiquity dressed the coffin,
Who cheerfully concealed the burnt ashes:
So, he too, whose tears melt,
Built his coffin from pictures of life.
The ashes rest–the spirit flies on paths
Of life, whose fullness we only suspect,
Where art also reaches its heavenly goal
And before the original, every image pales.

Hauff's literary legacy was small; the first edition of all his works was organized by *Gustav Schwab*, who had been in personal contact with him. Hauff's cheerful, imaginative spirit, his pensive disposition, his youthful, amiable nature speak vividly in all his works, which gained their value through this and through his skillful storytelling talent and became treasures of German literature.

Alfred Weile

TABLE OF CONTENTS

CONFIDENTIAL LETTER TO MR. WA SPÖTTLICH.

Retired Vice Battalion Surgeon and Toll Collector in Tempelhof near Berlin.

You will be obliged, dear Sir, if you read this preface, which I am having printed as a preface to a small collection of short stories. I am taking this opportunity to discuss a few things with you, partly because after six unanswered letters the postage to Tempelhof seemed too expensive, but also because you perhaps do not understand why I have written these short stories in this way and not otherwise.

In your usual way, when you read "novellas" on the title, you will close your little eyes a little, smile mysteriously and, if he happens to be there, assure Mr. Kohlhaupt, "I know the man, everything he writes is a lie," and yet you would be very wrong about these very novellas. The best and most famous novelists, Lopez de Vega, Boccaz, Goethe, Calderon, Tieck, Scott, Cervantes and even a Tempelhofer, certainly created their poems from an inexhaustible treasure of imagination, and the unfading bouquets they made were not picked from their neighbor's garden, but came from the evergreen paradise of poetry, to which, according to legend, fairies lay the invisible key in the cradle of their darlings. This is also why, through a mysterious power, everything they have lied about has become the most beautiful truth.

Lesser mortals, who have not been blessed with that magical spring root which not only opens the invisible paths of the imagination, but also opens the solid and impenetrable gates of the human breast, have to resort to all sorts of makeshifts if they want to write novellas. For that is precisely the annoying thing about the matter, that their truth often appears as a poorly invented lie; while the poetry of those fairy children is considered to be faithful, unadulterated truth.

So, we humble fellows often have no choice but to *spy* on a novella . Coffee houses, restaurants, Italian cellars, and the like are not very advisable for this purpose. Usually, only men are to be found there and you yourself know how poor restaurant people are at telling stories. They only throw out this or that fact quickly and hastily; pure asides, nothing picturesque; I would say they give no flesh to their stories, and how often have I been annoyed when someone talked about an execution and this or that person just threw out "beheaded" or "executed," instead of seeing the poor sinner, his confessor, the executioner's red cloak, his glittering sword, and even hearing the air whistle as his annoying arm strikes the blow, as is usual in proper stories.

There are certain wine bars where older gentlemen gather and do not like to see a "youngster" or a "stranger" among them. These men tend to tell better stories; because they have already told fifty times this or that robbery, the mysterious, inexplicable escape of a nobleman, a sudden death about which "all sorts of rumors" were made, their stories have acquired a finery, a stately dress, and they move on respectably, while the stories of the people in the restaurant industry glide by like shadows. Such gentlemen also have a kind of historical thoroughness, and it always gives me great joy when one says: "You've brought me to a strange incident," asks for another half bottle and then begins: "In the seventies there lived a gentleman of mysterious nature in my hometown." Such gentlemen can be found everywhere, and they are used a lot by several of our newer novelists. The well-known ** assured me that he owed a whole volume of his novellas to such old moths, and only from this confession could I understand why his novellas were so stiff and dry; afterwards they all seemed to me like old, withered bachelors who tell each other their love adventures, which all begin: "In my time."

But the richest source for novelists of our kind are women who are past sixty-five. The world calls Medisance, which is really just an excellent way of telling a story; young girls of sixteen or eighteen tend to get on well with such women and take care not to expose them to any weakness that could bring them into the mouths of the old novelists; women of thirty and their family friends prefer to walk a corner so as not to pass their field of vision, or if chance brings them together with their late grandmother's childhood friend, they tend to praise the old woman's good looks and patiently listen to a caustic praise of the old days, which regularly contains a gentle exordium, three parts on housekeeping, clothing and child-rearing, a practical application and a pious Amen. Such older women tend to adopt a certain mysterious and trusting tone towards younger men who pay them some attention. They have fine and descriptive nicknames for young girls and beautiful women who now occupy the same position in society that they once occupied themselves, and they tell the gentlemen who lend them an ear all sorts of "curious" things about the "little squirrel and his mother," and also "how things go in this or that house," "gallant adventures of that elderly, dignified gentleman who was not always like that," and once they are in the adventurous area of secret court stories and bad marriages, they spin out stories with trembling voices, fine smiles and the most expensive assurances that could be printed immediately in any almanac (with the names changed, of course).

No one knows how to convey the costume, the conversation, the customs "fifty years ago" as well as she does; I once thought I could hear the hoop skirts rustling, the high stilts clattering, the French words purring during such a conversation, the whole story smelled of amber and powder like the old ladies themselves. And so fresh and lively is their memory and facial expressions, that once, when one of these ladies was telling me about a long-dead minister and imitating her gait and her rasping tone, I involuntarily remembered that I had known this woman as a child, that she had given me a carrot with the same rasping voice. Several short stories that I have written down relate to secret family histories or strange, adventurous incidents, the true causes of which have rarely been made public, and I can assure you that I have heard them all, some in Berlin, some in Hanover, Kassel, Karlsruhe, and even in Dresden, from such old women, the chronicles of their surroundings, and have often retold them word for word.

Only in this way is it possible that, even without that key to the fairy kingdom, we can now produce such a significant number of novellas in Germany. The wonderful world of fairy tales no longer finds a receptive audience, lyrical poetry seems to only be uttered by a few sacred lips, and of the old drama, it is said, only the dramaturgists remain. In such miserable times, my dear friend, the novella is a very convenient thing. We have borrowed the title, like a mask, from the great novelists, and God and his dear critics may know whether the stories below are real and fair novellas.

I have said all this, my dear sir, to show you how I came to write novellas, how one goes about writing novellas, and that everything I have written is *faithful* truth, even if not poetic. Do you remember the good Mrs. von Welkerlohn, who always wore a dress of faded yellow velvet that seemed only a soft continuation of her hard, yellow features? I have given the story "Othello" to her. She was far too discreet to mention names and the residence where these strange scenes took place, but when I consider that she was a lady-in-waiting in Scherau at the same time that Jean Paul was living there, I cannot help believing that the story took place at that court. I got the second novella from the mouth of the old Countess Nelkenroth; she is generally considered a wicked woman, but I can assure you that I saw her shed tears over Joseph's fate. One might say that she often tells whiny stories in social gatherings because twenty years ago a Painter assured me that she had something of a Mater dolorosa ; but this much is certain, that she claimed to have known several characters in the play, and the woman with whom Mr. von Fröben lived in S. told me many oddities about him. I and many people in S. to whom I retold the story made a vain effort to find out more about Mr. von Fröben and the people he came into contact with. We only learned that the picture of the lady had been lithographed by Strixner after the painting in the Boisserée Gallery. In Ostend, where I made inquiries through several letters, I could find out nothing except that an English ship, the "Luna", Captain Wardwood, had indeed taken passengers on board for Portugal in August, and that the port director's register contained a Don Petro de Montanjo with his niece and servants. On the Rhine, where I asked about Mr. von Faldner and his family and explained why I was asking, I was told that everything was a fabrication, because all along the Rhine there were only civilized farmers who lived with their wives like angels in heaven.

You see, I have spared no effort to make the stories I tell as credible as possible. There are, of course, people who are angry with me because of this historical truth and claim that the real poet must not mention any street, any town, any well-known names or objects; everything and anything must be purely fictitious, not through external adornment, but gaining truth from within, and like Mohammed's coffin it must float in the lovely, blue air between heaven and earth. Others may also consider it "*an illegal deception of the public*" and may want to sue me for claiming that this and that happened here and there, and yet I cannot produce any testimony from the city court. But are we talking about real poetry, about real poets here? One should not apply this lofty standard to the stories of a few old ladies! Goethe said in Poetry and Truth that he saw a door and a beautiful garden in the Frankfurt city wall. Even today, all foreigners go there (I was there myself) and look at the wall and wonder why one cannot at least see the repair, even though the hole was only a dream and never was in the wall. Such poetic One might accuse Goethe of being an outrage against a sedate public; but one must allow such liberties to poor people *without the chamberlain's key of poetry, which opens walls even when they have no doors.*

Therefore, dear Sir, read these stories, however adventurous they may be, as pure, faithful *truth* ; it will annoy you less than if you thought you were *reading fiction,* and your keen eye found a confused web of improbable lies.

Wilhelm Hauff

OTHELLO.

1.

The theatre was packed; a newly recruited singer was playing Don Juan. Seen from above, the stalls heaved like the restless sea, and the ladies' feathers and veils emerged from the dark masses like shimmering fish. The boxes were richer than ever, for with the beginning of the winter season a little mourning had set in, and today for the first time the shimmering colours of the rich turbans, the waving bushes, and the colourful shawls broke through into the light. However brilliantly the rich wreath of ladies formed around the amphitheatre, the diadem of this circle seemed to be a magnificent, lovely image, which looked out from the princely box on the world around and below it, friendly and sweet. One was tempted to wish that this beautiful child had not been born so high, for this fresh complexion, this cheerful brow, these childishly pure, gentle eyes, this lovely mouth were created for love, not for adoration from afar. And it was wonderful, as if Princess Sophie had suspected this wicked thought-her dress also corresponded to this image of simple, natural beauty; she seemed to have left every adornment that art bestows to the proud circle of ladies.

"Look how lively, how cheerful she is," said a stranger in one of the first rank boxes to the Russian ambassador who was standing next to him, looking at the princess through the opera glasses; "when she smiles, when she closes her expressive eyes a little and then opens them again with indescribable charm, when she acts with her small, cute hand - one would think one could hear her witty speeches, her naive questions from such a great distance."

“It is astonishing!” replied the ambassador.

“And yet this heaven of joy should be only a mask? She should feel, feel painfully, she should love unhappily, and yet be so blooming, so cheerful? Madam,” the stranger turned to the ambassador's wife, "admit that you want to mystify me because I have taken some interest in this child of the gods."

"Mon Dieu! Baron," said she, shaking her head, "you still do not believe me? Upon my honour, it is true, as I told you; she loves, she loves beneath her station, I know it from a lady who does not miss anything of the sort. And what do you think, a princess, brought up from her youth to be a representative, will not have bustle enough to conceal such an improper relationship from the eyes of the world?"

"I cannot understand it," whispered the stranger, looking at her again thoughtfully; "I cannot comprehend it; this mirth, this almost mischievous jest—and silent, unhappy love? Madam, I cannot understand it!"

"Yes, why shouldn't she be cheerful, Baron? She probably doesn't suspect that anyone knows about her mischievous behavior; the Amoroso is nearby -"

"Is there anyone nearby? Oh please, Madame! Show me the lucky one, who is he?"

"What do you want? That would be against all the discretion that I owe the Grand Marshal; my friend, that will not happen. You can certainly tell people in Warsaw what you have seen and heard here, but names? No, to mention names in such affairs is very improper; my husband cannot stand that sort of thing."

The overture was nearing its end, the sounds roared up louder from the orchestra, the audience's eyes were fixed on the curtain, hoping to see the new Don Juan soon; but the stranger in the box of the Russian embassy had no ear for Mozart's sounds, no eye for the piece, he saw only the lovely, splendid child, who was all the more interesting to him because those beautiful eyes, those sweet, friendly lips were supposed to know secret love. Those around her, some older and younger ladies, had stopped speaking; they were listening to the music; Sophie's eyes glided through the packed house, they seemed to be missing something, to be searching for something. "Is she sending her eyes out for her lover?" thought the stranger; "Is she surveying the rows to see him, to greet him with a furtive smile, with a slight bow of the head, with one of those thousand signs which silent love, with which she makes her favourites happy and enchants them?' A quick, light blush now flew over Sophie's features, she moved her chair more to the side, she looked several times at the door of her box: the door opened, a tall, handsome young man entered and approached one of the older ladies, it was the Duchess F., the princess's mother. Sophie played indifferently with the glasses she held in her hand, but the stranger was connoisseur enough to read in her eyes that this and no other was the lucky one.

He could not yet see his face; but the figure and the movements of the young man had something familiar for him; the princess drew her daughter into the conversation, she looked up in a friendly manner, she seemed to have replied something piquant, for the mother smiled, the young man turned round, and "My God! Count Zronievsky!" the stranger cried so loudly, so anxiously, that the ambassador at his side was greatly frightened, and his wife convulsively seized the guest by the hand and pulled him down onto the chair beside her.

"For heaven's sake, what a scandal you are making!" cried the angry lady. "People are looking at us from right to left; who would be shouting so murderously? It is just as well that they were playing the violin and trumpet just as murderously down there, otherwise everyone would have heard your 'Zronievsky.' What do you want from the count? You know that we avoid knowing him!"

"I don't know a word," replied the stranger; "how can I know who you know and who you don't, since I've only been here three hours? Why do you avoid seeing him?"

"Well, you cannot be unaware of his relationship with our government," said the ambassador. "He has been banished, and it is most disastrous to me that he wants to be here and only here. He has had himself presented at court with the impudence of being presented, and so I see him at every step, and yet circumstances dictate that I ignore him. Besides, this disastrous man is giving me enough trouble; people in higher places want to know how he lives, and how he lives so splendidly, when his property has been confiscated; and I cannot find out. Do you know him, Baron?"

The stranger had only half heard these speeches; he looked intently at the princely box, he saw how Zronievsky spoke to the Princess and the other ladies, how his fiery eyes glide now and again to Sophie, how she eagerly caught this ray and returned it. The curtain flew open; the Count stepped back and disappeared from the box; Leporello began his lamentations.

"You know him, Baron?" whispered the ambassador. "Do you know anything about his circumstances."

"I served with him among the Polish Lancers."

"It's true; he served in the French army; did you see him often? Do you know his resources?"

"I have only seen him," said the stranger lightly, "when duty required it; I know nothing of him except that he is a brave soldier and a very learned officer."

The ambassador was silent; either because he believed these words or because he was too cautious to show his distrust of his guest by asking further questions. The stranger also showed no desire to continue the conversation; the opera seemed to occupy his entire mind; and yet it was a completely different subject that was constantly occupying his mind. "So, your unfortunate fate has finally brought you here?" he said to himself, "poor Zronievsky! As a boy you wanted to help Kosciuszko and free your fatherland; freedom and Kosciuszko have faded away and disappeared! As a youth you were enthusiastic about the glory of arms, the honor of the eagles you followed, but they were crushed; you had protected your heart from love for so long, it finally finds you as a man, and behold - the beloved stands so terribly high that you must forget or perish!"

The fate of his friend, for this was Count Zronievsky to him, made the stranger serious and gloomy; he sank into that brooding which forgets the world and all its circumstances, and when the first act of the opera was over, the ambassador had to rouse him from his reverie by asking him several questions, which were not even interrupted by the applause and shouts of bravo from the stalls.

"The Duchess has asked for you," said the ambassador; "she claims to know your family; come, wipe this seriousness, this melancholy from your brow; I will lead you into the box and present you."

The stranger blushed; his heart pounded, he himself did not know why; only when he walked down the corridor with the ambassador, As he approached the princely box, he felt that it was joy that set his blood in motion, the joy of being near that lovely being whose silent love attracted him so much.

2.

The Duchess received the stranger with remarkable kindness. She herself presented him to Princess Sophia, and the name of Larun seemed to ring familiarly in the ears of the beautiful child; she blushed briefly and said that she thought she had heard that he had formerly served in the French army. The Baron was only too certain that none other than Zronievsky could have told her this, and he was all the more certain because her eyes rested on him with a certain interest, as if he were an acquaintance, and she seemed to be glad to address the conversation to him.

"You are a stranger here," said the Duchess, "you have not been within these walls for a single day, so you cannot have been bribed by anyone; I challenge you, be the arbitrator; can there not be mysterious powers in nature which - which, how shall I express myself, which, if we wickedly invoke them, can bring us mischief?"

"You are not impartial, mother," cried the princess, animatedly. "You have already captured the Baron's mind by the way you asked the question. Tell me, if by chance, over the course of many years, six tiles had fallen from a house, one after the other, and killed several people, would you no longer pass by that house?"

"Why not? There must be mysterious powers in these bricks which – "

"How reckless," interrupted the Duchess, "you want to send me home with my mysterious powers, but just be patient; the analogy that Sophie brought forward doesn't quite fit -"

"Well, we will see who the Baron agrees with," she cried; "the thing is, we have a very pretty opera here, they perform all sorts of things, old and new mixed together, except for one thing, the most beautiful, most magnificent opera that I know; I had to hear it for the first time on foreign soil, the first thing I did when I came here was to ask that it be performed here, and my wish has never been granted! And not because it is too heavy - they make heavier pieces - no, the reason is actually ridiculous."

And what is the name of the opera? asked the stranger.

It's Othello!

"Othello? Certainly, a magnificent work of art; I, too, am rarely so moved by music as I am by this, and I feel solemnly, I might even say holy, moved for days when I have heard Desdemona's swan song sung on the harp."

"Do you hear it? He comes from Petersburg, from Warsaw, from Berlin, God knows where - I have never seen him, and yet he thinks so highly of Othello. We must see him again sometime. And why should he not be performed again? Because of a fairy tale that no one believes nowadays."

"Do not be wicked!" cried the Princess; "I know of facts which make me shudder to think of them; but we are speaking in riddles to our arbitrator; just imagine whether it would not be terrible if the theatre were to burn every time Othello was performed."

"Another parable," Sophie said, "but the fairy tale itself is even more amazing!"

"No, it will burn one day," continued the mother. "Othello was first performed as a drama based on Shakespeare, fifty years ago; the legend went, no one knows where or why, that whenever Othello was performed, a certain event took place; now our burning; it burned every time after Othello. An attempt was made, Othello was not performed for a long time; a new, ingenious translation came along, it was performed - that unfortunate case happened again. I still remember today when Othello, transformed into an opera, was performed for the first time; we laughed long before that we had deprived the unfortunate Moor of his sacrifice by making him musical

- Desdemona had fallen, a few days later the black man had another victim. The case happened again afterwards, and that is why Othello was never performed again; it is foolish, but true. What do you say to that, Baron, but honestly, what do you think of our dispute?"

"Your Highness is quite right," replied Larun, in a tone that was halfway between seriousness and irony; "if you will allow me, I will confirm your statement by an example from my own life. I had an unmarried aunt, an unpleasant, mystical person; we Children only called her the Feather Aunt because she wore large black feathers on her hat. As with your Othello, there was a legend in our family that whenever the Feather Aunt came, one or the other would fall ill. We joked and laughed about it, but the illness always came, and we were so used to the spook that whenever the Feather Aunt came to visit the farm, all preparations were made for the coming illness and even the doctor was called."

"A delightful figure, your feathered aunt!" cried the princess, laughing. "I can imagine her sticking her head with her feathered hat out of the carriage, how the children run as if the plague were coming because none of them wanted to get sick, and how a groom had to gallop to town to fetch the doctor because the feathered aunt had appeared. You really had a living white woman in your family!"

"Hush about these things," interrupted the Princess, gravely, almost angrily; "one should not speak so lightly of things which cannot be denied, and whose nature can never be explained. That is just how my Othello is," she added kindly. "And you will not see him, Baron, and must look for your favorite play elsewhere."

"And you shall see it nonetheless," Sophie whispered to him, "I must hear my Desdemona song once more, see and hear it properly on the stage, even if I should become a victim myself!"

"You yourself?" asked the stranger, concerned. "I hear that the ghostly Moor is only supposed to burn, not kill?"

"Oh, that was only the mother's parable!" she whispered even more quietly, "the legend is even more gruesome and much more dangerous."

The conductor knocked, the introduction to the second act began, and the stranger stood up to leave the prince's box. The Duchess had kindly dismissed him, but he looked around in vain for the ambassador; he had probably long since returned to his box. Undecided whether to go right or left, he stood in the corridor when a warm hand was placed in his; he looked up; it was Count Zronievsky.

3.

"So, I saw rightly, then?" cried the count, "my major, my brave major! How everything is coming back to life in me! I throw away these unhappy thirteen years; I am the happy lancer as ever! Vive Poniatowsky, vive l'emp- "

"For God's sake, Count!" the stranger interrupted him, "consider where you are! And why summon up these shadows? They are gone with their time; let the dead rest!"

"Rest?" he replied. "That is precisely what I cannot do. Oh, that I were among those dead! How gently, how patiently I would rest! They are sleeping, my brave Poles, and no voice, however powerful it calls, can startle them. Why am I alone not allowed to rest?"

A dark, unsteady fire burned in the handsome man's eyes, his lips closed painfully; his friend looked at him with anxious sympathy, he no longer saw the cheerful, heroic youth that he had seen at the head of the regiment in the days of prosperity; the trusting, winning smile that had previously attracted him so much had given way to a grim, bitter expression, the eyes that had previously looked around him freely and openly, full of proud confidence, full of joyful courage, seemed to want to examine every object suspiciously, to pierce it; the dull red that covered his cheeks was only the reflection of that bloom of youth that had earned him the name of the handsome Pole in the salons of Paris, and yet, even after this great change that time and misfortune had brought about, one had to admit that Princess Sophie was very much to be excused.

"You are looking at me, Major?" said the other, after a short silence. "You are looking at me as if you wanted to read the old days from my features? Do not make a point of trying; so much has changed. Should not a person change with his fortunes?"

"I don't think you've changed much," replied the stranger, "I recognized you at first sight. But there's one thing I don't see as I used to. A certain confidence that used to make me so happy has disappeared from those eyes. Alexander Zronievsky doesn't seem to trust me anymore. And "Yet," he added, smiling, "and yet my spirit was always with him; I even know the deepest thoughts of his heart."

"My poor heart!" replied the Count, melancholy; "I should hardly know whether I still have a heart if it did not sometimes beat with discontent! What thoughts do you think you have discovered, other than unchanging friendship for you, Major? Do not scold my eyes because they are no longer cheerful; I have withdrawn into myself; I have put my trust in my right hand; their pressure will tell you that I am still the same as before."

"Thank you; but what, I cannot understand the thoughts of your heart? You say it is only beating with discontent; what has a certain prince's child done to make your heartbeat so discontentedly?"

The count turned pale; he pressed his friend's hand firmly in his own. "For God's sake, be silent; never say another syllable on this point! I know, I understand what you mean, I will even admit that you saw correctly; the devil made your eyes, Major! But why am I asking a man of honour like you to be silent? No one from the Eighth Regiment has ever betrayed his comrade."

"You are right, and no more about it; but just this one more thing: none of the eighth will betray their comrades, but will not the good comrade betray himself?"

"Come up here to these stairs," whispered the count, for several people were approaching; "Jesus Mary, does anyone suspect anything except you?"

"If you will give trust for trust, well, I will confess."

"Oh, don't torture me, Major! I'll tell you what you want later, just quickly, if anyone else -"

Major von Larun told us that he had arrived in the city today, that his dispatches had soon been received by the ambassador, that he had been taken to the opera, and that there, as he was enchanted and looking at the princess from a distance, the ambassador had told him that Sophie was involved in a relationship beneath her station. "You entered the prince's box, and one look convinced me that no one but you could be the lover."

“And the ambassador?” cried the count in a trembling voice.

"She confirmed it. If I'm not mistaken, she also spoke of a Grand Marshal from whom she got the news."

The count remained silent for several minutes, staring straight ahead; he seemed to be struggling with himself, he looked shyly at the stranger several times from the side - "Major," he finally said in a dull, feeble voice, "can you lend me a hundred Napoleons?"

The major was surprised by this question; he had expected that his friend would lament a little about his misfortune, as was usual in such scenes and he could not immediately come to terms with the question and looked at the count in astonishment.

"I am a refugee," he continued, "I thought I had finally found a quiet place where I could rest a little, so I must love - must be loved, Major, how to be loved!" There were tears in his eyes, but he controlled himself and continued in a firm voice: "It is a strange request that I make of you here after such a long time of seeing you, but I do not blush to ask: Comrade, do you remember the last glorious day in the north, do you remember the day of Mosaic?"

"I remember!" said the stranger, his eyes shining and his cheeks coloring.

"And do you remember how the Russian battery lined up at the redoubt, how their grapeshot whizzed into our ranks and the traitor Piolsky blew the sound of retreat?"

"Ha!" the stranger interrupted in a booming voice, "and how you shot him down, Colonel, so that not a single vein in his body twitched, how the hussars turned to the right, how you shouted 'forward!' 'Forward, Lancers of the Eighth!' and the cannons were ours in five minutes!"

"Do you remember?" whispered the Count sadly. "Well, I am in command at the front again. I have to rescue a comrade. Will you save him? En avant , Major! Forward, brave lancer! Will you save him, comrade?"

"I want to save him!" cried the friend, and Count Zronievsky threw his arm around him, pressed him fiercely to his breast, and then hurried away from him along the corridor.

4.

"It's good that I've met you," cried Count Zronievsky, when he met the major on the street the next morning, "I was just going to come and ask you for a small favor -"

"I promised you yesterday," he replied. "Would you like to accompany me to my hotel? It has been waiting for you for a long time."

"For God's sake, nothing about money now," the count interrupted. "You are killing me with this prose; I am in a divine mood, blissful, supernatural. Oh, friend, I told the angel that we were being noticed; I told her that I was going to flee, for it is impossible for me to be near her, not to speak to her, not to worship her."

»And may I know what she said?«

"She is calm about it; she is greater than these bad people. 'What is it?' she said, 'no one can say anything bad about us and even if our relationship were discovered, I would gladly be forgiven for one stupid prank. Where is there a person who would not commit one at least once?'"

"A sound philosophy," observed the major. "One cannot think more sensibly of such circumstances; for those who believe they can deceive everyone are usually the worst advised. But may I ask one more question? It seems that you see your lady alone ? For what you told me was hardly discussed yesterday at the Don Juan."

"We'll see each other," he whispered, "yes, we'll see each other, but I can't say where, and as sure as I live, those people won't find out either. But I can see it myself, it can't last much longer. That's why I'm always on the move, comrade, and your help will save me if my money doesn't come through in the meantime. 'But if it's tomorrow, let us sip the last of this precious time today;' I still want to be happy, blessed, because it must soon come to an end."

"And how can I help you?" asked the major. "If I am not mistaken, you wanted to visit me."

"That's right, that's why I wanted to come," he replied after some thought. "Sophie knows that you are my friend, I have already told her about you, especially the story of the Beresina Bridge, where you took me on horseback. She spoke to you yesterday and about Othello, didn't she? The Princess will not allow it to be performed, because of some fairy tale that I no longer remember."

"You were very secretive about it," interrupted his friend, "and it seemed to me that the Princess would not admit it either."

"And yet, I got her there with a word. The princess begged and pleaded, and I cannot see that without coming to her aid; so, I assumed a somewhat serious expression and said: 'It is strange when something like this gets out into the public, it is like the wind in the embassies, and once it has got to that point, one must not worry that it will be told as a scandalous chronicle at all courts within a week.' The princess agreed with me; she said, albeit with a very worried and embarrassed expression, that the play should be performed; but as she was leaving she called out to me that she was not giving up on the play, because even if Othello was already on the list, she would let Desdemona fall ill."

"You have done well!" cried the major, laughing. "So, the fear of the Chronique scandaleuse has overcome the fear of ghosts and the horror of the mysteries of nature?"

"Yes, Sophie is overjoyed that she has got her way. I am on my way to the director of the opera; I am to bring him four hundred thalers so that the performance will not be subject to any financial difficulties, and you must accompany me to him."

"But won't it be noticed if you deliver this sum in the name of the princess?"

"That's taken care of; we're bringing it as a collection from some art lovers; introduce an amateur or an enthusiast or whatever suits our needs. The director lives not far from here and is an old, honest fellow who we're hoping to win over. Just around the corner, friend; do you see the little green house with the bay window over there?"

5.

The director of the opera was a small, gaunt man. He had once been famous as a singer and was now resting on his laurels in his old age. He received his friends with a certain artistic majesty and dignity, which was only slightly disturbed by his strange clothing; he wore a black Florentine cap, which he only took off when he put his wig on his bald head to go out. A modern, tight-fitting tailcoat and wide, pleated trousers stood out strikingly against the old man's comfortable home clothes; they showed that the director, despite his sixty years, was not dead to the vanity of the world. On his feet he wore wide, worn fur shoes, in which he skillfully skated around the room without visibly lifting his legs; it seemed to his friends as if he were skating.

"It has already been made known to me, the highest wish," said the director, when the count informed him of the purpose of their visit, "already knows about the matter; I shall not fail to be there, my only purpose is to delight the highest ears in an amusing manner, but - but I shall have to dare, most humbly, to exhibit some counter-representations."

"What? You don't want to perform this opera?" cried the count.

"God forbid, that would be an obvious assassination attempt on the very highest family! No! No! If my word on the matter is worth anything, this unfortunate play will never be performed."

"I would never have thought," replied the Count, "that a man like you would be seized by mob madness. Even in my earliest youth, in distant lands, I heard your celebrated name with astonishment and admiration; you were called the crown of singers and I burned with desire to see this man. Please do not diminish this venerable image with such absurdity."

The old man seemed to feel flattered; a charming smile spread across his weathered features; he put his hands in his pockets and walked up and down the room several times on his fur shoes. "Too good, too much honor!" he cried; "yes, we were something for our time, we were a good tenor! Now, of course, it has come to an end. Superstition, you may say? I would be ashamed to indulge in any superstition; but where there are facts, there can be no talk of superstition."

“Facts?” the friends cried in one voice.

"Oh yes, dear messieurs , facts. You do not seem to be from this town and region, since you do not know such things?"

"I have certainly heard of such a tale," said the Major; "if I am not mistaken, it is said to burn every time after Othello, and -"

"Burn? God forgive me; I would rather it burn all the time; you can put out fires, you have fire insurance, you can endure such fire damage if necessary; but die? No, that is a far more dangerous case."

"Die? Tell me, who should die?"

"Well, that's no secret," replied the director; "whenever Othello is performed, a member of the royal family must die eight days later."

The friends jumped up from their seats in alarm, for the prophetic, judgmental tone with which the old man said this had something horrible about it; but they immediately sat down again and burst into merry laughter at their own terror, which, by the way, did not disturb the singer.

"Are you laughing?" he said. "I must put up with it; if you don't mind, I will let you inspect the theatre chronicle which the prompter has been writing for the past hundred and twenty years."

"Give us the theatre chronicle, old man, let us inspect it," cried the count, who seemed to enjoy the whole thing; and the director slipped into his room with extraordinary speed and produced a folio bound in leather and brass.

He put on a pair of large bone-rimmed glasses and leafed through the chronicle. "Note," he said, "about what follows, first of all: it says here: 'In the year 1740, on December 8th, the actress Charlotte Fandauerin was suffocated in the local theater. The tragedy Othello, the Moor of Venice, by Shakespeare was being performed.'"

What? interrupted the Major, In 1740 Shakespeare's Othello was supposed to have been performed here? And yet It was, if I am not mistaken, Schröder who first and much later had the first Shakespeare play performed in Germany?'

"I beg your pardon," replied the old man. "The Duke saw this Othello performed in London on a trip through England, and because he liked it so much, he had it translated and performed here several times. My chronicle continues as follows: 'The aforementioned Charlotte Fandauer played Desdemona and perished miserably under the bedclothes with which she is to be killed in the play. God have mercy on her poor soul!' The story of this murder is told here as follows: Fandauer was said to have been very beautiful; things were very lascivious at court under Duke Nepomuk at that time; Fandauer became the Duke's mistress. But she is said not to have given herself over to him blindly and carelessly; she was put off by the example of so many whom he cast out after a few months or years and left to run around miserably. She is said to have made a terrible alliance with him and only surrendered to him after he swore to it. But as with the others, so it was with Fandauer. He soon grew tired of her and wanted to get rid of her in a gentle way. But she threatened to have the pact he had made with her printed and distributed throughout Europe, and she also showed him that she had already published this document in many foreign cities, where it would be distributed at her first hint.

The Duke was a cruel man, and his anger knew no bounds. He is said to have tried to poison her in various ways, but she ate nothing but what she had cooked herself. He therefore gave an actor a large sum of money and had Othello performed. You will remember that in Shakespeare's tragedy, Desdemona is suffocated in bed by the Moor. The actor did his job only too naturally, for the Fandau woman never woke up again.

The count shuddered. "And this is supposed to be true?" he exclaimed.

"Ask any of the older people in the town, and you will hear it told like this everywhere. The courts subsequently began an investigation against the murderer, but the Duke dismissed it, took the actor from the theater into his service, and declared that the Fandauer woman had suffered a stroke by chance. But eight days later his only son, a twelve-year-old prince, died."

“Coincidence!” said the major.

"You may call it that," replied the old man, turning the pages; "but listen, Othello was not performed for two years, because the Duke did not like the tragedy because of the memory of that murder. But after two years - every comedy is recorded in this book - after two years he was so wicked as to have it performed again. Here it is written: '28 September 1742 Othello, the Moor of Venice'; and here in passing it is noted: 'Strange! On the 5th October Princess Auguste died, exactly eight days after Othello, like the late Prince Frederick two years ago.' Coincidence, gentlemen?"

“It’s just a coincidence!” they cried.

Continue! 'The 6th of February 1748 Othello, the Moor of Venice.' I wonder if it will happen again? Look here, gentlemen! The prompter wrote that down, please note, it is the same hand that notes here in the margin: 'Terrible! The Fandauerin is haunting again, Prince Alexander died suddenly on the 14th, eight days after Othello.'" The old man paused and looked questioningly at his guests; they were silent, he turned the page and read: "'The 16th of January 1775, in aid of Mlle. Koller: Othello, the Moor of Venice.' Correct again! 'Poor Princess Elisabeth, you had to die so quickly! † January 24th, 1775.'"

"Nonsense!" interrupted the major. "I admit it is so; the obstinacy of chance has sometimes made it so; but give me one reasonable reason between cause and effect if you want to let these blessed souls die at Othello!"

"Sir," answered the old man, with deep earnestness, "I cannot; but I recall the words of that great mind from whom this unfortunate Othello is descended: 'There are many things between heaven and earth which philosophers cannot dream of!'"

"I know that" said the Count, "but I bet Shakespeare would never have uttered that saying if he had known how much ridiculousness lay behind it!"

"It is possible," replied the singer, "but listen further. I come now to a somewhat more recent example that I can remember, the Duke himself ."

"What," interrupted the major, "the very man who had the actress murdered?"

"The same one; Othello had not been performed for perhaps twenty years, when, as I remember it, foreign lords and ladies came to visit. They liked our play, and strangely enough, one of the foreign royal ladies wanted to see Othello . The Duke was reluctant to go, not out of fear of the horrible circumstances that usually followed this play, for he was a free spirit and believed in nothing of the sort; but he was old now; the sins and crimes of his youth weighed heavily on his heart, and he abhorred this tragedy. But whether it was because he did not want to refuse the lady anything, or because he was ashamed in front of the audience, the play had to be rehearsed headlong, and it was performed at his summer palace. Look, here it is: 'Othello, performed on October 16, 1793, at the summer palace H....'"

"Well, old man, and what happened next? Quickly!" cried the friends impatiently.

"Eight days later, on October 24, 1793, the Duke died."

"Not possible," said the Major after a short silence. "Let me see your chronicle, where is there anything about the Duke? There is nothing mentioned in the margin."

"No," said the old man, bringing two books; "but here is his life story, here is his eulogy, would you mind looking at them?"

The count took a small black book in his hand and read: "Description of the solemn burial of the Duke and Lord who died on October 24, 1793 - Nonsense," he cried, jumping up: "that could drive me mad! Coincidence! Coincidence! and nothing else! Well and do you know another story like that?"

"I could give you a few more," replied the old man calmly, "but you'll be bored by this strange conversation; just one more recent case. Rossini wrote his splendid opera Othello, in which he showed, as had been doubted, that he knew how to strike the deeper, tragic strings of the human heart. He was not required by the higher authorities here and therefore he was not rehearsed for the theatre. The orchestra, however, undertook to study this opera on its own, a few scenes were performed in concerts, and these few rehearsals ignited such a rapid enthusiasm for the opera in the public that it was generally in newspapers, at pubs, at singing teas and the like, nothing but Othello was spoken of, nothing but Othello was demanded. There was no mention of the horrific events that had accompanied the play Othello; it seemed that people imagined a completely different Othello when they saw the opera. Finally, the director of the time (I was still in the theater and sang Othello), he was given the task, I say, of staging the opera. The house was packed to overflowing, the court and the nobility were there, the orchestra made a superhuman effort, the singers left nothing to be desired, but I don't know - an eerie spirit came over all of us when Desdemona played her song on the harp, when she prepared for bed, when the murderer, the hideous Moor, approached. It was the same house, it was the same boards, it was the same scene as before, when a lovely creature in the same role ended her life so horribly. I must confess that, despite the devilish nature of my Othello, I was overcome by a slight tremor when the murder occurred. I looked anxiously towards the princely box, where so many blooming, strong figures were watching our performance. 'Will you allow yourself to be appeased by the sounds that accompany your death, bloodthirsty ghost of the murdered woman?' I thought. And so, it was. For five or six days there was no word of illness in the castle. People laughed that all it took was dressing up in an opera to drive that ghost mad, so to speak. The seventh day passed quietly, and on the eighth day Prince Ferdinand was shot while hunting.'

"I heard about it," said the Major, "but it was accidental; his neighbor's gun went off, and—"

"Am I saying that the ghost kills the blessed ones himself, squeezes their throats with his own hands? I am only talking about an inexplicable, mysterious connection."

"And didn't you tell us a fairy tale last but not least? Where does it say that Othello was performed eight days before that hunt?"

"Here," replied the director coolly, pointing to a passage in his chronicle; the count read: " Othello , opera by Rossini, March 12th," and in the margin was written, underlined three times: "On the 20th Prince Ferdinand fell while hunting ."

The men looked at each other in silence for a few moments They seemed to want to smile and yet the old man's seriousness, the strange coincidence of those terrible events, had moved them more deeply than they were willing to admit to themselves. The major leafed through the chronicle and whistled to himself, the count seemed to be pondering something, his forehead and eyes firmly propped up in his hand. Finally, he jumped up. "And all this still cannot help you!" he cried, "the opera must be performed. The court and the ambassadors already know that they would be disgraced if they were to allow themselves to be disturbed by these coincidences. Here are four hundred thalers, sir! Some friends and lovers of art are sending them to you so that your Othello can appear brilliantly. Buy whatever you like with it," he added with a smile, "send ghost spells, conjurers, buy a whole witch's apparatus, in short, whatever is necessary to drive away the ghost - just give us Othello."

"Gentlemen," said the old man, "it is possible that in my youth I would have laughed and joked about such things myself; age has made me calmer, I have learned that there are things which one must not reject outright. I thank you for your gift, I will know how to use it in a worthy way. But I will only give Othello on the strictest orders. Oh, God and Lord!" he cried piteously, "if the case should arise again, if the dear, sweet child, Princess Sophia, should be of the devil!"

"Be quiet," cried the Count, turning pale, "truly, your crazy stories are contagious, one could be frightened in broad daylight! Adieu! Do not forget that Othello will be performed in any case; do not play tricks on me with catarrh and fever, with making people sick and obstacles that have arisen. By the devil, if you do not give Desdemona, I will summon the ghost of the strangled woman to take a guest role this time."

The old man crucified himself and spun around impatiently on his shoes. "What impiety," he lamented, "if she were to appear like the stone guest? Stop such talk, I beg you; who knows how close each one is to his own ruin?"

Laughing, the two descended the stairs and for a long time the musical prophet with the Florentine cap and fur skates served as the butt of their jokes.

6.

There were times when the major could not find himself in the count, his old brother in arms. If he was otherwise cheerful, lively, radiant with wit and good humor, if he could entertain the company with apt anecdotes and stories from his life, if he knew how to connect everyone, no matter how humble they were, in a subtle and sensible way, so that he was the darling of all and adored by many, then at other times he was just the opposite. He began to become dry and silent, his eyes drooped, his mouth tightened. Little by little he became gloomy, played with his fingers, answered sullenly and impetuously. The major had already noticed that this was the time when he had to be removed from the company, for now only a few minutes were missing, and with his slightly agitated sensitivity he drew every innocent word to himself and began to rage and rage.

The major was often with him; he had a certain power and dominion over him from earlier times, which he now used to protect him from these outbursts of passion in company, and the more horribly they broke out in his rooms; he raged, he swore in all languages, he accused himself, he wept. "Am I not a miserable, depraved man?" he once said in one such fit; "to trample on my duties, to push away the most faithful love, to torture a heart that is so dear to me! I wander carelessly about the world, have squandered my happiness because in my madness I believed I was a Kosciuszko, and am nothing but a fool who was thrown away. And to repay so much love, this sacrifice, this loyalty in this way!"

The Major resorted to all sorts of consolations. "You yourself say that the Princess loved you first; could she ever expect any other love, any other loyalty from you than that which circumstances permit?"

"Ha, what are you admonishing me of!" cried the unfortunate man, "how your excuses accuse me! She too, she too, is beguiled! How childlike, how innocent she was when I, the wicked one, came, when I saw her with the lovely glow of innocence in her eyes, then my frivolity began again; I forgot all my good intentions, I forgot to whom alone I belonged. I plunged myself into a whirlpool of pleasure, I buried my conscience in oblivion!" He began to weep; the memory seemed to calm his anger. "And could I," he whispered, "could I leave her like that? I felt, I saw it in her every movement, I read it in her eyes that she loved me; should I flee when I saw that dawn of love rising in her cheeks, the first bright ray of understanding breaking out of her eyes, falling upon me, seeming to call upon me to return it?"

"I pity you," said his friend, pressing his hand; "where is there a man who would have resisted such sweet temptation?"

"And when I was allowed to tell her how much I admired her, when she confessed to me with proud joy how much she loved me, when that intimate, enchanting game of love began, where a glance, a fleeting pressure of the hand says more than words can express, where one lived for days only in the joyful anticipation of an evening, an hour, a lonely minute, where one reveled in the memory of that blissful moment until the evening came again, until I drank oblivion anew from the dizzy cup of her sweet eyes; how richly she knew how to give, how much love she knew how to put into a word, into a look; and I was supposed to flee?"

"And who is asking for this?" said the friend, moved. "It would have been cruel to reject such a beautiful love that sacrificed all circumstances. I would have wished for caution; I think all is not lost yet!"

He did not seem to listen; his tears flowed more violently; his shining eyes seemed to plunge deeper into the past. "And when she told me with a sweet blush how I could reach her, when she allowed me to kiss her princely brow, when the sweet mouth, whose wishes were the commands of a people, belonged to me, and the majesty of a princess was lost in the intimate whispers of love - then, then should I leave her?"

"How happy you are! There must be a charm of its own in the very mystery of this relationship; and why do you want to condemn this love so deeply? Pull yourself together! The judgment of the world can be of no interest to you if you are happy; for on the whole, this relationship really does not have anything so dark and guilty about it as you yourself imagine!"

The count had listened to him; his eyes rolled, his cheeks darkened, he gritted his teeth. "You must not judge me so leniently," he said in a dull voice, "I do not deserve it. I am a scoundrel who should make you shudder. Oh, if I could buy oblivion, if I could erase years from my memory! I want to forget, I must forget, I will go mad if I do not forget bring me some wine, comrade; I want to drink, I am thirsty, a flame is raging within me, I want to drown away my memory, my guilt!"

The Major was a prudent man; he was fairly calm about these desperate outbursts of remorse and self-accusation. "I have always known him to be reckless," he said to himself; "such people easily go from one extreme to the other. He sees great guilt in his love now, because it can harm his beloved in her circumstances and the next moment he is intoxicated again by the joy of memories." The wine arrived, the Major poured it; the Count quickly downed several glasses; he walked quickly up and down the room in silence, stopped in front of his friend, drank and left again. The latter did not want to interrupt his quiet feelings; he drank and watched his friend's expression and movements attentively over the glass.

"Major!" he finally cried, throwing himself down on his chair, "which feeling do you consider the most terrible?"

He sipped the wine carefully in small gulps, he seemed to be thinking, and then said: "Without doubt, that which gives the happiest feeling must also become the saddest - honor, injured honor."

The count laughed grimly. "Let me give you back the thalers you gave to a bad psychologist for his lessons, comrade. Injured honour! So, your art does not descend any deeper into the soul? Injured honour still feels itself; there is a feeling in the heart of the injured person that raises him high above the insult; he can wipe out the smear on the offender; he still has the opportunity to wash his honour clean and spotless again, but deeper, brother," he cried, grasping the major's hand convulsively, "deeper into the soul! What feeling is more terrible?"

"I have heard of one," he replied, "but which men like us do not know - it is called self-contempt."

The count turned pale and trembled. He stood up in silence and looked at his friend for a long time. "You've been hit, comrade!" he said. "That goes even deeper. Men like us don't usually know it; it's called self-contempt. But the devil also lays very fine snares on the earth; before you know it, you're caught. Do you know the torment of fickleness, Major?"

"Thank God, I never found out; my path always led straight to the goal!"

"Straight to the target? Who would be so lucky? Do you remember the morning when we rode out of the gates of Warsaw? Our feelings, our senses belonged to that great spirit that held them captive; but to whom did the hearts of the Polish lancers belong? Our trumpets sounded those arias from the Cracow's, those songs that had inspired us as boys to fury for our fatherland; those familiar sounds were pounding again at the gates of our breasts; comrade, to whom did our hearts belong?"

"For the fatherland!" said the major, moved; "yes, back then, back then I was certainly fickle!"

"It is fortunate for you that you have never been so before; the devil knows how to make it look pretty; here he lets us feel, make us happy, and there he shows us even greater bliss, even greater happiness!"

"Possible; but the man has the strength to remain true to what he has chosen."

"That's it," cried the Count, as if thundered down by this one word, "that's it, and from that self-contempt; and why appear better than I am? Comrade, you are a man of honor, flee from me like the plague, I am dishonorable, a man who forgets my honor, you are a man of strength, despise me, I must despise myself, you know, I am -"

"Stop, be quiet!" interrupted his friend, "there was a knock at the door - come in!"

7.

"I am very sorry, I am infinitely sorry," said the director of the opera, sliding into the room with a deep bow, "I am interrupting your Excellency?"

"What do you bring us?" replied the major, more quickly composed than his unfortunate friend. "Sit down and do not disdain our wine; what brings you to us?"

"The sad certainty that Othello will be performed after all. It's no use; all begging is in vain. I will only confess to you that I had the opera rehearsed but had already persuaded our prima donna to solemnly promise me that she would become hoarse; then yesterday evening Satan brought the singer Fanutti to town; she comes from the...theater, asks the highest theater management for guest roles, and just imagine, she is promised Othello for next Sunday. I almost cried when I was told; now no god can help me, and yet I have terrible premonitions!"

"Old gentleman!" cried the count, who had meanwhile had time to collect himself. "Just give up your belief in charcoal burners for once; I can assure you that not a hair on the head of any of the most high-ranking persons will be harmed. I will go out into the churchyard, have the grave of the strangled Desdemona shown to me, pay my respects to her and ask her to turn a blind eye this time and strangle me. Of course, then she will only have a count and no royal blood; but one of my ancestors also wore a crown!"

"Don't be so horrible," replied the old man, "how easily misfortune can drag you down with it! Such things are not to be trifled with. Moreover, last night in a dream I saw a great funeral procession with torches, such as one usually buries princes."

"Terrible visions, my good sir!" laughed the major. "Have you perhaps had a glass or two too many? And what is more natural than that you dream of such things, since you spend the whole day thinking of death?"

The old man did not allow himself to be talked out of his seriousness. "You, my dear sir, should not make fun of it," he said. "I never saw you until that hour when you visited me with the Count, and yet we both followed the coffin together last night, you wept bitterly."

"Ever more delightful! How vividly you dream; that is why I had to come here, to walk with you in your dreams, dear man!"

"Let us break off," he replied, "what must come will come, and we would perhaps give a lot if we had only dreamed it all. But I have come to you mainly to invite you to the rehearsal; you have shown yourself so generous to us that I shall take pleasure in showing you our staff, especially the new singer."

The friends accepted the proposal with joy. The Count, as always, seemed to regret his vehemence and this distraction was welcome; the Major had found these outbursts of self-accusation heavy and oppressive; he too therefore gratefully accepted this way out in order to escape a more detailed explanation from his friend, which he feared rather than desired.

8.

And indeed, from that moment on, the count seemed to no longer want to touch that chord; he did seem gloomy now and then, and indeed moments of deep grief returned, but not with them the confession of a great guilt that was already on his lips at that time; he was more reserved than usual. The major hardly saw him at all for several days; the business that had called him to this city left him few hours, and the count was in the habit of devoting these to the theater; for whether out of pleasure in the matter itself or to act in the spirit of his beloved and to make her favorite opera appear brilliant, he was present at every rehearsal; his good tact, his extensive travels, his fine, worldly-educated taste imperceptibly improved many things that would have escaped the eye and ear of even such a sharp critic as the director; and the old man often forgot for hours the dark forebodings that tormented his soul, so well did Count Zronievsky know how to capture his interest.

Thus, Othello had progressed to a perfection that was not thought possible at first; the opera had been hampered by the strange circumstances which had so far had prevented, became new not only to the audience, but even to the singers; no wonder that they did their utmost to meet such great expectations; no wonder that people looked forward with joyful anticipation to the day that would call ***The Moor of Venice*** to the stage.

But there were two other things that captured the public's interest. The singer Fanutti had a great reputation, and people were curious to see how she would perform in the theater, how she would play Desdemona, a role that required not only beautiful singing but also a high level of tragic acting. In addition, there was a faint rumor about the strange incidents that had always accompanied Othello; the older people told stories, the younger ones repeated them, doubted them, exaggerated them, so that a large part of the audience believed that the devil himself would take on a guest role in Othello.

Major von Larun had the opportunity to hear these things discussed in many places; what struck him most was that at court, where he spent a few evenings, no word was said about Othello; only Princess Sophie once said to him briefly and smiling: "We would have won Othello after all, thanks to your sick aunt, Baron, and the Count's diplomatic threat. How I look forward to Sunday, to my little Desdemona song; truly, when I die, it shall be my swan song."

"Are there premonitions?" thought the major at these hastily thrown words, which sounded involuntarily heavy and meaningful to him; "the legend of the ghostly Desdemona, the old director's fears, his dreams of the funeral procession and this swan song!" He watched the lovely, charming apparition as it glided happily and kindly through the halls, how, like the girl from abroad, it offered everyone a beautiful gift, a smile or a friendly word - if chance would have it again, he thought, if she died! He laughed at himself the next moment; he could not understand how such a thought could enter his unprejudiced soul - he tried with all his might to drive this ridiculous phantom from his memory - in vain! This thought kept returning, surprising him in the midst of the strangest speeches and objects, and he still thought he heard a sweet voice whispering; When I die – let it be my swan song.

Sunday came and with it a strange incident. The major had ridden out in the afternoon with the count and several officers. On the way home they were caught in a rain that soaked them to the skin. The count's apartment was next to the gate, so he asked the major to change his clothes at his place. Wearing one of his friend's hats and wrapped in one of his overcoats, the major left the house to hurry to his own apartment. He must have walked a few streets, and it always seemed to him as if someone was following his every step. He stopped, looked around, and close behind him stood a tall, gaunt man in a worn coat. "This to you, sir!" he said in a dull voice and with a piercing look, pressed a small note into the astonished man's hand and jumped around the next corner. The major could not understand where such a mysterious message could come from in a completely foreign city. He looked at the note from all sides; it was fine, shiny paper, artfully tied in a bow, sealed with a beautiful cameo. No inscription. "Perhaps they're trying to play a joke on you," he thought, and opened it carelessly in the street. He read and became attentive. He read on and turned pale. He put the paper in his pocket and hurried to his apartment, his room.

It was already dusk on the street, he thought he hadn't read correctly, he called for light. But even in the bright light of the candles the unfortunate words remained firm and threatening.

"Wretched man! You can let your wife, your little worms, languish in misery, while you appear before the world in splendor and magnificence? What do you want in this city? Do you want to insult a venerable royal house, make its daughter as unhappy as you have made your wife? Flee, the hour you read this, *Priest Sph.* will know the shameful secret of your deception."

The major had no doubt that these lines were addressed to the count, that they had come into his hands by chance, perhaps because he had been walking down the street in his friend's clothes. Now he suddenly became aware of those outbursts of despair; it was remorse and self-loathing that at certain moments broke through the brilliant veneer with which he had covered his deceptive game. Larun's eyes fell on the lines he still held in his hand; those codes Pr. Sph. could mean nothing other than the name of the lovely, now so unfortunate creature that that unscrupulous traitor had drawn into his net. The major was a man with a cold, calculating look, with a strong, consistent mind; he had seldom if ever allowed himself to be surprised or thrown off balance by an object, but at this moment he was no longer master of himself; anger, rage, and contempt alternately fought in his soul. He tried to force himself to look at the matter from a milder point of view, to excuse the count by his character, his boundless frivolity; but the thought of Sophie, the sight of the wretch's "wife and the poor little worms," drove away every lenient sentiment, roared through his soul like a storm; yes, there were moments when his hand convulsively reached towards the wall to pull down the pistols and punish the wicked man that very hour. But his contempt for him did what milder voices in his breast could not. "He must go, this very hour," he cried; "the unfortunate woman he has bewitched must not at any price learn to what wretch she gave her first love. She must weep for him, forget him; to have to despise him could kill her." He quickly through these thoughts on paper, gathered together a large sum, more than he could spare, enclosed the unfortunate letter and sent everything to the count through his servant.

It was time to go to the opera; how the major would have liked to have seen no one today, and yet he felt he owed it to the princess to protect her from the threatened warning. He thought about how he could make this possible, and there was nothing left for him but to implore her not to accept any letter from strangers. He threw on his coat and was just about to leave the room when his servant returned, still holding the package for the count. "His Excellency has just left," he said, laying the package on the table.

"Left?" cried the major. "Not possible!"

"His hunter is at the door. He has a letter for you. Shall I bring him in?"

The major waved, the servant led the hunter in, who handed him a letter, crying. He tore it open. Life You, forever! The letter which, as I have just learned, came into your hands an hour ago will excuse my departure without adieu. Will my comrade of six campaigns spare a beloved lady the pain of hearing my name in all the papers? Will he cover the few posts which I can no longer pay?'

"When did your master leave?"

A quarter of an hour ago, Major!

Did you know about his trip?

"No, Major! I believe that His Excellency did not know this afternoon, for they were going to the theater this evening. At five o'clock the Count went out on foot and had me follow him. He met a tall, gaunt man at the Reformed Church who was very frightened at the sight of him. He went up to my master and asked if he was Count Zronievsky? My master said yes; then he asked if he had received a note a quarter of an hour ago? The Count said no. The stranger then spoke to my master in secret for a while; he must not have given him good news, for the Count turned pale and trembled; he turned back home, sent the coachman for post horses, I had to quickly pack two suitcases; the carriage had to drive up. The Count referred me to you with the bills and everything and drove down the street out of the South Gate. Before he left, he said goodbye to me, I think for good."

The major had listened in silence to the huntsman's report; he ordered him to come back the next morning and drove to the theater. The overture had already begun when he entered the box; he threw himself down on a chair from where he could observe the princely box. Princess Sophie sat next to her mother in all her natural beauty and grace. Her eyes seemed to radiate with joy, a serene calm lay on her brow, a lovely smile wafted around her finely-cut mouth, perhaps the echo of a cheerful joke - she had now got her way, it was Othello who had filled the hall and the boxes of the house. Now she put her lorgnette to her eyes, as she had done before, she seemed to be eagerly searching for something else in the house - unsuspecting heart, you beat in vain for your beloved; your loving glances will no longer find him, your ear listens in vain to see if his footsteps are resounding in the corridor, you bend in vain his beautiful neck back, the door will not open, his tall, commanding figure will no longer approach you.

She lowered her glass; a cloud of disappointed expectation and sadness settled under her blonde curls, the beautiful arches of her eyebrows drew together and revealed a barely perceptible wrinkle of displeasure. Her fine, silky eyelashes drooped like a transparent curtain, she seemed to be pondering, she was drawing with her lorgnette on the parapet of the box. Are these perhaps his codes that she is writing down, lost in thought? How soon will she perhaps curse the name that now fills her soul!

Tears involuntarily came to the Major's eyes as he looked at Sophie. "She has no idea what awaits her," he thought, "but never, never shall she know how miserable the man she loved was." The thought of this wretched man took hold of him again; he closed his eyes and cursed human nature, which through frivolity and weakness could turn a noble spirit, a brave man, into an honorless, faithless deceiver.

The major has often confessed that one of the most terrible moments in his life was when he entered the prince's box during the first interlude of Othello. He felt as if he himself had offended Sophie, as if he were the one who must break her heart. The thought was unbearable to him, to see her before him, unsuspecting, happy, expectant, and yet knowing what nameless misfortune awaited her. He entered; her eyes met his immediately; she must have often looked towards the door. With hasty impatience she overlooked a prince and two generals who were about to approach her; she beckoned the major over. "Have we got our Othello now?" she said, "aren't you happy and expectant too? but I don't see any of our Othello sworn companions," she whispered more softly, blushing slightly. "The Count is surely behind the scenes, deserving warm thanks for having everything done so beautifully?"

"Forgive me, Your Highness," replied the major, struggling to regain his composure, "the count sends his apologies, he has gone away for a few days."

Sophie turned pale. "Away, not at the opera? Where did his business call him so quickly? Oh, that must be a joke that you two are playing together," she cried. "Do you think he will just leave so quickly without taking a leave of absence? No, no, that would be some fun. Now I know where a certain letter came from."

The major was frightened and had to hold on to the nearest chair. "A note?" he asked in a trembling voice, a terrible premonition rising within him.

"Yes, a pretty little note," she said, teasingly letting the end of a piece of paper peek out from under the broad brasselet that encircled her beautiful arm. "A little note that was slipped to me in a very mysterious way. I can see from your eyes that you are part of the plot. I have not yet found an opportunity to open it, for such a joke must not be made public, but as soon as I get into my boudoir -"

"Your Highness, I beg you for God's sake, give me the note," said the major, tormented by the most terrible agony, "it is not even intended for you, it has fallen into the wrong hands."

"So? So much the better; I won't give it away for the world, it's to tell me about the secrets of certain people! So it was definitely for a lady; it's really nice that it came into my hands."

The major wanted to ask and implore him once more, but the prince put his head in between, the two generals burst in with questions and news, and he had to withdraw. Pursued by terrible torments, he went back to his box, pressed his eyes into his hand so as not to see the unfortunate woman, and again and again he had to look, had to absorb the torments of fear, the certainty of approaching disaster, with his eyes.

The diamonds on the clasp of her bracelet shone with a thousand lights, their rays flashed towards him, they penetrated his heart like a thousand arrows. "What misery those diamonds lock! When she opens these bracelets in the lonely room, is she not at the same time opening the door to a terrible crime? Her pulse beats to these unfortunate lines as her heart beats for her lover; will it not stop when the seal bursts and the unsuspecting eye falls upon a terrible tidings?"

Desdemona tuned her harp; her melancholy chords whispered through the house, she raised her voice, she sang – her swan song. How wonderful, how powerfully moving these melancholy sounds touch every heart; this song is so simple, so childlike, and yet so tragically effective! One feels anxious and constricted, one senses what a terrible fate awaits her, one thinks one can hear the murderer creeping in the distance, one feels the inevitable power of fate coming closer and closer, it rustles around her like the wings of death. She has no idea; gently, innocently as a sweet child, she sits at the harp, only melancholy trembles in soft tones from her breast, from this full, warm heart for which the steel is already drawn. She whispers loving greetings into the distance to him who will crush her; her longing seems to call him into her arms, he will come - to murder her; she prays for him, Desdemona blesses him - who gives her death.

The Major divided his eyes between the singer and Sophie. She listened, lost in melancholy, to her favorite song, a tear hung in her eyelashes, she wept unconsciously over her *own fate* , the chords of the harp drifted away, Sophie looked before her, pensive, dreaming. "When I die one day, it shall be my swan song," the Major recalled. "Truly, she has spoken the truth," he said to himself, "it was the swan song of her happiness." Othello entered. Sophie's attention was no longer focused on the opera, she looked down at her bracelet, she played with the lock; a cheerful smile dispelled her melancholy, her eyes wandered over to the major's box, he strained his eyes anxiously - God in heaven, she pushes out the unfortunate paper and hides it in her handkerchief - he thinks he sees her secretly breaking the seal - in despair he rushes out of his box and down the corridor. He does not know why, he is driven by an invisible force towards the prince's box, he is only a few steps away - when he hears a noise in the house, someone is coming out of the box, servants and chambermaids rush past him anxiously, a terrible premonition tells him in advance what it means, he asks, he receives the answer: "Princess Sophie has suddenly fainted!"

9.

A few days after this incident, Major Larun sat in his room, gloomy and torn within himself. His forehead rested in his hand, his face was pale, his eyes half closed, the man who was usually so strong wiped away many a tear that tried to sneak over his eyelashes. He thought of the terrible fate into whose innermost fabric chance had thrown him; he saw all those fine threads that, visible to few eyes other than himself, were so loosely attached; he saw how they were spun further, how they were tied and doubled to form a net that was all too tight around a tender, unhappy heart. Invincible bitterness mingled with these gloomy memories; his old friend in arms, such a shining meteor on the horizon of honor, such a brave soldier, and now a wretch, a man who forgot his honor, who, without being able to remotely expect any other outcome, beguiled with all the arts of love the unguarded senses of a child who had barely blossomed into a virgin! The image of this angel suffering so infinitely was mixed with these thoughts, as was the fear of a scene which he was about to face in the next hour. A respected lady, the head maid of honour to Princess Sophie, had summoned him that afternoon. She revealed to him without concealment that Sophie was suffering from a serious illness, that the doctors offered little hope, for they called her illness a nervous attack. She went on to tell him that the princess had told her everything, that she had not concealed a word of this criminal relationship from her. She knew that there was only one person living in the capital who had known Count Zronievsky well, and that person was Baron von Larun. With a fear and a desire which bordered on despair, the unfortunate woman insisted on speaking to him without witnesses. The head lady-in-waiting knew how much this ran counter to the rules imposed on her by etiquette, but the sight of the whining child, who seemed to want to attend to only this one business on earth, raised her above the limits of her circumstances, and she dared to propose to the major that he should go secretly to the sick woman that evening, accompanied by her.

The major had not said no. He knew that he could not say anything comforting to her, but he felt that in such a[96] deep grief the desire for communication must become insurmountable.

But what should he say to her? Did he not fear that the sight of her, the sad memories of the last few days, would so overwhelm her that his sheer pain would make her even more unhappy? He was still lost in these thoughts when he was told that he was expected; the old lady-in-waiting stopped in front of the house in her carriage; he sat down silently by her side.

"You will find the Princess very bad," said this lady with tears. "I give up all hope. I cannot imagine that there is anything that can save us in a conversation with you, Baron. If you cannot give her comfort, she will go out like a lamp that has no oil left to feed its flame. And if you were to give her comfort and hope, these feelings are of such an unnatural nature in her circumstances that I almost wish she would die rather than bring disgrace to her house."

"So, I shall have to kill her," said the major, smiling bitterly; - - "does anyone in the family know about these stories? What do they think of the illness?"

"As I told you, Baron, the family, the court and the town know nothing but that she must have caught a cold; the foolish people even bring the fatal opera into play and let her die at Othello. What we both know is unknown to anyone else; there are a few ladies who suspected this relationship earlier but did not know for sure."

"And yet I fear," replied the Major, fixing his piercing gaze on the lady at his side, "I fear she will die as a result of a very daring prank. This relationship was suspected, it was investigated, it became a certainty; they tried to bring about a separation, they investigated the count's circumstances -"

"Do you believe it?" said the lady-in-waiting, pale and with trembling lips, as she tried in vain to meet the major's gaze.

"They investigated these circumstances," continued the major, "they tried to scare him away from here by threatening to tell the princess that he was married. Up to this point the plan was not bad; he belonged to such a wretch that they did not treat him more gently. But they went further: they also wanted to quickly get the unfortunate lady away from here of her love, they made her aware of the Count's secret, they believed she would forget everything overnight. And here the plan was calculated on the nerves of a dragoon, but not on the heart of this tender child."

"I must ask you to consider," replied the lady-in-waiting with her former coldness, but with piercing glances, "that this delicate child is a princess of the royal house, that she was brought up to overlook such imbalances with decency. If such a plan really existed, I cannot blame the people involved, they operated with real skill –"

"You have achieved your purpose; she will die," interrupted the major.

I have achieved my purpose? Sir, I must ask –

"You?" said Larun in an indifferent voice. "I was not talking about you, madam, I said: you, the actors, the operators."

The old lady bit her lip and said nothing. A few moments later they had reached a side gate of the palace. An old servant led them through a labyrinth of corridors and stairs. Finally, the passages were wider, the lighting more elegantly arranged, and the major noticed that they had reached the more inhabited wing of the palace. The old man waved at a side door. The path now led through several rooms to a drawing room that probably belonged to the princess's apartments, where the head lady-in-waiting whispered to the major that he should wait in an armchair for the time being until she called him.

After a deadly long quarter of an hour, she appeared again. She told him that, according to the patient's express wishes, he would be alone with her; she herself would sit at the door as dame d'honneur, where she would certainly not be able to hear anything unless one spoke too loudly. Moreover, he was not allowed to stay longer than a quarter of an hour. The major entered. The splendid room with its shimmering wallpaper and gold moldings, the rich drapery of the curtains, the bright colors of the Turkish carpet hurt his eyes, for the mind does not want to see a suffering heart, a sick body surrounded by the splendor of majesty. And how great was the contrast between this splendor of the surroundings and this delicate, lovely child, lying on a magnificent ottoman in a simple white robe.

The impression that her features, her figure, her whole being had made on him the first time returned to the Major's soul. It was her simple, unadorned beauty, her quiet greatness, hidden behind the magic of childlike amiability, that had attracted him. He was certainly dazzled then by the brilliance of her fresh, youthful colors, her bright, shining eyes, that winning, gracious smile that hovered around her fine, rosy lips. A night frost had stripped these blossoms; but did not this transparent pallor, this quiet sadness in her thoughtful eyes, this melancholy expression around her mouth, which never joked again, give her an even more sublime beauty, an even more dangerous charm? The Major stood still a few steps away from her and looked at her with deep emotion. She beckoned to him towards a stool that stood at her feet; she spoke; her voice had lost the bright metal that had formerly rang out in her cheerful jokes and her happy laughter, but these soft, touching tones penetrated deeper. "It would be foolish of me, Baron," she said, "to leave you in the dark for long as to why I had you summoned. I know that the Count, as his best friend, has informed you of a relationship that should never have existed. Do you remember the evening in Othello? I told you about a note that I received; I remember that you repeatedly asked me for it; why did you do that?"

"Why?" asks Your Highness, because I suspected the content, thought I knew it."

"So, it is!" she cried, and a tear came from her beautiful eye; "so it is! From the first moment I saw you, I thought you a man of honor. If you knew the count's circumstances, why did you not remove him sooner, why did you not spare me the pain of having to despise him?"

"I can swear by all that is sacred to me, by my honour," replied the Major, "that barely an hour before I entered the box before Your Serene Highness, I learned of these circumstances through a paper which by chance came into my hands instead of into the Count's. When I wanted to confront the Count about it, he had already heard of it and had left. I suspected from certain hints contained in that letter that you too would not be spared; I tried in vain to talk Your Highness out of the unfortunate little paper.

"So, you believe in this invention?" said Sophie, her tears streaming more violently; "Ah, it is only a device of certain people who wanted to remove him from us. Read this note, it is the same one I received; admit it yourself, it is slander!"

The major read:

"The Count of Z. is married; his wife lives in Avignon; three small children are crying for their father. Should a noble lady have so little sense of honour, so little pity, as to deprive him of these bonds any longer?"

It was the same handwriting, the same seal as the note he had received himself. He was still looking at those lines; he did not dare to look up, he did not know how to answer; for his strict notions of truth did not permit him to speak against his convictions, and his deep compassion for her pain did not let him crush her hope so cruelly.

"You see," she continued, as he was still silent, "when I opened this little note, innocent and curious, those terrible words, wife, father, surprised me like a voice of judgment. I lost my senses; I became very ill and miserable; but every time I feel better for just an hour, my hopes rise again; I believe that Zronievsky cannot have been so bad after all, that he cannot have deceived me so terribly. Smile, Major, be kind! I allow you to mock me for allowing myself to be so upset by these lines - but don't you think it's a lie, it's slander?"

The major was beside himself; what should he say to her? She hung on his every word so expectantly, it was as if a word from him would bring her back to life - her eyes shone again, that lovely smile appeared again on her lovely features - she listened as if to the message of a good angel.

He did not answer, he looked gloomily at the floor; then the happy hope gradually disappeared from her features, her eyes sank, her little mouth pressed together painfully, the delicate red that had once again colored her cheeks fled; she lowered her forehead into her beautiful hand, she hid her weeping eyes.

"I see," she said, "that you are too noble to flatter me with hopes that will vanish again after a few days. I thank you too for this terrible certainty. It is always better than the uncertain hovering between pain and joy; and now, my friend, take that little box there, try to deliver it to him, it contains many things that were dear to me but no, let me keep it for a few days, I will send it to you when I no longer need it.

I feel as if I shall not live long," she continued after a few moments; "I am certainly not superstitious, but why must I be ill after this fatal Othello?"

"I never thought that this thought could worry Your Highness for a moment," said the Major.

"You are right, it is foolish of me; but the night I was brought home from the opera, ill, I dreamed that I was going to die. A serious, gloomy young lady came to me with a red silk duvet, covered me with it and pressed it against me ever more tightly, so that I almost suffocated. Then suddenly my great-uncle, Duke Nepomuk, appeared, just as he is painted in the gallery, and freed me from the oppressive pressure, and the strangest thing is -"

"Well?" asked the Baron, smiling, "what did the painted duke do with Desdemona?"

The princess was astonished: "How do you know that the lady is Desdemona? I beseech you; how do you know this?"

The major was embarrassed and silent for a moment. "What is more natural," he then replied, "than that you dreamed of Desdemona? You had seen her die in a red bed the evening before."

"Strange that you thought of that right away! But the strangest thing is that I woke up when the Duke freed me, I actually woke up and saw that lady slowly walking out the door with the duvet under her arm. Since that night I have always had the same dream, her pressure became more and more constricting, the Duke came to my aid later and later, but I always saw her clearly from the room. float! And when I had the harp brought to me yesterday evening and played my dear Desdemona song , then - you always mock me! - the door opened, and that lady looked into the room and nodded to me."

She had told this half-jokingly, half seriously; she became more serious. "Isn't that right, Major," she said, "when I die, you will remember me too? The memory of such a man is precious to me." - "Princess!" cried the Major, trying in vain to control his melancholy, "put away these thoughts, which cannot possibly be beneficial to your recovery!"

The lady-in-waiting appeared at the door and signaled that the audience must be over. Sophie offered the major her hand for a kiss; he had never kissed a girl's hand with such deep feelings of pain, love and reverence. He raised his eyes to her once more and met her gaze, which rested on him full of melancholy. The lady-in-waiting approached with an official air; the major stood up; how difficult it was for him to part with cold social forms from a being who had become so dear to him in a few minutes.

"I hope," he said, "to see your Highness fully recovered at the next court."

"You hope, Major?" she answered, smiling painfully. "Farewell, I have ceased to hope ."

10.

For several days the residence was occupied with nothing but the illness of the beloved princess; sometimes she was said to be very ill, sometimes hope was given again; a fluctuation that was terrible for all who knew her well. One morning, very early, a servant brought the major a small box. A glance at this well-known container and at the servant's mourning clothes convinced him that the princess was no more. It seemed to him as if this lovely creature had died for him, for him alone . He had lost much on earth, and yet no loss had touched his soul so sensitively, so deeply, as this one. It seemed to him as if he had only one business left on earth, to pass on the legacy of the deceased to[102] to his place; he would have left this city, which had such heavy memories for him, at once, had he not been held back by the desire to see her mortal remains laid to rest. When the solemn sounds of all the bells, the mournful tones of the music and the long lines of torchbearers announced that Sophie was being led to the tomb of her ancestors, he left his house for the first time and joined the procession. He did not listen to the whispers of the people who were discussing the causes of her illness and her death; he had only one thought, only that moment when her eyes had once again rested on him, when his lips had touched her hand, stood before his mind. The insignia of her noble birth were taken from the coffin, they were slowly lowered down to the dust of her ancestors. The crowd dispersed, the attendants extinguished their torches and left the hall. The major cast one last glance at the place where she had disappeared and left.

An old man walked in front of him with uncertain, dragging steps, weeping violently. When the major was at his side, he looked around; it was the director of the opera. The old man came closer to him, looked at him for a long time, seemed to think about something, and then said: "Wouldn't you like it, Baron, that we had only dreamed, and that lovely child who was buried was still alive?"

"What are you warning me of?" cried the major, with involuntary horror; "yes, by God, it is as you dreamed; she is buried, and we are both walking side by side from her grave."

"Therefore, man should never joke with fate," said the old man with gloomy seriousness. "Is it not eleven days today since we gave Othello? She died on the eighth ."

"Coincidence, coincidence!" cried the major. "Do you wish to continue your madness now? I know only too well what she died of?

A dagger may have pierced her soul like Desdemona's breast; a wretch, blacker than your Othello, has broken her heart; but it is still superstition, madness, to reconcile this death with your opera!"

"Our quarrel will not bring her back to life," said the old man with tears. "Believe what you will, my dear sir![103] I will note it in my opera chronicle as I know it. It had to happen this way!«

"No!" replied the major, almost angrily, "no, it did not have to be like this; a word from me might have saved her. For God's sake, don't bring your Othello into the picture; it's a coincidence, old man; I want it, it's a coincidence!"

"There is no such thing as chance, if you please; there is only fate. But I have the honour to commend myself, for this is my dwelling. Believe what you will, however," added the old man, pressing the Major's cold hand in his own, "the fact is that she died— eight days after Othello ."

THE BEGGAR WOMAN FROM THE PONT DES ARTS.

1.

Anyone who in 1824 occasionally visited the King of England's Inn in Stuttgart in the evenings or strolled along the broad path in the grounds between two and three in the afternoons must, if his memory is not too short, still remember a few figures who attracted everyone's attention at the time. They were two men who did not fit in at all with the usual Stuttgart drinkers or people strolling through the grounds but seemed to belong more in the Prado in Madrid or in a café in Lisbon or Seville. Imagine an elderly, tall, gaunt man with blackish-grey hair, deep, burning eyes of a dark brown colour, with a boldly curved nose and a fine, pressed mouth. He walks slowly, proudly and upright. With his black silk trousers and stockings, with the large roses on his shoes and the broad buckles on his knee belt, with the long, thin sword at his side, with the high, somewhat pointed hat with a broad brim pressed askew against his forehead, you would wish, if you have any imagination, for a short, slit doublet and a Spanish cloak instead of the black tailcoat that the old man is wearing.

And the servant who follows him with equally proud steps, does he not remind you, with his mischievous, foolish face, his strange, garish clothing, the uninhibited way in which he looks around, gaping at everything and yet admiring nothing, of those servants in Spanish comedies who are like a shadow loyal to their master, far below him in education, next to him in pride, and above him in cunning and slyness? Under his arm he carries his master's parasol and raincoat, in his hand a silver box with cigars and a match.

Who did not stop to watch these two slowly strolling along the promenade? But it was, as we know, none other than Don Pedro di San Montanjo Ligez, the majordomo of the Prince of P., who was staying in Stuttgart at the time, and Diego, his servant.

As often happens, only a small, insignificant event is needed to make a person famous and conspicuous, and this was also the case with young Fröben, who for half a year (that is probably how long he had been in Stuttgart) had entered the grounds through the castle gates every day at two o'clock sharp, walked around the lake three times and up and down the broad path five times, passed all the splendid carriages, beautiful young ladies, a crowd of directors, councillors and lieutenants and was noticed by no one, for he looked like a completely ordinary person of about twenty-eight to thirty years of age. But ever since he had come across Don Pedro one afternoon on the broad path , who had greeted him very kindly, put his arm in his and had walked up and down with him several times, talking eagerly, people had looked at him curiously, even with a certain respect, for the proud Spaniard, who otherwise spoke to no one, had treated him with striking awe.

The most beautiful young ladies now found that he did not have a bad face at all, in fact there was something interesting, extremely attractive about him, something that one does not often see in the grounds; the directors and all sorts of councillors asked: "Who could the young man be?" and only a few lieutenants could give information that he occasionally eats beefsteaks in the museum, has lived in Schlossstrasse for six months and rides a beautiful Mecklenburg horse that belongs to him. They added a lot about the excellence of this horse, how it was built, what colour it was, how old it was, how much it might cost, and so they started talking about horses in general, which was said to have been very instructive to hear.

From this time onwards, young Fröben was often seen in Don Pedro's company, and he usually went to the King of England in the evenings, where he sat with the Sennor, somewhat removed from the other guests, and talked to him. Diego, however, stood behind his master's chair and diligently served both of them with rum and cigars. No one could really understand why how the two men came together or what interest they had in each other. People guessed back and forth, made conjectures, and in the end the young man himself could have given the best answer if only someone had asked him.

2.

And was it not the beautiful gallery of the brothers Boisserée and Bertram where they first met and recognized each other? These hospitable men had allowed the young man to visit their paintings as often as he wanted; and he did so whenever he could come at midday, when the gallery was open. It might rain or snow, the weather might tempt him to take the most wonderful excursions into the area, he came; he often looked quite ill and came anyway. But one would unfairly overestimate Mr. von Fröben's artistic sense if one thought that he had studied or copied the magnificent paintings of the old Dutch artists. No, he came quietly to the door, said his greetings in silence and went into a distant room to a painting that he looked at for a long time; and just as quietly he left the gallery again. The owners were too delicate to question him about his strange fondness for the painting; but of course, they must have noticed it too, because often when he went out he could hardly hide the tears that welled up in his eyes.

The picture had no great historical or significant artistic value. It showed a lady in half Spanish, half old German costume. A friendly, blooming face with clear, loving eyes, a fine, delicate mouth and a delicate, round chin stood out very vividly from the background. Her beautiful forehead was framed by thick hair and a small hat decorated with white bushy feathers, which sat somewhat mischievously to the side. The dress, which left only her beautiful, delicate neck free, was hung with heavy gold chains and testified as much to the lady's modesty as to her high status.

"In the end, he is probably in love with the picture," they thought, "like Calaf with that of Princess Turandot, although with far less hope, for the picture is probably three hundred years old and the original is no longer among the living."

After a while, however, Fröben no longer seemed to be the only admirer of the painting. One day, the Prince of P. visited the gallery with his entourage. Don Pedro, the majordomo, had left the crowd of spectators and was looking at the paintings, wandering alone from room to room; but, as if struck by lightning, with an exclamation of astonishment, he stopped in front of the picture of the lady. When the Prince left the gallery, they searched for the majordomo for a long time in vain. At last, they found him, with his arms crossed, his fiery eyes half closed, his mouth pressed shut, in deep contemplation in front of the painting.

He was reminded that the prince was already descending the stairs, but the old man seemed to have only one mind at that moment. He asked how this picture had come there. He was told that it had been made by a famous master several hundred years ago and had come into the hands of the present owners by chance.

"Oh, God, no!" he answered, "the picture is new, not a hundred years old; where did you get it from, say you, where did you get it from? Oh, I beseech you, where can I find it?"

The man was old and looked too venerable for this outburst of feeling to be considered ridiculous; but when he heard the same assertion again, that the picture was old and probably painted by Lucas Cranach himself, he shook his head in concern.

"Gentlemen," he said, placing his hand on his heart in reassurance, "Gentlemen, Don Pedro di San Montanjo Ligez considers you to be honorable people. You are not a salesman of paintings, and you do not want to sell me this picture as old; I am allowed to see these pictures through your kindness, and you enjoy the respect of this province. But I must be mistaken, or I know the lady who represents that picture."

With these words he walked out of the room, greeting everyone respectfully.

"Truly," said one of the gallery's owners, "if we did not know exactly who painted this picture, when and how it came into our possession, and how many years it had previously hung in K., we would be tempted to be confused about this lady. Doesn't even the young Fröben seem to have some memory of this picture almost daily?[108] to do, and this old Don, didn't a youthful fire flash in his eyes when he confessed that he knew the lady who is painted here?

Strange how often the imagination plays along with perfectly reasonable people; and I would be wrong if the Spaniard had been here for the last time."

3.

And it happened; the gallery had hardly been opened the following morning when Don Pedro di San Montanjo Ligez entered with a firm, dignified step and walked past the long row of pictures to the room where the lady with the plumed hat was standing. It annoyed him that the place in front of the picture was already taken, that he could not examine it alone and feature by feature, as he would have liked to do. A young man stood in front of it, looked at it for a long time, went to a window, looked out at the flight of the clouds and then went back to the picture. The old gentleman was a little annoyed; but he had to be patient.

He set to work on other pictures but filled with thoughts of the lady, he kept turning his head to see if the young man had not yet left, but he stood like a wall, he seemed lost in contemplation. The Spaniard coughed to wake him from his long dreams, the latter continued to dream; he scratched something lightly on the floor with his foot, the young man looked around, but his beautiful eye passed fleetingly by the old gentleman and then rested once more on the picture.

"San Pedro! San Jago di Compostella!" muttered the old man, "what a boring, silly dilettante!" He left the room and the gallery in a huff, for he felt that all enjoyment had been spoiled by annoyance and annoyance. He would have preferred to have waited! The next day the gallery was closed, and so he had to wait forty-eight long hours before he could go to the painting that interested him so much. Before the bells of the collegiate church had struck exactly twelve o'clock, he climbed the stairs with respectable haste, into the gallery, towards the well-known room, and hit it! He was the first, was alone, could look at it in solitude.

He looked at the lady for a long time with unblinking eyes, his eyes gradually filled with tears, he hand over his grey eyelashes. "Oh Laura!" he whispered softly. Then a sigh sounded quite audibly in his ears, he turned around in alarm, the young man from the day before yesterday was standing there again, looking at the picture. Annoyed at being interrupted, he nodded a fleeting compliment, the young man thanked him a little kindlier but no less proudly than the Spaniard. This time too, the latter wanted to wait for his superfluous neighbour, but in vain, he saw to his horror how the latter even took a chair and sat down a few steps in front of the painting in order to look at it with due leisure and comfort.

"The fool," murmured Don Pedro, "I think he wants to mock my grey hair." He left the room even more dejected than the day before.

In the anteroom he came across one of the owners of the gallery; he thanked him warmly for the pleasure the collection had given him but could not refrain from complaining a little about the young troublemaker. "Mr. B.," he said, "you may have noticed that one of your pictures in particular attracted me; it interests me infinitely, it has a meaning for me that - which I cannot express to you. I came as often as you allowed me to see the picture, and was very happy to see it undisturbed, because the crowd does not usually linger there for long and just imagine, a young, wicked man has overheard me, and comes as often as I come, and stays, in spite of me, he stays for hours in front of this picture, which does not concern him at all!"

Mr. B. smiled, for he could well imagine who might have disturbed the old gentleman. "I would not say the latter," he replied, "the picture also seems to have affected the young man, for it is not the first time that he has looked at it for so long."

"Why? Who is the man?"

"It is a Mr. von Fröben," he continued, "who has been staying here for five or six months, and since he first saw that picture, that very lady with the plumed hat, which you are also visiting, he has come every day regularly at this hour to look at the picture. So, you can at least see that he must be interested in the picture, since he has been visiting it for so long."

"Sir! Six months?" cried the old man. "No, I have done him a great injustice in my heart, may God forgive me! I even believe I treated him rudely in my anger. And is he a gentleman, you say? No, one cannot say of Pedro di Ligez that he treated a stranger rudely. Please tell him but don't do that, I will meet him again and speak to him."

4.

When he returned the next day and found Fröben standing in front of the painting, he also approached with a very friendly face; but when the young man respectfully moved aside to give the old man a better place, the old man bowed politely and said: "If I am not mistaken, Sennor, I have seen you lingering in front of this painting several times. You are probably in the same situation as me; I also find this painting very interesting, and I can never get enough of looking at it."

Fröben was surprised by this address; he too had noticed the old man's visits to the painting, he had found out who he was, and after the stiff, cold greeting of yesterday he was not expecting this friendly address. "I confess, sir!" he replied after some hesitation, "this painting attracts me more than any other because - because - there is something in this painting that is important to me." The old man looked at him questioningly, as if this answer was not entirely sufficient for him, and Fröben continued more composedly: "It is wonderful with works of art, especially paintings. Thousands of people often walk past a painting, find the drawing right, applaud the coloring, but it does not speak to them in any deeper way, whereas a single person discovers a deeper meaning in such a painting; he remains captivated, can hardly tear himself away from the sight, he returns again and again to look at it anew."

"You may be right," said the old man thoughtfully, looking at the picture, "but—I think this could only be said of larger compositions, of pictures in which the painter has put a deeper idea. Many pass before the meaning finally dawns on one who then admires the artist's deep sense. But can one say this of such minds?"

The young man blushed. "And why not?" he asked, smiling. "The beautiful forms of this face, the noble forehead, this thoughtful eye, this lovely mouth, has the artist not created them with deep spirit, is there not something so attractive in these features that -"

"Oh, please, please," interrupted the old man, kindly dismissing him; "she was indeed a very pretty woman who sat with the artist; the family has beautiful women."

"What? Which family?" cried the young man in astonishment; he doubted the old man's common sense, and yet his words seemed to excite him to the highest degree. "This picture is pure fantasy, sir; it is at least several hundred years old!"

"So, you believe the fairy tale too?" whispered the old man. "Between you and me, this time the owner's insight was deceived. I know the lady."

"For God's sake, do you know her? Where is she now, what is her name?" said Fröben, deeply moved, as he took the Spaniard's hand.

"I would rather say I knew her," he answered in a trembling voice, raising his moist eyes to the lady. "Yes, I knew her, in Valencia twenty years ago; a long time! It is none other than Donna Laura Tortosi."

"Twenty years!" repeated the young man sadly and dejectedly. "Twenty years, no, it is not her!"

"It is not her?" said Don Pedro, heatedly. "No, you say? So, you can believe that a painter has drawn these features from his own mind? But I will not be unfair; it was certainly a capable man who painted them, for his colours are true and faithful, true and fresh as the blooming of life. But do you think that such an artist does not create a very different picture from his imagination? Do you not think, without knowing the Tortosi family, that this lady must obviously have a family resemblance, family traits, clearly and distinctly expressed by nature, traits such as are never found in paintings of the imagination, but only in good portraits? It is a portrait, I tell you, sir, and by God no other than that of Donna Laura, as I saw her twenty years ago in lovely Valencia."

My dear Sir, Fröben replied, there are similarities, deceptive similarities; one often believes a To see him speaking to a friend, only in a strange, outdated costume, and if you ask, is it his ancestor from the Thirty Years' War or even a stranger. I also admit that this picture bears so-called family features, that it resembles the lovely Donna Laura, but this picture, this one is old and at least we know this much from registers and church books, that it has hung in the Magdalene Church in K. for a hundred and fifty years, that it came to the church by chance donation, not by order, and that by all indications was painted by the German painter Lukas Cranach."

"Then may the living Satan take my eyes!" cried Don Pedro angrily, jumping up and taking his hat. "It is a deception from hell, who wants to plunge me into melancholy and grief once more in my old age through this picture." Tears stood in the old man's eyes as he left the gallery with hasty, thundering steps.

5.

But even so, this was not the last time he would be there. Fröben and he often saw each other in front of the picture, and the old man grew fonder of the young man through his modest but firm judgment, through his amiable openness, through his whole being, which revealed a fine upbringing, excellent knowledge and a tact that was rare for his age. The old man was a stranger in this city, he felt lonely, but he was not so dead to the world that he did not want to speak to someone now and again. So it happened that he inadvertently became closer to the young Fröben; the latter also attracted him so indescribably because he shared a dear feeling with him, namely the love for that picture.

So, it came about that he gladly accompanied the young man on his walks, and that he often invited him to keep him company in the evenings. One evening, when the dining room at the King of England was unusually full and strangers were sitting around the two of them, so that they felt prevented from having a private conversation, Don Pedro said to his young friend: "Sennor, unless you have promised a lady this evening to appear before her gate with your lute, or unless some other promise prevents you from doing so, I would like to I invite you to open a bottle of genuine Ximenes with me in my chamber.

"You honor me immensely," answered Fröben, "I am not bound by any promise, for I know no lady here, and it is not the custom here to play the lute in the street in the evening or to talk to one's lover at the window. I will be happy to accompany you."

"Very well, then wait here for a minute until I have arranged things with Diego; I will send for you."

The old man had made this invitation with a kind of solemnity that struck Fröben as odd. Only now did he remember that he had never been to Don Pedro's room before, for they had always met in the common dining room of the inn. But from everything he thought he had to conclude that the Spaniard wanted to show him a special courtesy by introducing him to him. After a quarter of an hour Diego appeared with two silver candelabras, bowed respectfully to the young man and invited him to follow him. Fröben followed him and noticed as he walked through the room that all the drinkers were looking at him curiously and putting their heads together. On the first floor Diego opened a double door and beckoned the guest to come in. The guest stopped on the threshold in surprise. His old friend had taken off his tailcoat, put on a black, slit doublet with red puffs and a long sword with a gold handle; a dark red mantillo fell over his shoulders. He strode solemnly towards his guest and stretched out his thin hand from his rich cuffs to greet him. "Welcome, Don Fröbenio," he said, "don't be offended by this unpretentious room; when you travel, as you know, not everything is as it is at home. It is certainly softer in my hall in Lisbon, and my divans are genuine Moorish work; but always sit down with me on this narrow thing called a sofa, for Mr. Schwaderer's wine is genuine and good; sit down!"

With these words he led the young man to a sofa; the table in front of it was covered with jam and wine; Diego poured the drinks and brought matches and cigars.

For a long time, Don Pedro began, I have long wanted to speak to you in a truly confidential manner, Don Fröbenio, if you do not underestimate my confidence. Look, when we often met at midday in front of Laura's portrait, I looked at you attentively when you were so deeply absorbed in contemplation and forgive me if my old eyes committed a theft upon your eyes - I noticed that the subject of this painting must have an even greater interest for you and a deeper meaning than you have previously admitted to me."

Fröben blushed; the old man looked at him so sharply and penetratingly, as if he wanted to read the innermost depths of his soul.

"It is true," he answered, "this picture has a deep meaning for me, and you are right in thinking that it is not the *work of art* that interests me, but the *subject* of the painting. Ah, it reminds me of the strangest but happiest moment of my life! You will smile when I tell you that I once saw a girl who bore a deceptive resemblance to this picture; I saw her only once and never again, and therefore it is my happiness to at least see her lovely features again in this painting."

"Oh God! That's my case too !" cried Don Pedro.

"But you will laugh," continued Fröben, "when I confess that I can only speak of a part of this lady's face. I do not know whether she is blonde or brown, whether her forehead is high or low, whether her eyes are blue or dark, I do not know! But this delicate nose, this lovely mouth, these tender cheeks, this soft chin, I find in the beloved picture, just as I saw it in life!"

"Strange! And these forms, which are less impressed on the memory than the eyes, forehead, and hair, should, after you have only once seen them, remain so vividly in your soul?"

"Oh, Don Pedro!" said the youth, moved, "a mouth that one has *once* kissed, one does not easily forget *such a mouth. But I will tell you how it went for me.*"

"Stop, not a word!" interrupted the Spaniard. "You would think me very badly brought up if I tried to extract a gentleman's secret without first giving him mine as a pledge. I will tell you about the lady I recognized in that strange picture, and if, If you then consider me worthy of your trust, you may repay me with your story. But you are not drinking; it is real Spanish wine, and you must drink it if you want to visit Valencia with me."

They drank the inspiring Ximenes, and the old man began.

6.

"Sennor, I was born in Granada. My father commanded a regiment, and he and my mother came from the oldest families in that kingdom. I was educated in Christianity and all the sciences that a nobleman should learn, and when I was twenty years old and well-built, my father appointed me a soldier. But he was a man of strictness and ruthlessness in his service, and because he knew my mother's tenderness for me and feared that she would often prevent him from doing my duty properly, he decided to send me to another regiment, and he chose Pampeluna, where my uncle was commander. There I learned the service carefully and precisely, and in the next ten years I rose to the rank of captain. When I was thirty, my uncle was transferred to Valencia. He had influence and managed to get me to follow him as adjutant after only six months. But when I arrived in Valencia, much had changed in my uncle's household. He had long since become a widower, while still in Pampeluna. In Valencia he had met a rich widow and had married her a few weeks before I arrived. You can imagine how surprised I was when he introduced me to an elderly lady and called her his wife; but my surprise increased and grew in joy when he also brought a girl, beautiful as day, and called her his daughter Laura, my cousin. I had not loved until that day, and my comrades had often called me Pedro el Pedro (the stone Pedro), but this stone melted like wax before the fiery glances of Laura.

You have seen her, Don Fröbenio, that picture shows her heavenly features, if it is possible for an earthly artist to achieve the wonderful works of nature. Oh, she wore her hair just like that, she wore the little hat with the flowing feathers just as boldly as in that painting, and when she opened her dark eyes from beneath her long lashes, it was as if the gates of heaven were opening, and a shining angel was greeting her kindly.

My love, Sennor, was a joyful one; I could be with her every day; those barriers which in my country usually separate lovers and make love painful, anxious, sorrowful and sly, those barriers did not separate us. And when I looked into the future, how smiling it seemed to me! My uncle loved me like his son; if I understood his hints correctly, he did not think it unpleasant if I wooed his daughter; and I could expect no obstacle from my father, for Laura came from noble blood and her mother's wealth was well known. You can already see how powerful my love was from the fact that I loved where everything was so completely without need and misery. For love usually arises from the pleasant observation that one may not have displeased the beloved; just as fire creeps along under the roofs and, stopped by a wall, suddenly bursts down consumingly into the house and crackles up into the sky, so love. The small affection grows. The seemingly insurmountable obstacles spur you on; you believe you can feel a fire that can only cool down in the arms of your beloved. You speak to the lady at the gate, you send her letters through the maid, you paint her picture in your dreams and while awake, her figure so charming, because until now you had never seen her in anything but a veil and the concealing mantilla. Finally, whether by cunning or force, the barriers fall. You fly over, lead the woman you have won to the church and then take a closer look at the treasure. Just as on the beautiful meadow, which is only a carpet, covered over a swampy moorland, when you step out as if on firm ground, your feet sink in and springs trickle from the depths, so it is here. Every moment a new mood appears in the lady, every day she lifts the veil and mantilla of her heart more freely, and in the end you would rather stand at the gate again, singing love's laments, never to return."

7.

"By God, you are a sharp critic," replied Fröben, blushing. "There is some truth in what you say, but quite like that? No, that divine spark that ignites the heart, that blessed moment when half a minute is enough for understanding, would have to lie, and yet I believe in its heavenly origin. Oh, have I fared better?"

"I understand what you mean," said Don Pedro, "that moment is heavenly beautiful, but it is often based on bitter deception. Listen further. I was tempted and held back by no limits, and yet I loved as warmly as any young gentleman in Spain. The only obstacle could be Laura's heart, and her eyes had often confessed to me that they gladly met mine. All those little tokens of my tenderness, such as one gives in this state, were kindly received by Donna Laura, and after a quarter of a year she allowed me to confess my love to her. My parents had long since noticed the matter; my uncle gave me his consent and said that he had applied for a major's commission from the king for me because of the good services I had rendered. With the news of my departure, I was to confess my love to my father and ask his consent. I promised to do so; alas, why did I do it! Shouldn't we always believe that there is a demon behind us who gives us happiness like a beautiful toy, only to suddenly smash it?

Soon after I had become certain of my happiness, I made the acquaintance of a captain from a Swiss regiment, whom I grew fond of and took to my house every day. He was a handsome, fair-haired youth with clear blue eyes, white skin and rosy cheeks. He would have looked too soft for a soldier if the famous feats of arms he had performed had not been on everyone's lips. He was all the more dangerous for women. His whole appearance was so new in this country, where the sun darkens faces, where black eyes flash beneath black hair; and when he spoke of the icebergs and the eternal snow of his homeland, people listened to his talk with pleasure, and many a lady may have already tried to melt the ice of his heart.

One morning a friend came to me who knew about my love for Laura and, in all sorts of mysterious words, suggested that I should either be on my guard or marry my cousin without a major's commission, as otherwise many things could happen that would not be pleasant for me. I was embarrassed, inquired further and learned that Donna Laura occasionally met a man at a married friend's house who sneaked into the house covered in a coat. I dismissed the friend and thanked him. I did not believe any of it, but a thorn of jealousy and mistrust remained in me. I thought about Laura's behavior towards me, and I found it unchanged; she was as sweet and kind to me as before, let me kiss her hand and her beautiful mouth - but that was it; for only now did I notice how cold she always was when I embraced her; she did not squeeze my hand when I squeezed it, she did not give me a kiss in return.

Doubts tormented me; my friend returned, stoking the fire more powerfully with more definite news, and I resolved to watch my lady's steps more carefully. We usually dined together, my uncle, my aunt, my beautiful cousin, and I. On the evening of the day when my friend had warned me for the second time, my aunt asked her daughter at table whether she would keep her company on the balcony.

She replied that she had promised to visit her friend. I must have looked at her more closely, involuntarily, for she cast her eyes down and blushed. She went to the lady an hour before nightfall. When it was dark, I crept up to the house and kept watch; I was overcome with jealousy when I saw a cloaked figure creeping up the street, pressed close to the houses. I stood in front of the door, the figure came closer, and I wanted to gently push me aside; but I grabbed her by the garment and said: 'Sennor, whoever you are, at this moment I believe I have a man of honor before me and on your honor I demand that you answer me!'

At the first sound of my voice, I saw him start; he thought for a moment and then replied: 'What is it?'

'Swear to me on your honour,' I continued, 'that you are not going to this house on account of Donna Laura di Tortosi.

'Who dares to ask me to account for my actions?' he cried in a dull, disguised voice. From his accent I could tell that he must be a stranger; a dark premonition arose in my soul. 'Captain di San Montanjo dares to do it,' I answered and, before he knew it, tore the cloak from his face - it was my friend Tannensee, the Swiss.

He stood there like a criminal, unable to utter a word. But I had drawn my sword, and, speechless with rage, I motioned for him to do the same. "I have no weapons with me except a dagger," he replied. I was ready to run my sword into his body without hesitation; but as he stood before me so motionless, prepared for anything, I could not do the terrible thing. I kept enough composure to order him to give me an account the next morning at the city gate. I held the door; he agreed and left.

I kept watch for a long time until the sedan chair was finally brought for Laura, until I saw her get in; then I slowly followed her home. The torments of jealousy prevented me from sleeping on my bed, and so at midnight I heard footsteps approaching my door. There was a knock; surprised, I threw on my coat and opened the door; it was Laura's old servant, who gave me a letter and hurried away again.

Sennor! May God protect you from a similar letter! She confessed to me that she had loved the Swiss for a long time, even before she knew me; that she had always held him back from courting her out of fear of the anger of her mother, who hated all strangers; that she had accepted my proposals, compelled by my aunt's threats. She took all the blame on herself; she swore with the most solemn oaths that Tannensee had often wanted to confess everything to me and had only been held back by her pleading and her fear of being more strictly guarded afterwards. She hinted to me a terrible secret that would tarnish the honor of the family if I did not help her and the captain to escape. She implored me to give up my quarrel, because if he fell, she, his wife , would have no choice but to take her own life. She concluded by appealing to my magnanimity, saying that it would always respect me but never love me .

You will admit that such a letter, like cold water, can extinguish all the flames of love; it even partially extinguished my anger. But I could not forgive my honour for having been deceived, so I presented myself at the appointed hour on the field of battle. The captain must have felt deeply how much he had offended me; although he was a better fencer than I, he was only defending himself, and it is not his fault that I ran my hand between thumb and forefinger into his sword, so that I was unable to continue fighting. I gave him Laura's letter while I was being bandaged. He read it, he implored me to forgive him, I did so with a heavy heart.

The story of my love is over, Don Fröbenio, because five days later Donna Laura disappeared with the Swiss man."

“And with your help?” asked Fröben.

"I helped as best I could. Of course, my aunt's pain was great; but under the circumstances it was better that she never saw her daughter again than that dishonor came upon the house."

"Noble man! How infinitely much this must have cost you! Truly, it was a hard trial."

"That was it," answered the old man with a gloomy smile. "At first I thought that this wound would never heal; time does a lot, my friend! I never saw them again, never heard of them; only once did the newspapers mention Colonel Tannensee as a brave man who had offered long resistance to the enemy in Napoleon's troops at the Battle of Brienne. Whether he is the same man, whether Laura is still alive, I cannot say.

But when I came to this city, visited that gallery, and saw my Laura again after twenty long years, just as she was in the days of her youth, the old wounds opened up again and now you know that I visit her every day."

8.

With the elaborate gravity that befitted the steward of a prince of old Castilian descent, Don Pedro di San Montanjo had told Ligez his story. When he had finished, he drank a few Xeres, lifted his hat, stroked his forehead and chin, and said to the young man at his side: What I have learned in a few I have told you in detail, Don Fröbenio, about my trust in other people, not to entice you to return the same trust, although your secret rested as securely in my breast as the dust of the kings of Spain in the Escorial! - Although I am curious to know to what extent that lady interests you; - but curiosity is not fitting for old age, and that is enough."

Fröben thanked the old man for his information. "I will be happy to tell you my little novel," he said with a smile. "It does not contain any lady's secrets and ends where others begin. But if you allow me, I will tell you tomorrow, because it may be too late for today."

"According to your convenience," replied the Don, pressing his hand. "I will honor your confidence." So, they parted; the Spaniard politely accompanied the young man to the threshold of his antechamber, and Diego lighted his way to the street.

According to his custom, Fröben went to the gallery the next day; he stood in front of the picture for a long time, and on that day he actually thought more about the old man than about the painted lady; but he waited for over an hour - the old man did not come. He went into the grounds at the stroke of two o'clock, walked slowly around the lake, often took out his binoculars and looked down the long promenade, but the venerable figure of his old friend did not appear; in vain he looked at the thin, black legs, at the pointed hat, in vain at Diego and the brightly colored clothes, with parasol and raincoat, he was nowhere to be seen. "Could he have fallen ill?" he asked himself, and involuntarily he went to the castle square and to the inn of the King of England to visit Don Pedro. "The whole business is gone, up and away," answered the head waiter in answer to his question, "last night the Prince received dispatches, and this morning His Highness and his entourage left for W. in six carriages; the majordomo, who was travelling in the second, left a card here for you."

Fröben eagerly grabbed this last token of friendship. It only said *Don Pedro di San Montanjo Ligez, Major Rio di SA* etc. Sullenly, Fröben was about to pocket this cold farewell when he noticed a few words written in lead on the back. He read: "Farewell, dear Don Fröbenio; you must remain indebted to me for your story; greet and kiss Donna Laura."

He smiled at the old man's commission, and yet when he stood in front of the picture again in the next few days, he was melancholier than ever, for a gap had been left in his life by Don Pedro's departure. He had so enjoyed talking to the good old man, he had lived in a closer relationship with people for the first time in a long time, and he now felt more clearly than ever that only the lonely, the hopeless are completely unhappy. If it had not been for the picture, which held him back with its peculiar magic, he would have left Stuttgart long ago, which otherwise had no charms for him. So, when one day the Boisserée family showed him the faithful copy of that dear picture, a lithographed sheet, and gave it to him as a gift, he took it as a sign of fate, said goodbye to the original, carefully packed up the copy, and left the city as quietly as he had entered it.

9.

His stay in Stuttgart had been solely for the painting he had found in that gallery. When he arrived in the capital of Württemberg he had been on a journey to the Rhine, and that is where he was now travelling. He admitted to himself that the last few months had made him almost too soft. He felt, not without shame and a slight shudder, that his melancholy, all his thoughts and aspirations had already bordered on madness. He was independent and had planned to travel this year without setting himself any fixed plan or goal and wanted to put this long interruption in his journey down to the pleasant location of the city and its magnificent surroundings. But had he really found that city so pleasant? Had he sought out people, got to know them?

Had he not rather avoided them because they disturbed his solitude, which he had grown so fond of? Had he enjoyed the magnificent surroundings? "No," he said to himself, smiling, "one would be tempted to believe in magic! I have behaved like a fool! I locked myself in my room to read. And did I really read? Wasn't her picture on every page? Did my steps go further than to her or to get out of the crowd of[123] to walk up and down in a crowd? Is it not madness to chase a shadow over such long distances, to look attentively at every girl's face to see if I can recognize the lovely mouth of my unknown lover?"

Thus, the young man scolded himself, thought he was making firm resolutions, and how often, when his horse had gone uphill more slowly, he forgot to urge it on because his soul was wandering along other paths; how often, when he opened his luggage in the evening and the roll fell into his hands, he involuntarily unfolded the picture of his beloved and forgot to lie down to rest.

But the charming mountainous regions on the Neckar, the magnificent fields of Mannheim, Worms and Mainz did not fail to make a peculiar impression on him either. They distracted him, they filled his soul with new, friendly images. And when he set out from Bingen one morning, only one image stood before his eyes, an image that he was to see today. Fröben had travelled through France and England with a fellow countryman, and his companion had gradually become a friend. When he reflected on their friendship, he had to admit to himself that similar characters did not bring them together; but it often happens that the unlike love each other more than the similar. Baron von Faldner was somewhat coarse, uneducated; even that trip, the busy life of two capitals, such as Paris and London, had only been able to smooth and soften his exterior somewhat. He was one of those people who, because they spurned selected reading, finer, deeper knowledge and the educational hand of science, through their own or others' fault, came to the conviction that they were practical people, that is, people who had everything within themselves that others struggled to learn, who had a natural understanding of agriculture, animal husbandry, economics and the like, and who now considered themselves to be born farmers, practical housekeepers, who believed that they could achieve in the most natural way what the masses seek in books. This egoism made him happy, because he did not see the weak foundations on which his knowledge rested; he would have been even happier if this self-love had stopped at business, but he carried it with him wherever he went, gave advice without taking it, considered himself, although no one really said he was, a clever person , and became Because of all this he was an unpleasant companion and at home perhaps a little tyrant, for the simple reason that he was clever and was always right.

"I wonder if he still has his saying," asked Fröben, smiling, "the inevitable: 'I told you so!' How often, when he least expected that something would happen just like that, how often did he take me by the hand and call out: 'Friend Fröben, tell me, didn't I say four weeks ago that it would happen like this? Why didn't you follow me?' And when I proved to him so clearly that he had happened to say the exact opposite, he would not be dissuaded under any circumstances and grumbled for three or four days."

Fröben hoped that experience and the beautiful nature around him would have made his friend wiser. His estate was located in one of the most charming places in the Rhine valley, near Caub, and the closer the traveler came, the more joyfully his heartbeat at all the splendor of the mountains and the majestic river, and the more often he said to himself: "No! He must have changed; in these surroundings one can only be devoted, friendly and sympathetic, and in enjoying this view one must forget, even if one is really right, which is unfortunately the rare case with him."

10.

Towards evening he arrived at the estate; he gave his horse to a servant in front of the house, asked for his master and was shown into the garden. There he recognized the figure and voice of his friend from afar. At that moment he seemed to be arguing fiercely with an old man who was busy digging under a tree. "And even if you have done it a hundred years in the old sloppiness instead of fifty, the tree must still be taken out as I said. Just be quick about it, old man; the only thing that matters is that you think about it wisely." The worker sighed and put on his cap, looked at the beautiful apple tree once more with a wistful look and then quickly, apparently in annoyance, pushed the spade into the ground to dig. But the Baron whistled a little tune, turned around, and in front of him stood a man who smiled at him kindly and held out his hand to him. He looked at him in surprise. "What is on duty?" he asked briefly and quickly.

"Don't you recognize me anymore, Faldner?" replied the stranger. "Have you completely forgotten London and Paris while you were at your tree nursery?"

"Is it possible, my Fröben?" he cried, hurrying to embrace his friend. "But, my God, how you have changed, you are so pale and thin; it is from all the sitting and working; you do not follow any advice at all, I have always told you that it is not good for you."

"Friend!" replied Fröben, who was involuntarily reminded of his thoughts on the way: "Friend, think about it a little; have you not always told me that I am not suited to being a farmer, a forester, or anything like that, and that I should pursue a legal or diplomatic career?"

"Oh, my good Fröben!" said the other, smiling ambiguously, "so you are still suffering from a short memory? Didn't I say back then -"

"Please, you are right, let us not argue!" interrupted his guest. "Let us talk about something more sensible, how have you been since we last saw each other, how are you living?"

The Baron had wine put in an arbor and told of his life and activities. His story consisted almost of nothing but complaints about bad times and the foolishness of people. He made it clear that in the few years he had been involved in farming, with his bright mind and the knowledge he had gained on his travels. But soon his neighbors had advised him against this or that without being asked, and soon he had encountered incomprehensible recalcitrance among his own workers, who thought they knew everything better than he did and, in their blindness, relied on long experience. In short, he lived, as he admitted, a life full of constant worries and troubles, full of strife and anger, and a few lawsuits over border disputes embittered the few happy hours that the management of his estate left him. "Poor friend!" thought Fröben as he told this story, "so you are still riding the same hobbyhorse, and it runs away with you like the wildest racer, without you being able to control it."

But it was also the guest's turn to tell the story, and he was able to tell his friend in a few words that he, He said that he had been assigned to embassies at several courts, that he had had a bad time everywhere, that he had taken a long vacation and was now traveling around the world again.

"You're lucky!" cried Faldner. "How I envy your circumstances; today here, tomorrow there, you know no shackles and can travel wherever you want and for as long as you want. There's something wonderful about traveling! I wish I could go out into the world so freely again!"

"Well, what's stopping you?" cried Fröben, laughing. "But not your big farm? You can give it to a tenant every day, have your horse saddled and come with me!"

"Oh, you don't understand, my dear!" replied the Baron, smiling embarrassedly. "For one thing, as far as the economy is concerned, I can't be away for a single day without everything going wrong, because I'm the soul of the whole thing. And then - I've played a stupid trick but let it go; I'm not going to be able to travel anymore."

At that moment a servant came into the arbor and reported that the lady had returned and asked where the tea should be served.

"I think upstairs in the room," he said, blushing slightly, and the servant went away.

"What, you're married?" asked Fröben in astonishment. "And I'm only finding out now! Well, I wish you luck; but tell me - I would have dreamed of heaven's idea rather than this news; and since when?"

"For six months," replied the Baron sheepishly, without looking at his guest; "but how can this surprise you so? You can imagine, with my large household, where I take care of everything myself, so -"

"Well, I think it's quite natural and proper; but when I think back to your earlier comments on marriage, I never thought you would ever like a girl."

»No, forgive me! said Faldner, I always said and even then –

Well, you always said, even then, the young man cried, smiling, and even then and always I said, that you would not find any according to your pretensions, because they were based on an ideal that I did not want and probably could not be found. But once again my heartfelt Congratulations. But as there is a lady in the house who has invited us to tea, I really cannot appear in travelling clothes; just be patient a little, I will be with you again soon. Goodbye!'

He left the arbor, and the Baron watched him with gloomy eyes. "He is not wrong," he whispered.

But at that very moment a tall female figure entered the arbor. "Who just left you?" she asked quickly and hastily. "Who said that goodbye ?"

The Baron stood up and looked at his wife in surprise; he noticed how the otherwise delicate color of her cheeks had turned a glowing red. "No! This is unbearable," he cried out vehemently; "Josephe, how often must I tell you that Hufeland strictly forbids people of your constitution from moving too quickly; how you are glowing now! You must have walked a little way again and got hot, and now, against all reason, you are going down into the garden where it is already cool. I must repeat everything to you over and over again as if it were a child; shame on you!"

"Oh, I just wanted to pick you up," said Josephe in a trembling voice. "Don't get so angry right away. I've certainly driven the whole way and I'm not at all hot. Be good."

"Your cheeks contradict me," he continued sullenly. "Do I always have to preach to you? And you haven't put on your shawl, as I told you, when you go down to the garden in the evening. Why should I throw money out the window for such things when I don't even want to use them? Oh God! I often feel like going mad. You don't do me the slightest favor; your eternal obstinacy is killing me. Oh, I often feel like -"

"Please forgive me, Franz!" she pleaded wistfully, wiping away large tears from her eyes. "I have not seen you all day and wanted to surprise you here. Oh, I was no longer thinking about the handkerchief and the evening. Forgive me, will you forgive your wife?"

"It's all right, just leave me alone, you know I don't like such scenes and especially tears! For God's sake, get rid of the fatal weakness of crying over every little thing. We have a guest, Fröben, about whom I already told you, he traveled with me. Behave sensibly, Josephe, do you hear? Don't let anything go, so that I don't I also have to take care of the household. Tea is drunk in the drawing room."

He walked silently ahead of her along the avenue to the castle. Josephe followed him gloomily; a question hovered on her lips, but as much as she would have liked to speak, she locked the question deep in her breast.

11.

When the Baron accompanied his guest to his room late at night, the latter could not refrain from wishing him luck on his choice. "Truly, Franz," he said, squeezing his hand passionately, "you have been lacking such a wife. You have always been a lucky child, but I could never have dreamed that, with your strange maxims and demands, you would bring home such a lovely, wonderful child."

"Yes, yes, I am satisfied with her," replied the Baron dryly, as he brightened his candle; "one cannot have everything. One must, of course, get used to that idea in this imperfect world."

"Man! I hope you are not ungrateful for so many beautiful things. I have seen many women, but God knows, none of such impeccable beauty as your wife. Those eyes! What a touching expression! Can't you just read lovely dreams on her beautiful forehead? And that delicate, slender figure! And I don't know whether I shouldn't admire her fine tact, her correct judgment, her cultivated mind even more."

"You are quite enchanted," smiled Faldner, "but you have always read too much and paid less attention to practical matters. I always said it - women are a strange thing," he continued with a sigh, "believe me, in business, someone who understands and is quick to get things done is often better than a so-called educated mind. Good night: be glad that you are still free and - don't choose too quickly."

Fröben looked after him angrily as he left the room. "I believe that the monster is not satisfied with his fate even now; he has chosen an angel and is creating a hell in his house with his ridiculous pretensions. The poor woman!"

He had not failed to notice how anxiously she hung on his gaze in everything she did and said, how he often gave her a grim look when, in his opinion, she had made a mistake, how he often waved his hand at her, bit his lips and groaned when he thought the guest could not see him. And with what angelic patience she bore all this! She had made a deep, wonderful impression on him. The thick blonde hair that fell around a clear forehead suggested blue eyes, red cheeks, perhaps even a little nose that, with its delicate boldness, adorns blondes more than brunettes. But none of that. Under the blonde eyelashes rested, like moonlight behind thin clouds, a brown eye that surprised not with its glow or mere liveliness, but with a certain something of pensive melancholy that Fröben loved so infinitely in beautiful women, as rarely as he found it. Her nose was close to that of the Greek, her cheeks were usually pale, with only a slight shade of red under them, and the only thing that bloomed on her face, instead of the roses of her cheeks, were her lips, at the sight of which one could not help thinking of tender, red cherries.

"And this magnificent figure," Fröben continued in his thoughts, "so delicate, so tall, and as she walks across the room, almost floating! Floating? As if I had not seen that she has a very heavy burden to bear, that these lips hide so many words of grief, that these eyes only wait for solitude to weep over her brutal husband! No, it is impossible," he continued after some thought, "she cannot have married him for love. The world that lies behind this eye is too big for Faldner's understanding, his wife's heart too tender for the brutal pressure of her domestic tyrant. I pity her!"

While he was saying these words, he had gone to a cupboard in which the servants had put his travel gear. He opened it, his first glance fell on the well-known scroll, and he blushed. "Have I not been unfaithful to you this evening?" he asked. "Has not another image crept into my heart? Yes, and do I not find myself thinking about my friend's wife that do not suit me, that in any case cannot be of any use to her?" He unrolled the picture of his beloved and stood there, shocked. Like a thought that had been slumbering in him and dreaming confusedly, awakened it, suddenly occurred to him that Mrs. von Faldner bore a wonderful resemblance to this picture. Her hair, her eyes, and her forehead were indeed completely different from those in the picture, but he thought he found a surprising similarity in her nose, mouth, and chin, and even in the position of her delicate neck. "And that voice!" he cried. "Didn't that voice sound so familiar to me right from the start? How is it to me? Could it be possible that my friend's wife was the girl I saw only once, only half-seen, and loved forever, and have sought in vain since that moment? The figure - yes, it too was tall, and when I wrapped my coat around her, when she rested on my heart, I felt a fine, slender waist. And had I not met her eyes so often this evening, which rested searchingly on me? Should she recognize me too? But - fool I am! How could Faldner, with his distrust and his strict principles about nobility and reputation, have married an unknown beggar?'

He looked down at the picture again, examining it, thinking he was certain at one moment, doubting again at the next. He accused his faithless memory. Had not this picture become so mixed up with his earlier memories that he no longer thought of the unknown woman as anything other than this picture? And now that he had come across a new, striking resemblance, was he not faced with a labyrinth of doubts? He threw the picture aside and buried his hot forehead in the pillows of his bed. He wished for a deep sleep so that he could escape these doubts, so that the true picture would emerge with victorious force in his dreams.

12.

When Fröben entered the drawing room the next morning to have breakfast, his restless friend had already ridden out to inspect a dam on the edge of his estate. The servant who gave him this news added with importance that his master would hardly be able to return before midday because he still had to inspect his new steam mill, some fields in the forest, a new garden, and much more. "And the lady?" asked the guest.

"Was in the garden an hour ago picking beans and will be here soon for breakfast."

Fröben walked around the room and reflected on the previous evening. How different all the images appear in the morning light than they did to us in the scent of the evening! He felt the same way about the confused thoughts that floated up and down in his head yesterday; he smiled at himself, at the doubts that his active imagination had awakened. "The Baron," he said to himself, "is a good man after all; he has many peculiarities, of course, and some brutality, but that is more on the outside. But anyone who spends a long time with him gets used to it and knows how to deal with it. And Josephe? How hasty people often are in their judgments! How often have I thought I could read touching grief, deep suffering, resignation in the eyes and expressions of a woman, have allowed myself to be blinded by the devil into wanting to comfort and cheer her up very gently, and in the end the whole magic was in my imagination: then, upon closer inspection, it was a perfectly ordinary woman, who, with pensive eyes in which I saw melancholy, anxiously counted the eyes on her knitted stocking, or, behind her brow clouded with grief, considered what she was going to cook for the evening.' He pursued these thoughts in order to punish himself with irony, to suppress the more tender feeling, those echoes of yesterday, which today seemed foolish and exaggerated to him. Lost in these thoughts, he had gone to the mirror and read over the visiting cards that were pinned there. Then one fell into his hand, announcing Faldner's own engagement. He read the delicately engraved words: "Baron F. von Faldner with his bride Josephe von Tannensee."

"From Tannensee?" Like a flash of lightning, this name illuminated the dark resemblance he had found between his friend's wife and his beloved image. "What? Could she perhaps be the daughter of that Laura whom my good Don Pedro once loved? What joy for him if that were so, if I could give him news of the lost one. Did he not find in that wonderful image the most deceptive resemblance to his cousin? Can not the daughter resemble the mother?"

He quickly hid the card when he heard the door close; he looked around and - Josephe floated in. Was it the dainty morning dress that hugged her delicate figure, was the light of day more favorable to her than the candlelight? She seemed infinitely more charming to him at that moment than yesterday. Her curls still fluttered artlessly around her forehead, The fresh morning had brought a delicate blush to her cheeks, she smiled so kindly in her morning greeting, and yet at that moment he had to call himself a fool, for her eyes appeared dull and tear-stained.

13.

She invited him to sit down with her for breakfast. She told him that Faldner had ridden away at daybreak and had sent her his apologies; she described the various business he was undertaking that day, and which would keep him until noon. "He has a life full of cares and troubles," she said, "but I believe that this busyness has become a necessity for him."

"And is this only the case these days?" asked Fröben. "Is there a lot going on at the estates right now?"

"Not that," she replied, "everything is going on as usual, he has been like that ever since I knew him. He is restless in his work. This spring and summer not a day has passed when he has not been busy on the estate."

"You must often feel very lonely," said the young man, "all alone in the country, with Faldner away all day."

"Lonely?" she replied in a trembling tone and leaned towards a small table at the side; and Fröben saw in the mirror how her lips twitched painfully. "Lonely? No! Memories visit the lonely and -" she added, trying to smile: "do you think that the housewife in such a large household doesn't have a lot to do and worry about? One is not lonely there, or - one mustn't be."

You mustn't be? Poor thing! thought Fröben, does your heart forbid you the dreams of memories that visit you in solitude, or does your harsh friend forbid you to be alone? There was something in the tone with which she said those words that seemed to contradict her smile.

"And yet," he continued, giving a different direction to his feelings and her words, "and yet women seem to be expressly destined by nature for silence and solitude; at least among those peoples who generally had the most splendid men, the woman is mostly confined to her women's chamber, as was the case among the Romans and Greeks, and even in our Middle Ages."

"I would not have thought that you could give such examples," replied Josephe, her eyes lingering on his features as if examining them. "Believe me, Fröben, every woman, even the humblest, can tell very quickly whether a man has spent much time in the company of women or not, even before she has learned about his circumstances. And there is indisputably something in such circles that gives one that fine tact, that delicate feeling, to always select in conversation what is suitable for women, what appeals to us most; a level of education that no man should really lack. You will dispute this all the less," she added, "as you obviously owe part of your education to my sex."

"There is some truth in that," the young man observed, "and I will admit, especially the latter, that women have had less influence on my way of thinking than on the way I express my thoughts. My circumstances have compelled me to live a lot in the big world recently, especially in ladies' circles. But it is precisely in these circles that I realize how little women, or to put it another way, how few women, fit into this great life and activity."

"And why?"

"I will say it, even at the risk of making you angry with me. It is a nice development of modern times that in larger circles people have realized that gambling is really just a school disease or a fashionable cover for intellectual poverty. They have therefore left whist, Boston, Pharo and the like to the older gentlemen and a few ladies who simply cannot make conversation. In France, of course, men between the ages of twenty and thirty play in company; but it is only the poor wretches who have modelled themselves on an English dandy or who themselves feel that they lack the wit they should have in conversation. Since people, whether the circles are large or small, have made so-called conversation, that is, seated themselves around the fireplace or, in Germany, the sofa, drinking tea and having extremely witty conversations, women have obviously lost their way."

Please, you are being too strict, how could –

"Let me finish," Fröben continued eagerly. "A lady of so-called good society receives evening visitors every week; she sends them home six times a week. In such societies, only the young people dance a few times, unless they are at large balls, which are less common. The rest of the group, men and women, talk to each other. There are now extremely educated, really intelligent men who are mute and boring in men's circles, but extremely witty and talkative in front of women, and who display a wealth of social education and general knowledge that astonishes everyone. It is not vanity that makes these men brilliant or eloquent, it is the feeling that the more interesting aspects of their knowledge are more suitable for women than for men, who are more systematic and who set higher standards for themselves."

"Well, I can imagine such men, but let's move on."

"Through such men, the conversation takes on structure, background, life; women, especially intelligent women, will not have as lively a conversation among themselves as they do when there is only one man present as a witness and arbitrator. As such men bring all kinds of witty, interesting things into play, the women are unnaturally aroused. In order to say a word, to appear intelligent and educated, they have to give everything, to open all the taps of their minds, so to speak, in order to give their generous share to the general flood of conversation in which society bathes itself. But forgive me, this fund is usually soon exhausted; imagine having to be intelligent every evening for a whole winter, what torture!"

But no, you are making it too bad, you are exaggerating –

"Certainly not; I am only saying what I have seen and experienced myself. Since such conversation has recently become fashionable, girls are brought up quite differently than before, the poor creatures! What do they not have to learn now between the ages of ten and fifteen? History, geography, botany, physics, even so-called higher arts of drawing and painting, aesthetics, the history of literature, not to mention singing, music and dancing. Men usually do not really understand these subjects until after their eighteenth or twentieth year; they learn them little by little, and therefore more thoroughly; they learn some things by himself, and therefore knows how to use them better, and if he enters these circles at twenty-three or later, he has a great deal of self-confidence, provided he has at least a little wisdom and agility. But the girl? Come on, when such an unfortunate child enters the big world at fifteen, stuffed full of the most varied knowledge and tricks, how strange everything must seem to her at first! Although she would often prefer her lonely room, she is dragged along without mercy into all the circles, has to shine, has to chat, has to dig out her knowledge, and how soon will she be finished with it! Are you smiling? Listen further. She has no time now to expand on her school knowledge; soon even higher demands will be made of her. She must be able to talk about art objects and literature as well as her elders. So, she spends the day collecting all sorts of technical terms, reading journals to form an opinion about the latest book, and every evening is actually an exam, a school test for her, where she has to put into practice what she has learned in a skillful manner. You can imagine that a man of real education, of real knowledge, is horrified by such chatter, such half-education; he will find this bad habit ridiculous at first, then dangerous; he will curse this over-education which tears women out of their quiet circle and turns them into half-men, while men become half-women by getting used to discussing and applauding everything in a woman's way; he will wish for nobler women to return to that domestic silence, that solitude where they are at home and in any case shine more splendidly than in one of those intelligent circles!'

"There is some truth in what you have said here," replied Mrs. von Faldner. "I cannot judge it completely, because I have never had the good or bad luck to live in those circles. But it seems to me that there, as everywhere, the less good only arises from exaggeration. What you say is true, that we women are assigned to a narrower circle, that domesticity which is our calling. We will have no real support; we will enter an uncertain field if we leave this circle completely. But do you want to rob us completely of the joy of an intelligent conversation with men? It is true, seven such evenings a week must lead to something unnatural, to overeducation or lead to exhaustion; but isn't there a middle way to be found here?'

I may have expressed myself too strongly, I wanted to –

"Let me finish," she said, gently pushing him back. "You said yourself that women rarely carry on a so-called intelligent conversation for a long time among themselves. I know only too well how embarrassing a so-called intelligent lady is in a female society, to whom everything that is not general, not interesting, seems frivolous. We feel cramped and in the end we would rather blush in front of a man than in front of a woman with our little knowledge. Usually, when only women or girls are together, the economy, the household, the neighborhood, perhaps news or even fashions are discussed; but should we then be completely restricted to this circle? Should what is generally interesting and educational remain completely foreign to us?"

"God! You misunderstand me, is that what I meant to say?"

"It is true," she continued more eagerly, "it is true that men have that deep, more regulated education, that orderly clarity that excludes or disregards any half-education or even the appearance of knowledge. But how gladly we women listen to a conversation between men that borders on subjects that are not so far removed from us, for example about an interesting book we have read, about pictures we have seen; we certainly learn a great deal if we are allowed to listen or even join in the conversation; our judgment, which we have made in silence, develops and becomes more correct, and every educated woman must find such a conversation pleasant. Nor do I think that men will hold it against us if," she added with a smile, "we do not want to shine ourselves, do not want to leave the modest circle that has been assigned to us."

14.

How beautiful she was at that moment; the conversation had made her cheeks flush a deeper red, her eyes were shining, and the smile with which she concluded had something so magical and winning about it that Fröben did not know whether he should admire the beauty of this woman more or her spirit and the simple, beautiful way of expressing herself.

"Certainly," he said, lost in her gaze, "certainly, we should be very unjust if we were to demands; for I would have to consider the woman very unfortunate who, with an educated mind, with a love of reading and educated conversation, did not find such echoes in her surroundings; truly, so completely confined to herself, she would have to consider herself very unfortunate."

Josephe blushed and a dark cloud passed over her beautiful brow; she sighed involuntarily and Fröben was horrified to see that a woman like the one he had just described was sitting at his side. Yes, without meaning to, she had betrayed her own grief. For could her rude husband meet those tender demands? He, who saw in his wife only his first manager, who despised as impractical every intellectual thing that seems interesting or desirable to man, could he satisfy these demands for the enjoyment of educated conversation? Was there not a risk that he was even deliberately depriving her of this?

Before Fröben had regained enough composure to give his sentence a more general twist and to divert the whole conversation from this subject, Josephe said, without letting him feel his offense: "We women in the country, of course, enjoy this pleasure less often; but we are not as alone as the stranger might perhaps think; we visit each other all the more often; just look at the mass of visitors hanging on the mirror there."

Fröben looked at it and the card fell into his mind. "Oh yes," he said, pulling it out, "I committed a little theft just now." He pulled it out and showed it. "Can you believe that until yesterday I didn't even know that my friend was married? And I only found out your name just now from this card. Your name is Tannensee?"

"Yes," she answered, smiling, "and I exchanged this obscure name for the beautiful one of Faldner."

"Unfamous? If your father was Colonel von Tannensee, then your name was certainly not unfamous."

She blushed. "Ah, my good father!" she cried. "Yes, I was told that he was considered a brave officer of the Emperor, and they buried him as a general. I did not know him; I only saw him once, when he returned from the campaign, and then never again."

“And wasn’t he a Swiss?” Fröben asked.

She looked at him in amazement. "If I'm not mistaken, my mother told me that some of his relatives live in Switzerland."

And your mother, isn't her name Laura and does she come from a Spanish family?

She turned pale and trembled at these words. "Yes, her name was Laura," she answered, "but my God, what do you know about us, how come? From a Spanish family?" she continued more composedly. "No, you are mistaken, my mother spoke German and was a German."

"What? So, your mother is dead?"

"For three years," she replied wistfully.

"Oh, don't scold me if I ask further questions; did she not have black hair, and, like you, brown eyes? Did she not resemble you very much?"

"You knew my mother," she cried anxiously, trembling more violently.

"No, but listen to a strange coincidence," replied Fröben. "I would be mistaken if I had not met an excellent relative of your mother." And then he told her about Don Pedro. He described to her how she found herself in front of the picture, he had the copy brought from his room and showed it to her; he told her how she had become better acquainted and how Don Pedro had told him his story. But he repeated the latter with great care; out of a certain delicacy he even dated those events and Laura's flight back a whole year and finally concluded by saying that if Josephe did not call her mother a German, he would definitely believe that Mother Laura and the Spaniard's Donna Laura Tortosi, the Swiss captain Tannensee and her father, the colonel, were the same people.

Josephe had become thoughtful; she laid her forehead in her hand, pondering; she seemed unable to answer him immediately when he had finished.

"Oh, do not be angry with me," said Fröben, "if I allowed myself to be carried away into giving this interpretation to the strange play of chance."

"Oh, how could I be angry with you?" she said, moved, and tears welled up in her beautiful eyes. "It is only my difficult fate that has brought this darkness back. How could I ever imagine that I would be completely happy?"

"My God, what have I done!" cried Fröben when he saw her tears streaming more violently. "It's all just a foolish assumption on my part. Your mother was a German, and your relatives and you will know all this better"

15.

"My relatives?" she said, weeping. "Ah, it is my misfortune that I have none. How happy are those who can look back on many generations, who are bound to good people by the ties of kinship; how pleasant are the words uncle, aunt; they are like a second father, a second mother, and what magic lies in the name brother! Truly, if I were capable of envying a person, I should often have envied this or that girl who had a brother; he was her closest, most natural, most sincere friend and protector."

Fröben shifted anxiously back and forth; he had, without meaning to, touched a chord in Joseph's chest that resonated painfully; he was about to be told something that he involuntarily feared. He was silent as she dried her tears and continued:

"Fate has sometimes tried me in a very strange way. I was my parents' only child, and so I was deprived of the great blessing of having siblings; we lived among strangers, and so I had no relatives. My father did not seem to live on the best terms with his family in Switzerland, for my mother often told me that they were angry with him because he had married them and not a rich young lady in Switzerland who they had tried to force on him. I also saw my father very little; he was in the army, and you know how turbulent times were under the Emperor. So, I had nothing left but my good mother; and truly, she replaced all my relatives. When she died, of course, I was very alone in the big world; for there was no one among millions to whom I could have gone and said: Now those who fed and protected me are dead, you are now my parents!"

“So, your mother’s name wasn’t Tortosi?” asked Fröben.

I called her nothing but mother, and she never spoke to me about her former circumstances; oh, when I grew up she was always so ill! My father[140] called her only Laura, and in the few papers that were found after her death and given to me, she is called Laura von Tortheim."

"Well," cried Fröben cheerfully, "that is as clear as day; Laura was your mother's name, Tortheim is nothing other than Tortosi, which the dear refugees changed, Tannensee was the name of that captain in Valencia, he is your father, Colonel Tannensee, and what's more, don't you say yourself that this picture is exactly like your mother Laura, and didn't my dear Don Pedro recognize his Donna Laura in the original? Now you are no longer lonely, at least you have an excellent cousin, Don Pedro di San Montanjo Ligez! Ah! how happy my friend will be about the famous relatives!"

"Oh God, my husband!" she cried painfully, covering her face with her handkerchief.

Fröben could not understand how she could see all this so differently from him; he saw nothing in all this except Don Pedro's joy at finding a daughter for his Laura. He was rich, unmarried, and still bore the old enthusiasm for his beautiful cousin, so Fröben also combined a beautiful inheritance from this wonderful relationship. He took Joseph's hand and pulled it away from her eyes; she was crying violently.

"Oh, you don't know Faldner very well," she said, "if you think that these assumptions will surprise him with joy! You don't know his mistrust. Everything should just go on as usual, everything should be proper and orderly, and he hates anything out of the ordinary with all his heart. I had to," she continued, not without bitterness, "see it as a blessing that the rich, respected man married me, that he was satisfied with the few documents I could give him about my family. Must I then," she cried, weeping more violently, "must I not hear every day that he has made alliances with the most respected families, that he could have married this or that rich young lady? Doesn't he tell me as often as he is angry with me that my nobility is new, that no one knows anything about my mother's family, and that even some Tannensees in Switzerland have given up their title and become merchants?"

Only now did the young man realize a terrible light "So I have come into a house of misfortune, into an unhappy marriage," he said to himself. "Ah, she did not marry him out of love, but out of necessity, because she was alone; and Faldner, as I know him, took her because she was beautiful, because he could shine with her. The unfortunate woman! And the barbarian reproaches her for her misfortune, even makes her feel what she owes him?" A mixed feeling of anger at his friend, of pity and respect for the beautiful, unfortunate woman drew him to her; he tried to inspire her with courage and confidence. "Consider all this as unsaid," he whispered; "I see it is causing you grief; what use is it to Faldner? Let us keep quiet about the foolish suspicions I had, which can lead to nothing anyway."

Josephe looked at him with surprise as she said these words; her tears were extinguished in her wide-open eyes, and Fröben thought he could read a kind of pride in her expression. "Sir," she said, and her figure seemed to straighten up, "I cannot possibly believe that you can mean what you said; in any case, you will know that Baron von Faldner's wife shares no secret with you that her husband may not know."

With these words she had roughly pushed the tea things away from her, stood up and - after a brief bow - left the astonished guest. Fröben wanted to follow her, to apologize for what he had done, to make amends for everything at once, but she had already disappeared through the door before he had even had enough composure to pull himself up from the sofa. He went down into the garden in a huff; he did not know whether he should be angry with himself or with the lady's sensitivity, which seemed to him to be excessive at that moment. But as is usually the case in such cases, his agitated blood gradually calmed down and his mind gained space to reflect on itself. And here he found many things that served as an excuse for Josepha. "She does not love him," he said to himself, "perhaps he treats her roughly, and shows himself more like a master than a husband. She softened when I spoke to her about the higher pleasures of life, I saw how frightened she was when she had betrayed herself to me, when she expressed the lack that weighed on her even in the midst of external happiness. And must she not have felt anxious that she was revealing this lack to a friend of her husband? And further, when I told her everything, everything, when I spoke with a certain certainty of her origins, when I touched, perhaps somewhat indelicately, on strings that no one else had touched in her, did she not lose her temper? And when she considered the Baron's suspicions and doubts, did she not become more and more anxious, more and more embarrassed, and I," he continued, hitting his forehead, "could I expect her to share a secret with me that she must not reveal to her closest friend, her husband? Should she not fear that if she kept it secret she would be completely in my hands? Shouldn't the whole offer seem strange and indelicate to her?" How noble, how noble did this woman's character seem to him now? Where did she get such strength, such prudence, such unusual education, such fine social manners from, given her youth, for she could only be nineteen at the most? He felt, perhaps for the first time in his life, that women had something of delicacy, cunning, strength, and self-control; in short, that they had a secret within them that no man, even a proud, powerful man, could match.

16.

Baron von Faldner had returned for lunch and Josephe had received him with her usual grace, perhaps a little more serious than usual. But he hastily tore himself out of her embrace. "Isn't it enough to drive me mad, Fröben?" he cried, paying no further attention to his wife. "I have a steam engine brought from England at horrendous expense, have it blackened at the risk of ruining everything - you know the laws about this and now, when I think I'm in the clear, when I've already calculated eighty, even a hundred percent, now it won't work!"

“Franz!” cried Josephe, turning pale.

“She’s not going?” Fröben called after her.

"It doesn't work!" repeated the unfortunate farmer. "The joints don't engage, the gears are stuck, something must have gone missing. As you know, Josephe, I paid a lot of money for it, I had a mechanic come from Mainz; I showed him the drawing. 'Nothing could be easier,' said the dog, and now that I've given him A to A, B to B, because everything is numbered and described, no devil can put it together; oh, it's enough to drive me mad!"

They sat down to the table in a bad mood. The Baron bit back his inner anger at the failed hope and the probable loss of the capital, he drank a lot of wine and indulged in bad jokes. Josephe was even paler than usual; she was quietly going about her duties as housewife, and only Fröben knew how to interpret her feelings, because she avoided looking at him. The mouthful of food swelled in his mouth; he saw the displeasure of disappointed hope in his friend's face, he saw the courage, the determination and yet again the unmistakable fear on the beautiful woman's face; it sometimes seemed to him as if misfortune had befallen this house with him. The conversation during the meal was laborious and halting, but when the dessert was served and the servants had left at Josephe's signal, she took a few labored breaths, her cheeks turned redder, and she said:

"You missed a rather strange conversation between me and your friend this morning. As you know, we have often complained about the lack of relatives on my side, but now a new light seems to have dawned on me, for he is bringing many distinguished relatives into our house."

Faldner looked at his friend in surprise and questioning; the latter was a little taken aback at first, but he had to act with caution. At that moment he felt wonderfully the superiority of a man of the world over the low, almost crude way of thinking of Baron Faldner, and with more composure, making wise use of the circumstances, he told the strange story of the picture and his acquaintance with Don Pedro.

Contrary to all expectations, the Baron became noticeably more cheerful during the story. "Oh, strange," were the only words that escaped him here and there, and when Fröben had finished, he exclaimed: "What is clearer than this? Donna Laura Tortosi and Laura von Tortheim, the Swiss Captain Tannensee and your father are the same. And you say, dear Fröben, that the majordomo is rich? Wealthy, unmarried and still harbors the old affection for his Dulcinea of Valencia? Oh, my goodness! Josephchen, there could still be a rich inheritance of piastres!"

Josephe had not expected this statement; the guest could see that she preferred to say this nasty word without witnesses but a heavy burden seemed to be released from her breast, she pressed her husband's hand, perhaps only because this time he had said less bitter things to her than usual, and she said, somewhat cheered up: "I myself think that there is a peculiar twist of fate in the strange encounter between our friend and the Spaniard; yes, I even believe that they were Spanish songs that my mother sang on the lute now and then when she was lonely. Yes, perhaps it is precisely because I was not brought up in your faith, although my father, as I am sure, was of the Reformed faith. Well, the best thing is for our friend to write to Don Pedro."

"Yes, do me a favor," said Faldner, "write to the old Don and say you haven't found his Laura, but you have evidently found her daughter; it could lead to something, you understand me; who else would he leave his money to but you, you golden child? I have always said it, and I also said it to Countess Landskron when I asked you to marry her, even if she doesn't have much, actually nothing at all, with her comes blessing into my house. And don't we have blessings? How highly did you say you value the Spaniard?"

17.

The Baron had ordered fresh bottles, and Josephe stood up at the last words and left. Fröben could not understand how unkindly his friend was treating the lovely, noble creature. He felt how ashamed she was of her husband's meanness in front of him. He felt it and therefore answered rather angrily: "What do I know? Do you think I ask the people I associate with like an Englishman. How much do you weigh?"

"Ah, I know your strange whims on this subject," laughed the Baron. "You think a poor fellow, if he has only what is called sentiment and savoir vivre , is as good as one who has two hundred thousand pounds in pension; but seriously, we must settle things with the Don, and I am counting entirely on you."

"Yes, you can count on me completely. But what was it like with Countess Landskron? You didn't even tell me how you met your wife."

"Well, that's actually a short story," replied Faldner, pouring more wine into his and his friend's glasses. "You know my practical sense, my good tact in such matters. I had a free choice among the daughters of the country; rich, well-to-do, beautiful, pretty, everything was at my disposal. But I thought: all that glitters is not gold, and I looked for a capable housewife. And so, I came by chance to the estate of Countess Landskron. Josephe was then still her companion as Fraulein von Tannensee. I liked the industrious, busy child; pouring tea, peeling apples, breaking beans, watering flowers, in short, she knew how to do everything so gracefully and nicely that I thought this one or no one would make a good housewife. I spoke to the countess about it. At first I was put off by the brief information that the Landskron was able to give me about Joseph's circumstances. She told me that she knew Joseph's mother and that she had taken the girl in after her death. She had no fortune, but the countess provided a decent endowment. Her parents' certificate of marriage and her baptism certificate were correct - well, one is usually a fool in love, and so I took her in."

And you are certainly infinitely happy with this lovely creature?

"Well, well, that's how it goes; she's not practical at all, and I have to confiscate her stupid books properly, just to get her used to the house and garden; because how can you get by in the country if the housewife sits elegantly on the sofa, reads novels and almanacs, feels, which she has a great penchant for anyway, and neither looks after the kitchen nor the garden?"

"But my God, you could keep maids for that?" remarked Fröben, who had become even more heated and angry with the wine and the conversation.

Maids? Faldner asked, laughing, and looked at him with a wide eye. Maids! There you see the theoretician again! Friend, you don't understand anything about this! Wouldn't the maids secretly sell me half the garden, the beautiful vegetables, fruit and salad? And especially in the kitchen. Where can I get enough wood and butter when everything is entrusted to the maids! No, the woman has to rule and rule, and unfortunately! I am I had a bad time with Josephen; but come, toast; the Don will make everything right!

Fröben, as much as his heart and his tenderer senses were hurt by everything he saw and heard here, dared not say anything against him. He followed the master of the house when he now stood up, endured his embrace patiently and even accepted his invitation to accompany him to the new steam mill, more so as not to see Josephine so soon after this incident than out of joy in the Baron's company. The horses were brought out, the men swung themselves onto their feet, and Fröben was about to turn the corner when he cast another glance back and saw Josephine's figure in the window; she pulled her handkerchief from her eyes, she looked after them wistfully, she greeted them with her dainty hand. "Your wife is waving to us to say goodbye," he called to Faldner; but Faldner laughed at him. "What do you think?" he said as he rode on. "Do you think I have accustomed her to being so tender and gentle that we can part with an afternoon of kisses and hugs, greetings and waving handkerchiefs? God forbid, that's how women are spoiled, and if you ever get married, for God's sake do as I did. Not a word about a trip or a ride beforehand. The horse is brought out - 'Where are you going, my dear?' she asks for the first or second time. No answer, just the gloves on. 'But are you going to leave me alone like that?' she asks further, stroking your cheeks; you confidently take the riding whip and say: 'Yes, I want to go to the farm this evening, there are this and that to do. Goodbye! And if I'm not home by nine o'clock, you don't have to wait for the soup.' She is frightened, you pay no attention; she wants to follow, you wave her back with the riding crop; she rushes to the window, hangs herself and the handkerchief out and calls adieu! and waves the white flag back and forth. Let it blow and pay no attention to it. Put the spurs into the horse's body and away; I can swear to you, that will make the women respect her. The third time, mine didn't ask any more, and thank God! The whining is over!'

During this excellent speech, the Baron had filled a pipe with the greatest composure, lit a light, and was now smoking, surveying his fields and forests, without expecting an answer from his guest; but the latter pressed his lips together, and the rude man's speech pressed even more strongly, his full heart. "Oh, you dog of a man," he said to himself, "worse than a dog, for the Lord has given you reason. You have learned how to break a horse or plant a tree in better soil, but to treat a beautiful soul, to understand a loving heart, is beyond your limits. How she looked after him, so full of sadness, for he had not said goodbye to her, so full of angelic patience, for she had already forgiven him for his harsh words, with a look so full of love! Love? Can she love him? Is not her tender mind insulted a thousand times by him? Does she not see how he shows more tenderness to his hunting dog than to her? Or how," he continued in his reverie, "shall she, because she has once become his wife, feel tenderness for the one whom she surpasses so far in spirit and yet whom she - fears? Or should it always and forever be the fate of these poor creatures that among hundreds only one can truly love that the others, equipped by nature to be a splendid vessel of tender, noble love, grow, blossom, and wither without knowing true love? But that thought would be even more bearable to me than that she could really love him! No, it cannot, it must not be!" At the last thought he had involuntarily spurred his horse with a quick movement, which pulled itself up and flew away. "Ho, ho, boy! Do you want to ride a race with me?" the Baron called after him, putting his pipe in his pocket. "I'll give you two hundred paces and still catch you." He then skillfully calculated the gap, and when he thought that Fröben had covered the set pace, he let his horse run out and, to his no small triumph, arrived at the steam mill at the same moment as his friend.

18.

The mechanic, a modest man who, however, enjoyed a general reputation for great skill, received them at the door. "Still no progress?" asked Faldner, his face darkening. "Truly, either my correspondent in London is a villain and deserves to be hanged, or you, Master Fröhlich, may know how to turn pocket watches together, but you cannot open a steam mill, as you made me believe."

The man seemed deeply offended by the Baron's words; a deep blush spread over his face and a bitter word hovered on his lips, but he suppressed it and ran his hand over his straight hair, as if he wanted to smooth out his inner discontent as well as his hair. "Your grace, Baron," he replied, "if someone shows me the plan and calculations of a machine, and the gears and screws are drawn up so precisely, I will put a machine together, even if I have never seen it before. But then I must have free rein and then I am also responsible for making sure that everything turns out right, but like this"

"Well, that I helped a little myself, you mean? Is that what is to be blamed on? You yourself say that you have never seen such a machine in your life, and I have seen one, two, three, in France and England, and I know very well that the larger wheels engage in the middle of the cylinder and the smaller ones are mounted on top -"

"But my God, if you please," replied the artist impatiently, "this steam mill of yours is of a different structure, as you can see from the drawing -"

"Drawing or no drawing, steam engines are steam engines, and one looks like the other. I've been cheated; I've been led astray from all sides, and my money has been thrown out the window!"

Meanwhile, Fröben had taken the drawings in his hand and looked through them. He found that the structure of this mill was very simple and beautiful, and if the wheels and screws indicated fit, it was very easy to open. He had studied mathematics and physics thoroughly in the past, and together with his friend he had seen and become acquainted with the most famous machines, but because he rarely spoke about them, he was suspected by Mr. von Faldner, who was extremely knowledgeable, of understanding little or nothing about mechanical engineering. When Faldner's displeasure threatened to grow even greater, he turned to the mechanic, asked about this and that part that was shown on the drawing, and when the mechanic showed them to him, when it was clear how well they fit together, he said to Faldner: "I'd bet you weren't deceived at all, because as well as F and H fit into P here - you see, these are the main features by which the stamping mill is connected to the oil press – the rest must fit together just as well.

"Ah, our Lord has sent you here," cried the mechanic joyfully, "how you got rid of it so quickly! Yes, the F is the main pulley, H here engages the rod work, here the wheel KL is attached."

"The machine is very simple," continued Fröben, "and my friend's whole error comes from the fact that he has in mind the structure of larger works, which, however, look different. You will remember, by the way, that we saw an oil mill in Devonshire at Sir Henry Smith's which was built almost entirely according to this plan."

The Baron hid his astonishment behind an ironic smile, with which he looked first at his friend and then at the mechanic. "Do what you like," he said indifferently, "I give up the whole story; it would have been more sensible if I had sent an English mechanic with me. Try your luck at the hopeless screw-work; I think that when I come to fetch you in a few hours, you will already be sick of this machine ABC; for I know that you are only an ABC-shooter." Whistling, he left the building, mounted and rode into the forest.

But Fröben immediately had what had been put together according to the Baron's arbitrary plan taken apart again. The numbers were put in order, and he gradually became more cheerful as he did this, for it dispelled the gloomy images in his soul, and not without a smile he noticed how the mechanic looked at him with shining eyes, how his journeymen and boys looked at him with awe, like an old master of their art. Joy and life had come into the workshop, where that morning one had only heard the Baron's orders, the curses, the master's requests and counter-arguments; everything was soon in order, and when the Baron returned from the forest in the evening to fetch his guest, he was astonished and at first did not even seem to be pleased about the visible progress of the work. He had expected to find everyone in dismay and confusion, but the mechanic handed him the drawing with a smile, led him to the cylinder and, pointing now to the paper, now to the work, showed him with proud joy what they had already achieved. "If it continues like this," added the mechanic, "and if; If the strange gentleman there helps us so well tomorrow, I guarantee that we will finish before Sunday."

"Great stuff!" was all the Baron replied as he returned the drawing, and Fröben was uncertain whether it was curses or thanks that his friend muttered now and then as they rode back to the castle together.

The successful progress of the machine construction, and perhaps also the bright prospect of Don Pedro's Spanish quadruples, had put the Baron in a more cheerful mood over the next few days. Fröben had written to the Spaniard in W., and his host made him promise to stay with him until he received a reply from W. He also behaved a little more humanely towards Josephe, and he had even allowed her, probably more out of consideration for his friend than for her, to cut her housework short and to have Fröben read to her or to go for walks with him in the mornings or evenings when he had business to do. And she visibly perked up in those few days. Her posture became stronger, her cheeks flushed with a shimmer of quiet pleasure, and at times, when a lovely smile played on her lips, when those fine dimples appeared in her cheeks, Fröben admitted to himself that he had rarely seen a more beautiful woman; indeed, the sight of her often confused him so much that he believed a beloved image of his dreams had come true, that half-sunken memories resurfaced in him, that even her voice, when it was moved, touched, seemed so familiar to him, as if he had not heard it here for the first time. Less often during those days did he pull out the picture that he had otherwise looked at for hours, and when it happened to fall into his hands, when he unrolled it, when he looked into the eyes of his unknown lover, he felt ashamed, he felt he had to apologize to her lifeless image for this neglect. "But," he then said to himself, as if he had to apologize, "is it wrong to make a few days of the joyless life of our poor friend more pleasant? And how little it takes to please this lovely creature, to make her happier! Reading a good book with her, talking to her, accompanying her on a walk to her favorite places - this is all she needs to be cheerful and happy. What heaven could Faldner have in his house if he only occasionally shared one or other of these little joys with her!"

The young man, without admitting it to himself, felt pleasantly touched and flattered by Joseph's devotion to him. Didn't every morning and every evening seem like a new celebration to her? When he came down to breakfast, she had already prepared everything elegantly and nicely; sometimes she chose the hall, which opened up a magnificent view of the distant Rhine, sometimes the terrace, from where they had the rural picture of the workers in the fields and vineyards before them, so close that they could see everything like a faithful tableau, and yet far enough away not to be disturbed in the quiet enjoyment of the morning, sometimes she had chosen an arbor in the garden, where the world around was closed off by thick plane trees and only the fresh morning air or the early dawn was allowed in.

So, she always appeared new and surprising, and when his friend approached, how joyfully she stood up, how sweetly she offered him her hand in greeting, how lively she knew, when he was still completely absorbed in the sight of her without saying a word, how to start a conversation, to tell this and that, to give everything she said its own character, its own charm through whim and keen observation! And then afterwards, when she quickly and busily put the breakfast utensils to one side, when he took out his book, when she sat down opposite him with the work that she seldom put aside and hung expectantly on his every word, he often felt as if he had to forget everything, the whole world, and for a small, brief, blissful moment he dreamed that he was a happy husband and was sitting here at the side of a beloved woman.

19.

In the eyes of her friend, Josepha was not a little proud that she had chosen as her favorite the very poet who also attracted him above all others. It is true that he often had to help her during readings from Jean Paul's magnificent poems in order to explain this or that obscure parable; but she quickly grasped the point; her natural tact and her delicate sense, which lived so completely in the poet, allowed her to guess many things before her friend had given her any certainty.

"There is," she said one day, "a world full of thoughts in this Hesperus! Every human feeling, joy and pain, love and grief, lies dissected before us; us there; he knows how to describe to us, as we breathe in the sweet scent of a flower, its innermost parts, its delicate petals, its finest stamens, without destroying them or stripping them of their leaves. For I believe that is the great, deep secret of this master, that he does not describe every deeper feeling, but rather hints at it, and yet again does not hint at it fleetingly, but rather lets us take a deep look into the human soul, as if through the fine microscope of a parable, where thought after thought arises and the eye, surprised but delighted by the wonderful creation, turns into a tear."

"You have," replied the host, "it seems to me that you have really expressed his secret in these words. I confess openly that there is nothing I find so repugnant in my innermost soul as the visible effort of an author to make quite clear and obvious to the reader what his hero or heroine or a third or fourth person felt or thought here or there. But our poet! How wonderful, how rich is his invention in this too; we live, we think, we weep involuntarily with Victor, and Clothilde's paler cheeks, her uncomplaining grief touch us more deeply than any description can express, and in the warm, soft happiness of the lovers we would like to be a ray of the evening sun that plays in the arbor around their embrace, that nightingale that rang in the pious celebration of their bliss with its bell-like voice."

"It is strange," observed Josephe, "that the thread of this novel, what is called its skeleton, would not seem in the least interesting to us in any other case, perhaps even contrived and boring. Six sons lost, exchanged, found again, instead of Walter Scott, for example, usually having only one , and even the author of Walladmor in his parody being content with two; a young lady who is tormented by her brother's love, but who loves his friend herself; a small, simple farm in Duodez, a parsonage full of rats and children, and a noble house where ignobles live; imagine these common things in sequence, and you have one of our common novels of lost sons, etc., and not even a real pity, to put it this way, such as La Beau's murder by the court squire, or the tragic end of the lord in the fifth act. But what a life, what a world, becomes of this story when that poet puts his flowered cloak around it! What spiritual air, higher and purer than any earthly air, comes to us from the adoring love of Victor and Clothilde for their teacher Emanuel, what melancholy cannot be found in the deceptions of a cold life, when Victor and that lovable being do not recognize each other; what bliss, finally, when their souls, under the nightly, starry sky, open up in the pain of separation and overflow with love!

"Yes," cried the young man, "our poet is a great musician! He has a well-played, old theme before him that we have long heard; but by keeping to the flow of the old song, he develops the ideas in a way that seems so surprising, so new, that we forget the theme and only listen to the turns into which he passes, in which he goes up and down the celestial ladder of tones like an angel and shows us an open, blessed heaven in our dreams, while in reality we are perhaps lying on a very hard bed like Jacob. Then he is sometimes soft like a flute, piercing like the oboe, sometimes full, touching like the French horn from afar, sometimes he roars along as if with the mightiest, deepest basses, majestic, sublime, sometimes only gently whispering like the Aeolian harp or dissolved in melancholy like the tones of the harmonica."

"How I thank him," said Josephe softly, "for reconciling us, for healing the wounds of our sadness! It would have been in his power to let Klothilde perish in the pain of unrequited love; before she died, Victor would have called out to her: 'I loved you more than anything,' and she would have fallen asleep smiling. Imagine the immense pain, the bitterness against fate, if we had seen these people perish like that, without hope, without consolation! But it would not have been possible; Victor would not have loved for so long, would have given himself to Joachime or the Princess, for a man cannot love for long without requited love!"

"Do you really believe that?" replied Fröben with a wistful smile. "Oh, how little you must know us, how little you must think of us if we did not even have the courage to love faithfully throughout this short life, even without being loved!"

"I think it is possible with women," said the beautiful woman. "Love without love in return is a great misfortune, and women are more made to endure silent suffering throughout their lives than you. A man would throw off such grief, or the burning sorrow would consume him!"

"Neither - I am still alive and in love," said Fröben, looking absentmindedly ahead.

"You love me!" cried Josephe, and in such a peculiar tone that the young man looked up in alarm; she cast down her eyes when she met his gaze, a deep blush passed over her face and just as quickly changed into a deep pallor.

"Yes," he said, struggling to say it in jest, "the case you have set is mine, and I still love, perhaps more calmly, but no less fervently than on the first day; I even love almost without hope, for the lady of my heart knows not of my love, and yet, as you see, sorrow has not yet killed me."

"And may we ask," she said trustingly, but, as it seemed to Fröben, with a trembling voice, "may we ask who the lucky one is?"

"Ah, you see, that is precisely the misfortune, I do not know who she is or where she is, and yet I love her; yes, you will think me a second Don Quixote when I confess that I have only seen her a few times, and can only remember a few parts of her face, and yet I roam about the world to find her, because I cannot rest at home."

"Strange," remarked Josephe, looking at him thoughtfully, "strange; it is true, I can imagine such a case, but nevertheless you are a rare exception, dear Fröben; do you know whether you are loved? Whether the girl is faithful to you?"

"I know nothing of all this," he replied, earnestly and with concealed grief. "I know nothing except that I would be happy if I could call that being mine, and I know only too well that I may have to do without it forever and never be completely happy!"

The less often the young man spoke of these feelings, the more powerfully all the pain of memories of sad hours and a melancholy overcame him that he felt unable to cope with. He quickly stood up and left the arbor and went towards the castle. But Josephe watched him with eyes full of infinite love, tear after tear falling from her twitching eyelashes, and only when...When they fell like a spring upon her beautiful hand, they awoke Josepha from her dreams. And ashamed, as if she had overheard herself in the act of some secret sin, she blushed and pressed her handkerchief over those treacherous eyes.

20.

The old mechanic's prediction had come true, for by the last day of the week the steam mill's machinery had been fully installed. The Baron, however disgruntled he had been at first, had, in the joy of his heart when the first attempt had been a success, sent the old man and his journeymen away with a generous gift and invited all his neighbours in the area to celebrate the inauguration of his mill on Sunday with a small party. As happy and cheerful as he was that day, as cheerful and jovial as he received his numerous guests, it did not escape Fröben's watchful eye that he was tormenting poor Josephe with a hundred different orders and instructions, so that she could not thank him for anything. Now she was to be in the kitchen to encourage the servants and help out herself, now he was improving this or that in her finery, now he would despair with impatience if she did not fly down the stairs quickly enough to meet the new arrivals with him at the entrance, now he wanted the table to be set in one way or another, now he wanted to drink coffee in the garden, now in the drawing room. She bore all these hardships with angelic patience and a resignation that was incomprehensible to her friend. She was everywhere, took care of everything and even knew how to find a moment to ask her host why he was so gloomy today, to cheer him up, to share in the general merriment.

Everyone was delighted by the beauty and the nimble attention of the housewife; the men praised the Baron for being lucky to have such a treasure in the house, and several of the older ladies openly expressed their admiration for the rare talent for housekeeping, for the insight and order of such a young woman. "Do you see," whispered the happy man to Fröben, "do you see what a breeding like mine can do wonders? I am quite happy with it all today, but if I did not secretly help out everywhere myself, what would the economic honor of the housewife be like? But it will work out, I always said it, it will work out." The general[156] Cheerfulness and wine increased Faldner's mood more and more, and it was finally high time to clear the table, for he and some gentlemen from the neighborhood were already making jokes and allusions that would offend any sensitive ear.

They drove to the new steam mill, it was officially inaugurated with jokes and laughter, and then they returned, amazed once again at the tasteful and yet so comfortable arrangements that Josephe had made in the garden. She had dared to have a large, spacious arbor built quickly, according to her own invention; all kinds of refreshments awaited the guests there, and her general praise worked a miracle: the Baron was not even annoyed that young ash and fir trees from his forest had been used for the arbor, that his own plan of putting up a tent made of boards and carpets had not been followed. He kissed his wife on the forehead and thanked her for the pleasant surprise.

They sat around in colorful rows. The men drank the old wines of the host diligently, and soon a general cheerfulness had taken hold of the company. They played witty, clever games, and when the men's mischievous moods rose even higher, they even did not shy away from games of pledge. So, it came about that when they were redeemed, Fröben also had to redeem his pledge with a penalty, and Josephe, who was in charge of determining this penalty, ordered him to tell a true story from his life. Their choice was generally applauded, the Baron clapped his hands in delight at his clever wife, and when Fröben hesitated and thought for a moment, he called out: "Now shall I tell you something from your life? Perhaps the piquant story of the girl from the Pont des Arts ?"

Fröben blushed and looked at him disapprovingly; but the company, who perhaps suspected a funny secret, called out: "The story of the girl, the story of the Pont des Arts!" and perhaps only to avoid the indiscretion of his friend, who had already been pushed somewhat beyond his usual limits by the wine, he deigned to tell it; but the Baron promised the company that as soon as the narrator deviated from the exact truth, he would give marks to the story, for he himself had been there.

21.

"I do not know," began Fröben, "whether the company is aware that several years ago I travelled with our Faldner, and in particular lived with him for some time in Paris, even sharing a house with him. We had more or less joint studies, attended the same circles, introduced our former acquaintances to each other and thus lived inseparably. We had a mutual friend, the equally amiable and learned Doctor M., a fellow countryman who lived in the Rue Taranne, which, as we know, leads to the Rue St. Dominique and lies on the left bank of the Seine. Our usual evening walk was through the Champs Élysées, over the beautiful bridge to the Champ de Mars and from there through the Faubourg St. Germain to our friend's apartment, where we often chatted until late at night about our homeland, about France, about what we had seen, about all sorts of things. We lived, to add, in the Place des Victoires, quite a distance from the Rue Taranne and usually chose the Pont des Arts for our return journey, so as to cut through the Louvre and avoid a detour through the side streets. One evening, it was perhaps after eleven o'clock - it had rained a little and the wind was very cold and biting, especially near the river - we also walked from the Quai Malaquais to the Louvre across the Pont des Arts. The Pont des Arts is only accessible to pedestrians, and so it happened that at this time there was not much life around and on the bridge. We crossed the bridge in silence, pulling our coats tighter around us; I was just about to hurry down the steps on the other side when a surprising sight stopped me.

Leaning against the bridge stood a slim, rather tall female figure. A black hat was tied low over her face and, to top it all off, a green veil; a black silk cloak fell around her body, and the wind, which clung to the garments more tightly at that moment, revealed an extraordinarily delicate, youthful waist; a small hand protruded from the cloak, holding a plate; in front of her, however, stood a small lantern, the light of which flickered restlessly, its glow falling on a dainty base.[158] Perhaps nowhere else does the deepest misery coexist with the greatest splendor and luxury as much as in that city, but nevertheless one sees relatively few beggars. They rarely push themselves up shamelessly, and one never sees them running after strangers, pursuing them with requests. Old men or blind people sit or kneel at the corners of the streets, holding their hats calmly in front of them, and leave it up to the passer-by whether he wants to heed their pleading glance.

The most horrifying, at least to my mind, were always those shamefaced beggars who stand in a corner at night with their heads covered and a burning candle in front of them, motionless, almost as if dead; many of my acquaintances in Paris had assured me that one could count on these being mostly people from higher classes who had fallen so low through misfortune that they either had to look for work, or if they were too shameful, perhaps too weak, to work for bread, they took this last resort before they, like so many unfortunates, gave up their lives to oblivion in the Seine.

The female figure on the Pont des Arts was one of this class of beggars, and the sight of her captivated me irresistibly. I looked at her more closely; her limbs seemed to be trembling with frost even more violently than the flame in the lantern, but she was silent and let her misery and the cold night wind do the talking. I searched in my pocket for a little change, but there was not a sou, not even a single franc. I turned to Faldner and asked him for some change; but, annoyed at being exposed to the biting cold because of my hesitation, he called out to me in our language: 'Then leave the beggars alone and hurry up so we can get to bed, I'm freezing!' - 'Only a few sous, my dear!' I begged; but he grabbed me by the coat and tried to pull me away.

Then the veiled woman called out in a trembling but melodious voice and, to our surprise, in good German: 'Oh, gentlemen! Have mercy!' This voice, these words and our language had something so moving for me that I asked for some more coins. He laughed: 'Well, here you have a few francs,' he said, 'try your luck with the young lady, but let me get out of the train.' He pressed the money into my hand and walked on, laughing. At that moment I was really embarrassed about what I should do; she must have heard what Faldner said and insulted her.[159] I like an unhappy person the least of all. I approached hesitantly. 'My child,' I said, 'you have chosen a bad position here, not many people will pass by here this evening.' She did not answer immediately. 'If only,' she whispered after a while, barely audibly, 'these few had a feeling for unhappiness!' This answer surprised me, it was so spontaneous and yet so apt. The girl's noble bearing, the tone in which she said those words, betrayed education. "We are fellow countrymen," I continued, "may I not ask you to tell me whether I can perhaps do more for you than is usually done in passing?" "We are very poor," she answered, somewhat more courageously, it seemed to me, "and my mother is ill and without help." Without further consideration, driven only by the vague feeling that I was very attracted to the girl, I said: "Take me to her!" She was silent; the suggestion seemed to surprise her. "Do not take this as anything other than my honest desire to help you if I can." "Then come," replied the veiled woman, picked up her lantern, extinguished it and hid it and the plate under her coat."

22.

"What?" cried the Baron, laughing loudly, when Fröben was silent, "you don't want to tell him anymore? Do you want to do it again today as you did to me back then? That is, up to this point, gentlemen and ladies, he has told the story entirely according to the pure historical truth. He may have thought I was far away, and I was standing under the portal of the palace, not ten steps from the edifying Samaritan scene, watching him; I don't know whether the dialogue really took place like that, because the shameful wind blew the words away, but I saw the lady extinguish her lamp and walk back over the bridge with him. The night was too cold for me to follow him on his gallant adventure, but at the end, I would bet that he saw neither a sick mother nor anything like that, but the lady from the Pont des Arts had just sung the old siren song in a different way."

He laughed at his own joke, and the men joined in the rude laughter, but the ladies looked down, and Josephe seemed as dissatisfied with her husband's words as with her friend's strange story, for pale[160] She held her cup in her hands like death, so that it clinked, and gave the young man a look which at that moment he could not interpret in any other way than one which was deeply humiliating. "I believe," he said, breaking off the laughter of the men with a strong voice, "that I have redeemed my pledge, but my own interest requires that I do not accept the interpretation of this incident which my friend seems to be putting forward. You will therefore allow me to continue, and on my life," he added, blushing and his eyes lighting up, "I will tell you the plain truth.

The girl turned over the bridge from whence I had come. As I walked silently, more behind than beside her, I had time to look at her. Her figure, as far as her cloak allowed her to see, her whole bearing, and especially her voice, were very youthful. Her gait was quick, but light and floating. She had refused my arm when I offered it to guide her. At the end of the bridge, she turned into the Rue Mazarin. 'Has your mother been ill for a long time?' I asked, going back to her side and trying to catch a glimpse of her features through the veil. 'For two years,' she answered with a sigh, 'but for the last week she has become very miserable.' - 'Have you often been to that place?' - 'Where?' she asked. - 'On the bridge.' - 'This evening for the first time,' she replied. – 'Then you haven't chosen a good place, other passages are more frequented.' But even as I said this, I regretted having said it, because it must have hurt her. With suppressed tears, she whispered: 'Oh, I am so unknown here and - I was ashamed to go into the crowd like that.'

How boundless must the misery have been that forced this creature to beg. I admit that I too had thoughts like those Faldner had, but they always disappeared again because they were absurd and unnatural. If she belonged to that depraved class of girls, why should she stand in a lonely place covered up? Why should she deliberately conceal a figure that, as far as the outlines showed, was certainly one of the more beautiful? No, there was certainly real misery and that tender shame in the face of involuntary poverty that makes misfortune so indescribably touching.

'Does your mother have a doctor?' I asked again after a while. 'She did; but when we could no longer buy medicine, he wanted to have her taken to the Hospital des Incurables, and - I could not bear that. Oh God, my poor mother in the hospital!' How much deep pain lay in the last words of this girl!

She was crying, she put her handkerchief under her veil to her eyes, and the lantern and plate she carried in her other hand prevented her from holding her cloak together; the wind blew it wide open, and I saw that I had not been deceived; she had a fine, slender waist, she wore a simple dress that was, as far as I could see at first glance, very clean. She grabbed at the cloak, and as I helped her to put it back on, I felt her soft, delicate hand.

We had already walked through the Rue Mazarin, Rue St. Germain, Rue Ecole de Médecine and from there through a few small side streets, when she suddenly stopped and complained that she had lost her way. I asked her in which district she lived, and she said St. Severin. I was at a loss, for I could not find the street myself. Was it fear or cold? I saw her trembling more violently. I looked around; I noticed a light still in a basement where brandy was sold; I asked her to wait, went down and asked. I was shown the way, and I thought I could find my way. As I came up, I heard loud conversation nearby; by the dim light of a lantern, I saw the girl violently resisting two men, one of whom had taken hold of her hand, the other of her coat; they were laughing, they were speaking to her; I guessed what was happening, jumped up and snatched away the hand that one of them had taken; speechless and crying, she clung tightly to my arm.

'Gentlemen,' I said, 'you see that you are mistaken here, you will immediately let go of Mademoiselle's cloak!'

'Ah, pardon me, sir!' replied the man who had taken hold of her cloak. 'I see you have senior rights to Mademoiselle!' And laughing they went on their way.

We continued walking, the poor child was shaking violently, she was still holding my arm, she was close to collapsing.

›Be brave!‹ I said to her, ›St. Severin is not far away, you will soon be home.‹ She did not answer, she was still crying. When we were in the street which, according to the description, must have been St. Severin, she stopped again. 'No, you must not go any further with me, sir!' she said. 'It must not be.' - 'But why not, since you have taken me so far; please do not suspect me of any bad intentions!' As I said these words, I had, without knowing it, taken her hand and perhaps squeezed it; she hastily withdrew it from me and said: 'Forgive me for committing the impropriety of taking you so far; please leave me now!' I felt that the scene had hurt her deeply, that it had perhaps made her distrust me, and this moved me indescribably; I took the silver Faldner had given me and wanted to hand it to her; but the thought of how little this small gift could help her drew back my hand, and I gave her the little gold I had about me.

Her hand twitched as she took it; she seemed to think it was silver, but she thanked me in a trembling, touching voice and started to go.

'One more word,' I said, stopping her. 'I hope your mother will get well, but she may still be ill with something, and you, my child, are not made for such evening walks as today. Would you not like to be at the Ecole de Médecine at the same time in a week, so that I can inquire about your mother?' She seemed undecided, and finally said, 'Yes.' - 'And put the hat with the green veil back on so that I can recognize you,' I added. She said yes, thanked me again, hurried down the street, and quickly disappeared into the night.

23.

When I woke up the morning after this incident, it seemed to me as if I had only dreamed of it all. But Faldner, who soon came over and began to screw me in his gentle manner, tore me out of my doubts. The matter, viewed so clearly in the morning light, seemed to me too fabulous for me to want to tell it to my unbelieving friend. In recent times, people have reached a level of refinement that borders on immorality; in some cases, people prefer to appear wild, somewhat dissolute and bad, they prefer to give an ambiguity. just to avoid being considered a fool, an oddball, a person of weak intellect and limited views on life.

But what hurt me more than Faldner's fiddling was a restlessness, something I didn't know how to interpret. I reproached myself for not even having seen her face. 'Why,' I said to myself, 'why this excessive discretion? If I give away a couple of Napoleons, can I ask for the favor of lifting the veil a little?' And yet, when I recalled the girl's entire behavior, which, simple as it was, had not the slightest touch of meanness, when I considered how I was attracted by her noble bearing and the sophisticated tone of her answers, I had to justify myself, half to my annoyance. There is something in the human voice that tells us, before we know the features and eyes, before we know the status of the speaker, the tone in which we must speak to him. How infinitely, not so much in the form as in the sound of language, the educated differ from the uneducated, and the girl's tones were so soft and tender, her short answers often spoken from the depths of her soul. I could not get rid of these thoughts all day long, even in the evening, when the poor girl with the black hat, the green veil and the inconspicuous coat accompanied me to a brilliant company of ladies.

In the next few days, I was angry at my foolishness, which meant that I could only see the girl again after eight days. I counted the hours until the next Friday, and it was as if that capital of the world, as its inhabitants call it, had nothing more charming about it than the beggar woman from the Pont des Arts. Finally, finally Friday arrived. I used every possible trick to get away from Faldner and the rest of my friends that evening, and when it got dark I set off on my way. I had more than an hour to walk, and enough time to think about my course. 'Today,' I said to myself, 'today you will come to terms with what you think of this person; you will offer to go with her; if she accepts, you will have already deceived yourself for the first time. She must also show her face today.'

I had left so quickly that it was not even ten o'clock when I arrived at the Place de l'Ecole de Médecine arrived, and - I had only set it at eleven o'clock. I went into a café, thoughtlessly leafed through a bunch of newspapers -; finally, it struck eleven o'clock.

There were few people in the square, and as far as I could see, no green veil was to be seen. I always stayed on the side of the medical school, because there were several lanterns burning there. The moments of such expectation are painful. 'What if she had enough of your gold and didn't come at all? What if she laughed at your kindness?' I thought, after I had already walked up and down the square ten times. It struck half past eleven, and I was already beginning to grumble about my own folly, when something green waved in the light of a lantern about thirty paces away from me; my heartbeat faster, I hurried over - it was her. 'Good evening,' I said, offering her my hand, 'it's good that you've kept your word after all; I was beginning to think you wouldn't come.' She bowed without taking my hand and walked by my side; she seemed very moved: 'Sir, my noble countryman,' she said in an emotional voice, 'I must keep my word to thank you. I certainly do not come today to take advantage of your kindness again. Oh, how richly, how generously you have given us gifts! Can the heartfelt thanks of a daughter, can the prayers and blessings of my sick mother compensate you?'

"Let's not talk about it," I replied. "How is your mother?" "I think I can be hopeful again," she replied. "The doctor hasn't said anything definite, but she herself feels stronger. Oh, how I thank you! With your gift I was able to prepare her some hearty food again, and believe me, the thought that there are still such good people has strengthened her almost as much."

'What did your mother say when you got home?' - 'She was very worried about me because it was already so late,' she replied, 'ah, she had so reluctantly given me permission to go on this journey and was now imagining some misfortune that had befallen me. I told her everything, but when I opened my handkerchief and took out the gifts I had collected and there was gold among them, gold among the copper and silver pieces, she was astonished and -' She stopped and seemed unable to speak any further; I thought to myself that my mother had accused her of something bad and continued to inquire, but with touching frankness. she confessed: her mother had said that the generous countryman must have been either an angel or a prince.

'Neither one nor the other,' I told her. 'But how far did you go? Do you still have money?'

"Oh, we still have some," she replied, courageously as it seemed, but I could not help noticing that she perhaps sighed involuntarily.

'And what else do you have?' I said more firmly and urgently.

'We paid a bill at the pharmacy with it and a month's rent, and I cooked for my mother with it, but there was still some left over.'

'How poorly must you have lived if you could pay a chemist's bill, a month's rent and cook for eight days with this money? But I want to know exactly,' I continued, 'what and how much you still have.'

'Sir!' she said, taking an insulted step back.

'My dear child, you do not understand,' I replied, coming closer to her; 'or you do not want to admit it to yourself out of excessive delicacy; I ask you seriously: if you are short of a few francs, can you expect help?'

'No!' she said shyly and softly; 'none!'

'Think of your mother and do not despise my help!' As I said these words I offered her my hand; she took it hastily, pressed it to her heart and praised my goodness.

'Well then, come on,' I continued, putting her arm in mine. 'Unfortunately, I had not just come from home when I came here and had not expected it. So please be so kind as to accompany me a few streets to my house, so that I can give you something for your mother.'

She let herself be led on in silence, and although the thought of being able to support her further was pleasant to me, I was almost offended when she went with me without any resistance, into a man's house at night; but how different it turned out to be from what I had imagined. We had probably gone about two or three hundred paces when she stopped and took her arm away from me. 'No, it cannot, it must not be,' she cried, bursting into tears. 'What is troubling you all of a sudden?' I asked in surprise, 'what must not be?'

'No, I'm not going, I'm not allowed to go with you.'

'But my God,' I replied, acting somewhat annoyed, 'you really have very little confidence in me; if it weren't for your mother, I would certainly leave you now, for you offend me.'

She took my hand and pressed it with emotion. 'Have I insulted you?' she cried. 'Oh, God knows, I did not mean to; forgive a poor inexperienced girl; you are so generous, and should I insult you?'

'Well then, come,' I said, drawing her on, 'there is no time to lose, it is late, and the way is long.' But she stopped, weeping, and whispered, 'No, I will not go any further at any price.'

'But who are you afraid of? No one knows you; no soul sees you; you can safely come with me.'

'I beg you, for God's sake, let me go! No, no, it must not be, do not press me any further!' She trembled; I felt that if I once again presented her mother's distress to her in a very urgent manner, she would go along with it, but the girl's fear touched me deeply.

'Well, stay here,' I said. 'But tell me, can you perhaps work?'

'Oh yes, sir,' she replied, drying her tears.

›Could you perhaps get my finer linen?‹

'No,' she answered very firmly. 'We are not equipped for that.'

'Here is a white cloth,' I continued. 'Can you perhaps get me half a dozen and get them ready?'

She looked at the cloth and said: 'With pleasure, and I will sew it very neatly!' To my own shame, I was now forced to take out money, although I had previously denied it.

'Buy six of these shawls,' I continued, 'and can you finish three of them by Sunday evening?' She promised I gave her some more for her mother and told her that I was not ready for it today but could do more on Sunday. She thanked me sincerely; she seemed pleased that I had given her work, for she chatted about it again, how beautifully she wanted to make the cloths, and if I am not mistaken, she even asked me whether she could sew an English hem in? I agreed to everything, but when she wanted to take her leave, I held her tight. 'There is one more thing you must do to please me,' I said, 'you can certainly do it and easily.'

'And what?' she asked. 'How gladly I would do anything for you.'

'Let me lift this veil of envy and see your face, so that I may have a memory of this evening.'

She moved away from me and held her veil tighter.

"Please, stop that," she replied, and seemed to be struggling a little with herself; "you have the lovely memory of your kindnesses; my mother has strictly forbidden me to lift my veil, and I assure you," she added, "I am as ugly as night, you would only be frightened!"

But this resistance only irritated me more; a really ugly girl, I thought, does not speak of her ugliness in this way. I wanted to grab the veil, but she had escaped like an eel: ' Dimanche à revoir! ' she cried and hurried away. I looked after her in astonishment. About fifty paces away from me she stopped, waved my white handkerchief at me and called in her silvery voice: 'Good night!'

24.

In the next few days, I was preoccupied with the thought of what class the girl might belong to. The more vividly I recalled her sophisticated language and her delicate nature, the more I raised her up in my thoughts. She had to give me certainty about that at least, I decided, and resolved not to let myself be fobbed off again like I had been with the veil. Sunday came; you will still remember that afternoon, Faldner, when we sat with our friends in Montmorency in the garden of the great poet. You wanted to go home late at night, and I always insisted on an early return, and when you stayed anyway, I left despite your scolding. Of course, you did not believe then what I claimed, that I could not stand the night air, but you also could not have imagined that I was hurrying to a rendezvous with the beggar woman from the Pont des Arts? This time she was the first on the square and because she had to bring me the handkerchiefs, she was already afraid that I might have missed her and think that she would not keep her word. With almost childish joy and, as it seemed to me, even greater confidence than before, she chatted away, showing me the handkerchiefs by the light of a streetlamp.

She seemed to like hearing me praise her fine work. 'Look, I've signed your name too,' she said, showing the elegant E. v. F. in the corner. Then she wanted to give me back a lot of silver money as surplus, and only my firm declaration that she was insulting me by doing so could persuade her to accept it as wages.

I ordered more work because I saw that the girl's delicate mind was more inclined to use my gifts in this way, and this time I ordered jabots and cuffs. Her mother had not become any sicker but was still unable to leave her bed; but even this intermediate state seemed comforting to her. When the mother had been dealt with, I dared to ask her directly what her situation was.

The story which she told me in a few words is so commonplace in France that it must serve as a showcase for almost every poor person. Her father had been an officer in the Grand Army, had been reduced to half pay after the first restoration of the Bourbons, had then taken the side again during the Hundred Days and had fallen with the Guards at Mont St. Jean; his widow lost her pension and lived from then on in poverty and misery. During the last two years they had mostly eked out a living by selling their meager possessions and had now reached that extreme degree of misery where the poor have no choice but to leave the world.

I asked the girl whether she could have improved their relationship if she had tried to support her mother in other ways.

'You mean if I had taken a job?' she replied without any sensitivity. 'You see, that was not possible. Before my mother's illness I was much too young, barely fourteen years old, and then she suddenly became so miserable that she could not leave her bed; so, she always needed someone around her, and could I then leave her care to a stranger? Yes, if she had stayed healthy, I would have gladly renounced all our previous relationships, perhaps I would have gone into a dress shop or become a governess in a respectable house, for I have learned a lot, sir! But it didn't work out like that!'

This time too I begged her to lift the veil, but in vain. The hints she had given about her age only made me more anxious to see the face of this girl, who could not have been more than sixteen years old; but she begged me so earnestly to desist, saying that her mother had given her such compelling reasons that it could never be done.

From then on we met every three days. I always had a few small jobs for her to do and she finished them on time. The more I stuck to the behavior I had once adopted towards her, the more strictly I kept myself within the limits of decency, the more trusting and open the good girl became. She even confessed to me that when she was at home for the three days she was always thinking about the next evening. And was I any different? Day and night I occupied myself with this strange creature, who became more and more interesting to me through her cultivated mind, her lovable delicacy and her peculiar relationship with me.

Spring had meanwhile fully arrived, and the time had come when I had long since decided to travel to England with Faldner. Some may think what I am saying is foolish, but it is true that I only thought of this trip with reluctance; Paris itself no longer had anything of interest for me; but that girl had so captured all my senses that I only looked forward to a longer separation with sadness. I could not avoid it without making myself ridiculous, for there was no other compelling reason to postpone the trip; I was even ashamed of myself and imagined the folly of my actions; I decided to leave, but surely no one has ever looked forward to England less than I did.

25.

Eight days before, I told the girl; she was frightened and cried. I asked her to ask her mother if I could visit her, and she agreed. The next time, however, she brought me the very sad answer that her mother had asked me to; to give up this visit, which would be too damaging to her state of mind. I had actually only asked for that visit so that I could see my girl in the daytime and without a veil; so; I asked for this again; but she asked me to come again the evening before my departure, saying that she would pester her mother until she received permission to lift the veil. I will never forget that evening. She came, and my first question was whether her mother had given permission; she said yes and lifted the veil of her own accord. The moon shone brightly, and I looked under my hat, trembling and eager. But permission seemed to have been only partially granted, for my beauty had what were known as Venetian eyes, which covered the upper part of her face. But how beautiful, how charming were the parts that were exposed! A fine, delicate nose, beautifully formed, blooming cheeks, a small, lovely mouth, a chin as if made of wax, and a slender, dazzling white neck. I could not quite make out the eyes, but they seemed dark and fiery to me.

She blushed as I looked at her for a long time, delighted. 'Don't be angry with me,' she whispered, 'for putting on this half-mask; my mother wanted to refuse it completely from the beginning, but later she only allowed it on this condition. I was quite annoyed about it myself, but she gave me some reasons that made sense to me.'

'And what are these reasons?' I asked.

"'Ah, sir,' she replied wistfully, 'you will live forever in our hearts, but you yourself shall forget us entirely; you shall never, never see me again, or even if you see me, you shall not recognize me.'

'And do you think that I will not recognize your beautiful features if I am not allowed to see your eyes or your forehead?'

'Mother thinks,' she replied, 'that is not possible, because if you have only seen half of a face, it is difficult to recognize it.'

And why shouldn't I see you again, shouldn't I recognize you?

She cried when I asked her this question, she pressed my hand and said: 'It must not be! What could it matter to you to recognize an unhappy girl? And - no, the mother is right; it is better this way.

I told her that my trip would not last long; that I might be back in Paris in two months, and that I hoped to see her again. She cried more violently and said no. I pressed her to tell me why she thought I would not see her again.

'I suspect,' she replied, 'that I will see you today for the last time. I believe my mother will not live much longer, the doctor told me so yesterday, and then it will all be over! And even if she lives longer, in London you will long forget such a poor creature as I am.'

Her pain made me infinitely tender; I encouraged her; I promised her that I would never forget her; I made her promise to come to this place every first and fifteenth of every month so that I could find her again; she agreed, smiling with tears, as if she had little hope. 'Well, farewell, goodbye,' I said, taking her in my arms and putting a small, simple ring on her hand, 'farewell and think of me and do not forget the first and fifteenth!'

'How could I forget you!' she cried, looking up at me, weeping. 'But I shall never see you again; you say goodbye forever.'

I could not refrain from kissing her beautiful mouth; she blushed, but let it happen patiently; I put a safe deposit box in her little hand, she looked at me once more very attentively and pressed herself more tightly against me. 'Goodbye!' I said, as she gently pulled herself out of my arms. The last moment of farewell seemed to give her courage: she drew me to her heart once more, I felt a hot kiss on my lips. 'Forever! Farewell forever!' she cried painfully, tore herself away and hurried across the square.

I never saw her again! After a stay of three months, I returned from London to Paris; on the fifteenth I went to the Place de l'Ecole de Médecine, I waited for over an hour, my girl did not appear. I repeated these visits many times on the first and fifteenth; how often I walked through the Rue St. Severin, looked up at the houses, and even asked about a poor German woman and her daughter, but I never heard anything from them again, and the charming creature was right when she called out to me as I left: Forever! "

26.

The young man had told his story with a passion that gave it great truth and seemed to make a deep impression on at least the female part of the company. Josephe was crying violently, and the other young ladies and women also wiped their eyes now and then. The men had become more serious and seemed to be listening with great interest, only the Baron smiled now and again and whispered his remarks to him. Now, when Fröben had finished, he burst into loud laughter: "I'll tell you how to get out of this affair!" he cried. "I've always said it, my friend is a clever fellow. Just look how he knew how to move the ladies, the rogue! Truly, my wife is crying as if the priest had denied her absolution. That is delicious, on my honour! Fiction and truth! Yes, you overheard that from your Goethe, fiction and truth, it is wonderful fun."

Fröben felt hurt again by these words. "I already told you," he said angrily, "that I left aside all fiction and invention and only told the truth; I hope you will see it as such."

"God save me!" laughed the Baron. "Truth, you have been entertaining the girl, my dear, that is the whole story, and you have made a little novel out of the evening visits to her. But well told, well told, I will accept that."

The young man blushed with anger; he saw Josephe staring at her husband, staring anxiously; he thought he could see that she too perhaps shared his suspicions and thought badly of him; he did not want to let this woman's respect be taken away from him by these mean jokes. "Please, let us keep quiet about it," he cried, "I have never had reason in my life to cover up or distort anything, but I cannot tolerate it if others try to take this job away from me. I tell you for the last time, Faldner, that, on my word, everything is as I have said."

"Well, then, God be blamed," replied the other, clapping his hands. "Then, out of sheer exaggerated nobility and theoretical delicacy, you have thrown away a few hundred francs on a cunning prostitute who with a common story of misery and a sick mother; you got nothing out of it but a poor kiss! Poor devil! To let yourself be made a fool of like that by a whore in Paris."

Even more than the previous accusation, the young man was irritated by this mocking pity and the laughter of the company, who applauded the Baron's bad joke at his expense. He was just about to leave the company, deeply offended, when a strange, terrible sight stopped him. Josephe, pale as a corpse, had slowly got up; she seemed to want to say something to her husband, but at the same moment she collapsed, unconscious, as if dead. Everyone jumped up in dismay, everyone ran around in confusion, the women picked up the unconscious woman, the men asked themselves in confusion how this had happened so suddenly, Fröben had almost fainted himself from the shock, and the Baron muttered curses about the delicate nerves of women, cursed the boundless decency, the anxious observation of decency, which makes one faint, now trying to calm the company, now running back to his wife; everyone spoke, guessed, shouted together and no one heard, no one understood the other.

Josephe came to after a few minutes, she asked for her room, they took her there, and the girls and women crowded around curiously and busily; they suggested a hundred different remedies that could be used to combat fainting, they told how the same thing had happened to them here and there, they agreed that the great exertion of Mrs. von Faldner, the many worries and business that day had inevitably brought about this accident, and the concern that the Baron might perhaps disgrace himself, since he had already been quite indecent, had accelerated the matter even more.

The Baron, meanwhile, tried to restore the previous order among the men. He diligently poured out the wine, drank bravely to this or that person, and tried to calm himself and his guests with all sorts of comforting arguments. "It is due to nothing," he cried, "except the mischief of modern times; every woman of standing has weak nerves nowadays, and if she does not have them, she is not considered noble; fainting is considered good form; the devil invented these crazy arrangements. And that is also why one cannot[174] I can no longer call them by their proper names. Everything should be so extremely delicate, subtle, refined and well-mannered that it makes you want to get mad. Now she has changed her mind, so that I risked a few jokes, which is the spice of society; that I was not beside myself with emotion and pain at such tender, sensitive stories and allowed myself a few practical conjectures. What! Such things must be allowed among friends! And I would have thought you were smarter, friend Fröben, than to take offense at such things."

But the person to whom the Baron addressed the latter part of his speech was no longer among the guests; Fröben had gone to his room in anger, resentful of himself and the world. He could not yet fully understand this strange scene; his soul, still half agitated by anger at his friend's brutality, half seized by horror at his girlfriend's accident, was still too full, too stormy to allow room for calmer thoughts and reflection. "Will she not believe me either," he said to himself sorrowfully, "will she also give more weight to her husband's vile words than to the simple, unadorned truth that I told? What did those strange looks mean with which she sometimes looked at me during my story? How could this event have affected her so deeply that she turned pale and trembled? Could it really be true that she is good to me, that she cares deeply for me, that she was hurt by the scorn of her friend, who must have degraded me so deeply in her eyes? And what did she want when she stood up, when she wanted to speak? Did she want to put a stop to Faldner's inappropriate speeches, or did she even want to defend me?'

As he said these words he had paced up and down the room, his eyes now fell on the roll containing the picture, he unrolled it, and looked at it with a bitter smile. "And how could I let myself be carried away by a feeling of shame, opening my heart to people who do not know how to talk about things that are so foreign to such extremely noble people; the bad, the common, is dearer to them, seems more natural to them than the extraordinary; how could I speak of your lovely cheeks, of your sweet lips to these dolls? Oh, you poor, poor child; how much nobler are you in your misery than these fox hunters?[175] and you rabble, who know true misery and shameful poverty only by hearsay and laugh at every virtue that rises above the common as a fairy tale! Where are you now? And do you still remember your friend and those evenings that made him so happy?'

His eyes filled with tears as he looked at the picture, as he considered the bitter injustice that people had done to this poor creature today. He tried to suppress his tears, but they only flowed more violently. There was a place in the young man's chest where, as in a deep grave, all his melancholy, all his repressed tears of grief, were gathered silently and for a long time; but moments like this, when the pain of memory and his hopelessness came so heavily upon him, burst the ceiling of this grave and allowed the long-held grief to overflow all the more powerfully, the more his broken courage turned into melancholy.

27.

The next morning, Fröben reflected on the events of the previous day and was unsure whether he should not leave a house immediately, where a longer stay might expose him to such unpleasantness even more often, when the door opened and the Baron entered, dejected and ashamed. "You did not come to dinner last night, you have not shown yourself today," he began, coming closer, "you are angry with me; but be reasonable and forgive me; you see, I have been feeling strange; I had drunk too much wine during the day, was heated, and you know my weak side, so I cannot stop teasing him. I have been punished enough that the beautiful day ended so miserably, and that my house will now be the talk of the neighborhood for four weeks. Do not make my life completely embittered and be friendly to me again as before!"

"Let the whole story rest," replied Fröben grimly, offering him his hand. "I don't like to talk about such things any further; but tomorrow I want to go away, farther away; I'm not staying here any longer."

Don't be a fool! cried Faldner, who had not expected this and was seriously frightened. Wanting to leave immediately because of such a scene! I always said that you are such a hothead. No, nothing will come of it; and didn't you tell me promised to wait until letters arrived from the Don in W.? No, you must not leave me again; and you have nothing to be ashamed of because of the company, everyone, especially the women, are making fun of me, they agreed with you completely and said that I was to blame for everything."

“How is your wife?” asked Fröben, trying to avoid these memories.

"All right, it was just a little fright because she was afraid we were going to have a serious argument. She's waiting for you with breakfast.

Come down with me now and be sensible and come to your senses. I have to go riding, don't take it amiss, the mill is going to start today. So, you're just as you were before?"

"Well, yes," said the young man angrily. "Let the whole story rest for a moment." With strange feelings that he himself did not quite know how to interpret, he followed the Baron, who, delighted at his friend's quick reconciliation, hurried ahead of him, quickly reported to his wife what he had accomplished, and then left the castle to start his mill.

Had everything suddenly become so different today, or had he just changed himself? Joseph's features, her whole being, seemed to Fröben to have changed when he entered her room. A quiet melancholy, a gentle sadness seemed to have spread over her face, and yet her smile was so sweet, so intimate as she welcomed him. She attributed her illness from yesterday to too much exertion and did not seem to like to talk about the whole incident. But Fröben, who cared so much about his friend's good opinion, could not bear the fact that she almost deliberately avoided mentioning his story. "No," he cried, "I will not let you slip away like that, madam! I care little about what others think of me; what do I care if such everyday people judge me by their common standards! But, in truth, it would pain me infinitely if you too were to judge me wrongly, if you too were to give space to thoughts which would degrade me so deeply in your eyes, if you too were to doubt the truth of that story which I certainly should never have revealed to such ears. Oh, I implore you, tell me quite honestly what you think of me and that story?"

She looked at him for a long time; her beautiful, large eyes filled with tears, she pressed his hand: "Oh, Fröben, what do I think of that?" she said. "And if the whole world doubted the truth, I would still know for sure that you spoke the truth! You don't know how well I know you!"

He blushed with joy and kissed her hand. "How kind you are not to misunderstand me. And I am sure I have told you everything, everything, exactly according to the truth."

"And this girl," she continued, "is probably the same one you told me about the other day? Don't you remember, when we were talking about Victor and Clothilde, that you confessed to me that you were hopelessly in love? Is she the same one?"

"It is she," he replied sadly. "No, you will not laugh at me for this foolishness; you feel too deeply to find it ridiculous. I know everything that can be said against it; I often call myself a fool, a dreamer, chasing after a shadow; I do not even know whether she loves me -"

"She loves you!" Josephe exclaimed involuntarily; but, blushing at her own words, she added: "She must love you; do you think that such generosity cannot make a deep impression on the heart of a girl of seventeen? And in all the statements you have told us, I must be deceiving myself, or there is certainly a considerable degree of love in them."

The young man seemed to listen to her words with delight. "How often have I called this out to myself," he said, "when I was so without consolation and looked sadly into the past; but why? Perhaps only to make myself even more unhappy. I have often fought with myself, sought distraction in the throes of people, numbness in the pressure of business, but I could never succeed. That lovely, unhappy creature was always before my eyes; my only wish was to see her just once more. It is still my wish, I may confess it to you, for you know how to appreciate my feelings; I only undertook this journey because my longing drove me out to seek her, to see her once more. And when I think about this wish, I often even find myself thinking of possessing her forever! - Are you looking away, Josephe? Oh, I understand; You think that I should never choose a creature who was in such deep misery, whose circumstances are so ambiguous; you think of the judgment of men; I have often thought of all this, but as sure as I live, if I found her again as I left her, I would ask no one but my heart. Would you judge me so harshly, Josephe?'

She did not answer him; still turned away, her forehead resting on her hand, she offered him a book and asked him to read it. He took it hesitantly, he looked at her questioningly; it was the only time he was not quite sure what to make of her behavior; but she beckoned him to read, and he followed, although he would have liked to have let his heart speak for longer. He read absentmindedly from the beginning; but little by little the subject attracted him, carried his thoughts more and more away from the previous conversation and finally carried him away, so that in the flow of the speech he did not notice how the beautiful woman turned to him with a face full of melancholy, how her gaze was fixed on him with tenderness, how her eyes often filled with tears, which she only suppressed with difficulty. It was late in the reading, and Josephe had recovered herself sufficiently to be able to speak calmly about what she had read, but it still seemed to the young man as if her voice trembled here and there, as if the former kind familiarity which she had shown to her husband's friend had given way; he would have felt unhappy if that bright ray of warmer feeling which burst forth from her eye had not confused his observation.

28.

Since the Baron did not want to return until the evening, but Josephe had retired to her room after this lecture, Fröben decided to sleep away the hot midday hours at the table in order to escape these tormenting thoughts for at least a few hours. In the arbor, which had become dear to him through so many beautiful hours that he had spent there with the lovely woman, he lay down on the mossy bench and soon fell asleep. He had left his worries behind; they did not follow him through the gate of dreams; only lovely memories merged and mixed to create new, charming images; the girl from St. Severin Street with her melting voice floated over to him and told him about her mother; he scolded her for making him wait so long, when he had come on the first and fifteenth; he wanted to kiss her as punishment, she resisted, he raised his hand. He lifted his veil, lifted his pretty little face by the chin, and behold - it was Don Pedro, who had put himself in the girl's clothes, and Diego, his servant, wanted to die laughing at the wonderful joke. Then, with a bold leap of dreaming imagination, he was back in Stuttgart in that painting collection. They had rearranged them, he searched all the rooms in vain for the precious painting; it was not to be found; he cried, he began to call out and lament loudly; then the gallery attendant came and asked him to be quiet and not to wake the paintings, which are now all asleep.

Suddenly he saw the painting hanging in a corner, not as a half-length portrait as before, but life-size; it looked at him teasingly, with mischievous glances, it came alive out of the frame and embraced the unfortunate man; he felt a hot, long kiss on his lips. As often happens, when one thinks one has woken up in a dream and, in the dream, says to oneself that one was only dreaming, the same thing seemed to be happening to the young man now. He thought he had opened his eyes, awakened by the long kiss, and behold, a blooming, rosy face that seemed familiar to him was leaning down on him. He closed his eyes again, delighted by the sweet breath and the loving kisses that he was breathing in; he heard a noise, opened them again and saw a figure in a black coat, black hat with a green veil floating away; just as she was about to turn a corner, she turned her face to him once more; it was the features of the girl he loved, and, jealous as before, she had put on the half-mask. "Oh, it's only a dream after all!" he said to himself, smiling, as he was about to close his eyes again; but the feeling of being awake, the rustling of the wind in the leaves of the arbor, the splashing of the fountain were too clear for him not to be completely awake and alert. The strange, vivid dream image was still before his mind; he looked at the corner where she had disappeared; he looked at the spot where she had stood, leaning over him; he thought he could still feel the kisses of the beloved girl on his lips. "So, it has come to this with you," he said to himself, frightened, "that you dream even when you are awake, that you see her around you when you are in your right mind? What madness could this lead to? No, I would never have believed that one could dream so clearly. It is a disease of the brain, a fever of the imagination; yes, it is not far off, I would even say, Dream images can leave footprints behind; for these steps here in the sand are not mine." His gaze fell on the bench where he had been lying, he saw a neatly folded piece of paper and picked it up in surprise. It was uninscribed, it was exactly in the shape of a billet-doux; he hesitated for a moment, wondering whether he could open it; but curious as to who could write in such a form, he unfolded the paper - a ring fell towards him. He held it in his hand and skimmed through the letter, he read: "I am often close to you, my noble knight and benefactor; I surround you with that infinite love which kindled my gratitude, which will not die out even with my life. I know that your generous heart still beats for me, you have roamed lands to seek and find me; but your efforts are in vain - forget such an unfortunate creature; what did you want with me? Even if my greatest happiness lies in the thought of belonging to you completely, it can never be! Forever! I told you then, yes, I love you forever, but – fate wants us to be separated forever, that I may never live by your side, perhaps only in your kind memory

The Beggar Woman from the Pont des Arts.

The young man still thought he was dreaming or was dreaming again; he looked around suspiciously to see if his imagination had seduced him so completely that he was living in a dream world; but all the objects around him, the familiar arbor, the bench, the trees, the castle in the distance, everything was still as it had been before; he saw, he was awake, he was not dreaming. And so; these lines really existed, were they not a dream image of his imagination? "Did someone want to play a joke on me?" he then asked himself; "yes, of course; it all comes from Josephe; perhaps that apparition was only a mask?" As he rolled up the paper, he felt the ring that had been hidden in the note in his hand. Curious, he pulled it out, looked at it, and turned pale. No, at least that was not an illusion; it was the same ring that he had given the girl that night when he said goodbye to her forever. As much as he was tempted at first to believe in supernatural things, the thought that he had a sign from the beloved being, that she was near to him, filled him with such great Delighted that he no longer thought about the words of the letter, he did not doubt for a moment that he would find it, he pressed the ring to his lips, he rushed out of the arbor into the garden, and his eyes wandered along every path and into every bush for the beloved figure. But he looked in vain; he asked the workers in the garden, the servants in the castle if they had seen any strangers; they had not been noticed; dismayed, almost incapable of reflection, he came to the table; in vain did Faldner search for the reason for his disturbed looks, in vain did Josephe ask him whether he was perhaps still in such a gloomy mood from the day before. "Something has happened to me," he answered, "that I would have to call a miracle, if my reason did not rebel against superstition."

29.

This strange incident and the words of the note, which he read over at least ten times a day, had made the young man very thoughtful. He began to ponder whether it was possible for supernatural beings to intervene in the lives of mortals. How often had he laughed at those enthusiasts who believed in apparitions, in messengers from another world, in protective spirits that hover around people, as if it were a gospel. How often had he even demonstrated to them the physical impossibility of incorporeal beings appearing visibly, of being able to do this or that. But how could he interpret what had happened to him? Often he resolved to forget everything, to stop thinking about it altogether, and the next moment he would struggle to bring his memory to life; then her features would appear more clearly than ever; he had seen her when she turned around at the corner; he had seen the lovely mouth, those rosy cheeks, that chin, that slender neck again! He brought that picture before him, he compared them feature by feature, he covered the lady's eyes and forehead with his hand, and it was the lovely little face that looked out from under the half-mask!

Because Josephe was too busy at home the next morning to entertain him, he had sat down in the arbor again. He read, and while he was reading he was always preoccupied with the thought of whether she would appear to him again. The midday heat had a numbing effect on him; he tried hard to stay awake, he read more eagerly and with more effort but little by little his head sank back, the book fell from his hands, and he slept.

He awoke at almost the same time as yesterday, but no figure with a green veil was to be seen far and wide. He smiled at himself for having expected her. He got up, sad and discontent, to go into the castle, and then he saw a white cloth next to him that he could not remember having put down. He looked at it, and it must have belonged to him, for his signature was sewn into the corner. "How did this cloth get here?" he exclaimed, moved, when on closer inspection he discovered that it was one of the cloths that the girl had made for him and which he had carefully sealed up like holy relics. "Is this supposed to be another sign?" He unfolded the cloth and looked to see if there were perhaps a few more lines inserted? It was empty; but in another corner of the cloth; he discovered a few more letters that were sewn in like his name; there, delicately and neatly, were the words: Forever! "So, she was here after all!" cried the young man angrily. "And I was able to sleep through her lovely appearance? Why is she giving me a new sign? Why repeat those sad words that made me so unhappy then and again yesterday?" Today, too, he asked the servants in turn whether there had been a stranger in the garden? They all said no, and the old gardener said that no one had walked through the garden for three hours except the lady. "And what was she wearing?" asked Fröben, strangely surprised. "Oh, sir, you're asking too much," answered the old man. "She was dressed in elegant clothes, but I don't know how to describe it. As she passed in front of me, she nodded friendly and said: 'Good day, Jakob!'"

The young man led the old man aside: "I beseech you," he whispered, "was she wearing a green veil? Did she not have large black glasses on?"

The old gardener looked at him suspiciously and shook his head. "Black glasses?" he asked. "The lady has large black glasses? Oh, my God, what are you thinking, she has such sharp, clear eyes as a chamois and is supposed to wear glasses on her nose, with respect, large black glasses, like the ones the old women clip onto their noses in church so that they make a softer noise when they sing? No, Sir, you must get such bad thoughts out of your head, it's nothing; and don't take it the wrong way, but you should wear a hat in this heat, it's because of the sunstroke." So said the old man and walked on, shaking his head; but with a very suspicious gesture of his forefinger to the brains of the other servants he indicated that there must not be something quite right about the young guest up here.

30.

Even now Fröben came to no other conclusion than that the behavior of the girl he loved so dearly was incomprehensible, and this mysterious game with his pain, with his longing, occupied him so exclusively that he missed many things that he would otherwise have noticed. Josephe came to the table with tear-filled eyes; the Baron was upset and monosyllabic and seemed to have to vent his inner discontent, which lay on his forehead and spoke clearly from his eyes, now and then by cursing the bad cooking and the even worse housekeeping. The unfortunate woman bore everything quietly and patiently, occasionally casting a fleeting glance at Fröben as if seeking help and comfort; alas, she did not notice how her husband was watching these glances, how his forehead turned redder when he met her eyes in this way.

This passed by Fröben's eyes and ears as something he had already become accustomed to; he did not even bother to ask Josephe the reason for this outburst. He did not notice that she was more reserved towards him in Faldner's presence; he put it down to his friend's usual busyness that in the next few days he forced him to go here and there on the estate with him and often spent a large part of the day in the woods and fields doing measurements and calculations. But when one morning, when Faldner was already waiting for him, booted and spurred, he feigned a minor indisposition in order to avoid these unpleasant field visits, when he innocently mentioned that he must read to Josephe again sometime, he found it strange that the Baron called out angrily: "No, she must not read me anything anymore, nothing at all. Everything has been going the other way for some time anyway. I could really use that if she spent the whole morning reading and had such novel ideas in Heads, as I have seen some haunting. In God's name, read it to yourself, dear Fröben, and don't take offense if I place my wife somewhere else. You go into the garden after breakfast, Josephe, today we are going to dig up vegetables, then you will be so kind as to go to the pastor's, you have owed him a visit there for a long time." With these words he took his riding whip from the table and walked away.

"What's going on? What's wrong with him today?" Fröben asked the young woman in amazement, who could hardly hold back her tears.

"Oh, he is much as usual," she replied, without looking up. "Your presence has thrown him out of his usual routine for some time; you see he is now as he was before."

"But for goodness' sake," he cried angrily, "send a maid into the garden!"

"I mustn't," she said firmly, "I must see for myself; he wants it."

And the visit to Pastors-?

"I must do it; you have heard that I must do it ; let's leave it at that, it is as it is. But you," Josephe continued, "you, my friend, seem to me to have changed in the last few days, not as cheerful, as trusting as before. Perhaps you no longer like being here? Could my husband, perhaps I, be the cause of your displeasure?"

Fröben felt embarrassed; he was on the point of confessing to his friend the strange events in the garden, but the thought of exposing himself in front of the clever young woman held him back. "You know," he said evasively, "that I have received letters from S. in the last few days. And if I seem upset, it is only those letters that are to blame." She looked at him doubtfully; an answer seemed to be on her lips, but as if she had read the lack of trust in the young man's look and felt hurt by it, her beautiful lips twitched and pushed back the answer; she rang the bell in silence, ordered her maid to bring her, her hat and umbrella, and then, without inviting him to go on this trip, went to work in the garden.

When the young man also went down into the garden a few hours later and asked for Josephe, he was told that she had gone to the pastors. He hurried to the arbor and sat down with a pounding heart. Today he had resolved not to fall asleep. "I want to see," he said to himself, "whether this being that hovers so mysteriously around me has a third sign for me? I will lie down as if to sleep, and as sure as I live, if it appears again I will catch it and see what nature it is." He read until midday arrived, then he lay down and closed his eyes. Often slumber really did want to descend upon him, but expectation, restlessness and his strong will, which kept the poppy seeds away from him, kept him awake. He must have lain like that for half an hour when the branches of the arbor rustled. He opened his eyes barely a little and saw two white hands carefully parting the branches, presumably to open a view of the slumberer. Then soft, soft footsteps crackled in the sand. He glanced furtively toward the entrance of the arbor and his heart almost burst with joyful impatience when he saw his girl in her black cloak and hat, her green veil thrown back, her black masked eyes tied over the upper part of her beautiful face.

31.

She approached on tiptoe. He saw her face turn a deeper red as she came nearer. She looked at the sleeper for a long time; she sighed deeply and seemed to be drying her tears. Then she came close; she bent over him, her breath touching him like a messenger from heaven announcing the approach of her sweet lips, she sank lower, and her mouth rested on his as gently as the dawn falls on the hill.

Then he could not hold back any longer; he quickly wrapped his arm around her body, and with a short cry of fear she sank to her knees. He jumped up in alarm, he thought she had fainted, but she was only speechless and trembling violently; he picked her up, he pulled her down onto the bench by his side, filled with the joy of seeing her again, he covered her mouth with burning kisses, he pressed her tightly to him: "Oh, so I have you again, finally, finally again, you beloved being!" he cried; "you are not an illusion, you are alive, I hold you in my arms as I did then and love you as I did then and am happy, blissful, because you love me too!' A great flush covered her cheeks, she did not speak, she tried in vain to wriggle out of his arms. 'No, now I will not let you go,' he said, and tears, tears of happiness, clung to his eyelashes; 'now I hold you tight and no world can tear you away from me. And come, away with this envious mask, I want to see your beautiful face in full, ah, it has always lived in my dreams!' She seemed to want to keep her hand from the half-mask with the last of her strength, she breathed heavily, she struggled with him, but the young man's drunken joy at knowing that he was so inexpressibly happy after so long deprivation granted him an easy victory. He held her arms with one hand, trembling, he pushed back the hat with the other, untied the mask and saw - his friend's wife.

"Josephe!" he cried, as if he had been thrown into an abyss, and his thoughts were spinning in a circle. "Josephe!"

Pale, frozen, tearless, she sat next to him and said with a wistful smile: "Yes, Josephe."

" So, you have deceived me?" he said bitterly, as all the hope and happiness of the previous moment passed before him. "Oh, you could have spared us this farce. But" he continued, a thought flashing through his mind, "for God's sake, where did you get the ring, where did you get the handkerchief?"

She blushed again, burst into tears, and hid her head on his breast. "No," he cried, "I must have an answer; it is my ring, the handkerchief - I implore you, how did both come into your hands, where did you get the ring?"

"From you!" she whispered, pressing herself closer to him in shame.

Then a ray of light fell into Fröben's soul; the too bright light still blinded him, but he gently lifted her head and looked at her with eyes full of wonder and love. "It's you? Am I dreaming again?" he said after looking at her for a long time. "Didn't you say you were my sweet girl? Oh God, what veil lay over my eyes? Yes, those are your lovely cheeks, those are your charming mouth, which kissed me today, not for the first time!"

A high glow covered her cheeks. She looked at him full of joy and rapture. "What would have become of me without you, you noble man!" she cried, her eyes turning into tears. her eyes broke. "I bring you the blessing of my good mother, you have made her last days easier and lifted the blanket of misery that lay so heavy on her sick breast. Oh! How can I thank you? What would I have become without you! But" she continued, covering her face with her hands, "what have I become, the wife of another, the wife of your friend!"

He saw how an infinite pain rose and fell her bosom, how her tears trickled down like springs through her delicate fingers. He felt how deeply she loved him, and no thought of reproaching him for belonging to anyone but him entered his soul. "It is so," he said sadly, pressing her tighter to him as if he could not lose her. "It is so; let us think that it was meant to be so, that it had to be so because we were perhaps so happy. But at this moment you are mine, imagine you coming over to the square of the medical school and I am waiting for you: oh, come, embrace me as you did then, oh, just one more time!"

Lost in memories, she hung around his neck; behind her gloomy eyes the thought of reality seemed to disappear; brighter and brighter, friendlier and friendlier the memory seemed to emerge; a lovely smile moved around her mouth and sank into delicate dimples on her cheeks. "And didn't you know me?" she asked, smiling. "And you didn't know me?" he asked, looking at her tenderly. "Ah!" she answered. "I had listened to your features very carefully and written them deep into my heart, but truly, I would never have recognized you. It may also have been because I only ever saw you at night, wrapped in your coat, your hat pulled low over your brow, and how could I have thought - Of course, when you called out to Faldner on the first evening: 'Goodbye!' the tone seemed so familiar to me, as if I had heard it before; but I always laughed at myself at the foolish assumptions. Afterwards, I sometimes thought that you must be the person I meant; but I kept doubting it; but when you mentioned Pont des Arts on Sunday, a sun of its own suddenly appeared on your face; you seemed to be living in memory and with the first words it became clear to me that it was you, you! But of course, you couldn't recognize me, could you? I turned quite pale?"

"Josephe," he replied, "where were my senses? Where were my eyes, my ears, that I did not recognize you? At the very first sight of you, a joyful shock flew through my soul, you were exactly like the image that, through a true cycle of things, I had found and loved as resembling you; but the discovery of your mother's sex led me astray; I saw in you only the similar daughter of the beautiful Laura, and often, while I was sitting beside you, my mind wandered far away, far away, to you!"

"Oh God!" cried Josephe, "is it true, is it possible? Can you still love me?"

"Can I? - But may I? Good heavens, your name is Mrs. von Faldner; for heaven's sake, tell me how all this came about? How could you not wait for me even once more?"

32.

She stopped her tears, she forced herself to speak with difficulty. "See," she said, "it was as if a hostile fate had arranged everything just to make me very unhappy. When you were gone, I had no joy. Those evenings with you had meant so much to me. See, from the very first moment when you asked your companion for money in your beloved mother tongue, from then on my heartbeat for you; and when you looked after us with such infinite nobility, with such tenderness, oh, I often wanted to hold you close to my heart and confess to you that I adore you as a higher being. I do not know what would have been too difficult for me to do for you; and how great, how nobly you behaved towards me! You left, I wept for a long time, for a painful feeling told me that it was over forever; eight days after you left, my poor mother died very quickly. What you gave me at that time was enough to bury my mother and not to dishonor her memory. A lady, Countess Landskron, who lived in our neighborhood and heard about us poor people, sent for me. She examined me in everything, she looked carefully through my mother's papers, which I had to give her; she seemed satisfied and took me on as a companion. We traveled; I will not describe to you how my heart bled when I left Paris had to; there were only fourteen days left until the time you had set for your return was up; then I would have gone to the square on the first, spoken to you once more, said goodbye to you once more! It was not to be like this; as we drove from St. Severin Street across the well-known square of the Ecole de Médecine, my heart wanted to break, and I said to myself: 'Forever!' Eduard! I have never heard from you again, your name was unknown to me, you must have long since forgotten the beggar woman; I lived on the mercy of strangers, I had to endure many bitter things, I bore them, they were not the most painful. But when the Countess moved to her estate in this area, when Faldner asked me to marry her, when I noticed that she good-naturedly considered it a good place to be, and perhaps was tired of me - well, I had only been happy once, and could never hope to be happy again; the rest was so unimportant – so I became his wife.

"Poor child! to this Faldner, why you of all people, with such a soft soul, with such a delicate mind, with so much valid claim to a fate that is at least nobler, why you of all people, his wife? But it is so; Josephe, I cannot, I must not spend another day here; despite all the harsh things he may have, I once called him a friend, and now I am his guest, and even if all this were not the case, we must not be happy together!" There was an infinite pain in his words; he kissed the beautiful woman's eyes, only to keep the grief that lived in them from softening them any further. "Oh, just *one* more day," she whispered tenderly;

"I have only just found you, and you are already thinking of escaping. Look, when you are gone, the door to my happiness will close again forever; I will have to endure hardships, and I must save a few memories for myself that I can draw on in the endless desert."

"Listen, I will confess everything to Faldner," said the young man after some thought, "I will paint everything for him so that it will move him. He does not love you, you do not love him, and you are unhappy; he must give you up *to me* . My house is not as beautifully situated as this castle; you can overlook my property from the Belvedere on the roof, you are leaving great wealth here, but if you were to move into my house, I would lay my hands under you as a carpet, on the hands I wanted to carry you, you should be the queen in my house and I your first faithful servant!

She looked up to heaven in pain and wept more violently. "Ah yes, if I were of your faith, it would be fine, but we were married in a good Catholic marriage, and only death separates us! Oh, great God, how unhappy these laws often make us! What a bliss to be with you, to always care for you, to hold your gaze, and every day to give you, through tender love, a thousandth of what you have done for my dear mother and for me."

"So, forever after all," he replied sadly; "so only tomorrow, and then we'll part forever?"

"Forever!" she breathed barely audibly, pressing him more tightly to her lips.

"So here they find you, you vile whore!" shouted a third man, who was standing next to the group. They jumped up in alarm; the Baron stood there, trembling with anger, grinding his teeth with rage, holding a piece of paper in one hand and the riding whip in the other, which he had just raised to let fly over the unfortunate woman's beautiful neck. Fröben fell into his arms, with difficulty wrested the whip from him and threw it far away. "I beg you," he said to the angry man, "don't make a scene here; your people are in the garden, you are disgracing yourself and your house with such a scene."

"What?" cried the other, "hasn't my house been sufficiently disgraced by this vile person, by this pack of beggars that I had in my house? Do you think I don't recognize your handwriting," he continued, holding out the paper to her; "this is a sweet little letter to the gentleman here, the hero of the novel. So, I had to marry a prostitute that you supported, and when you were tired of her, the honest farmer was supposed to make her your lady; then after six months you come by chance to visit to put a few more ends to your husband's horns. You shall pay me for that, you scoundrel; but this beggar woman can always stand on the Pont des Arts with a plate and lantern or live off the wages of your sins. My servants shall drive her from the courtyard with whips!"

33.

In such moments, the man of solid education has a decided advantage over the brute who is carried away by rage to recklessness and is unsure what to do. A glance at Josephe, who was sitting pale, trembling, speechless on the mossy bench, convinced Fröben what to do. He offered her his arm and led her out of the arbor to the castle. The Baron watched them furiously; he was about to call his servants together to carry out his threat, but the fear of making his disgrace even greater held him back. He ran up to the hall, where Josephe was lying on the sofa, hiding her weeping face in the pillows, where Fröben was standing at the window as if absentmindedly, staring out. The Baron ran around the hall, scolding and cursing; he cursed himself for having tied his life to such a whore. "There would be no justice left in the land if I didn't get rid of her!" he cried. "She has a baptism certificate and everything else is false; she claimed to be an equal, the beggar woman; this marriage is null and void!"

"That will certainly be the most sensible thing to do," interrupted Fröben; "it just depends on how you approach it so as not to embarrass yourself even further -"

"Ha, sir!" cried the Baron in wild anger, "are you still mocking me after you have brought all this disgrace upon me by your boundless impudence? Follow me, we need no more assizes for our divorce; that can be arranged immediately. Follow me!"

Josephe, who understood these words, jumped up; she threw herself down before the angry man, she implored him to let her endure everything, for his friend was completely innocent; she pointed to the piece of paper in his hand, which she recognized; she swore that Fröben would only find out who she was today. But the young man himself interrupted her intercessions, picked her up and led her back to the sofa. "I am accustomed," he said coolly to the Baron, "to make my arrangements first on such trips, and you will do well not to neglect to do so either. First of all, your wife is leaving the castle now, for I do not want her here anymore if I am not there to protect her from your mistreatment."

"You are acting as if it were your own property," replied the Baron, laughing angrily; "but Madame was your property before, I had almost forgotten, where should the sweet angel be taken? To a poorhouse, to a hospital, or to the nearest fence to continue her trade?"

Fröben did not listen to him; he turned to Josephe. "Does the countess still live nearby?" he asked her. "Do you think you can find somewhere to stay there for the next few days?"

"I want to go to her," she whispered.

"Good; Faldner will have the grace to let you go there, and there you can await the further course of events, whether he realizes how wrong he has done to both of us, or whether he insists on separating from you."

34.

Josephe had gone to the countess; her friend had advised her to pretend that she was only visiting for a few days when she arrived, but that he would inform her of his friend's mood and, if possible, persuade him to reconcile himself with her. "No," she cried passionately, as she climbed down from the terrace to the carriage, "I will never return to this door, I will turn my back on these walls forever. Believe me, a woman can endure a lot. I have had to endure it for a long time and my heart often wanted to burst, but today he has offended me too deeply for me to forgive him. And if I have to return to the Pont des Arts to beg people for a few sous, I would rather do it than endure such low treatment from this rude man any longer. My father was a brave soldier and a respected officer of France; his daughter must not degrade herself to the point of being a maid to a falconer."

The young man had written a few letters after their departure and was busy arranging his small luggage when Faldner entered the room. Fröben looked at him in surprise and expected new attacks and outbursts of anger. But Faldner said: "The more I read these unfortunate lines that I found in your room this afternoon, the more I believe that you are actually innocent of this miserable story, namely that you did not know anything before and did not know the person; I forgive you for finding my wife in your arms, for that person had ceased to be mine when she wrote that foolish letter to you."

"I wish it because of our old relationship," answered Fröben, "if you look at it that way, and mainly because it gives me the opportunity to speak to you sensibly and calmly about Josephe. First of all, I give you my holy word that up to this afternoon, and not before, anything has ever happened between her and me that would have been in the least detrimental to her honor; that she was poor, that she was once compelled to call on people for help -"

"No, tell me instead that she was begging," cried Faldner heatedly, "and wandered around the streets and bridges of the dissolute capital at night to earn money; I could have had the pleasure of getting to know her better even then, I was there at the touching scene on the Pont des Arts. No, even if I believed everything you said, I am still insulted; the Faldner family and a beggar!"

Her father and mother were from good families –

"Fables, poetry! How I let myself be caught like that! I might as well have married the waitress from the tavern if she had a beer glass with a coat of arms on it and brought a false certificate of her birth!"

"That is the least of the matter in my eyes; the main thing is that from the very beginning you treated her like a servant and not like your wife; she could never love you; you are not suited to each other."

"That's the right word," replied the Baron, "we are not suited to one another; Baron von Faldner and a beggar woman can never be suited to one another. And now I am even more pleased that I followed my own mind and treated her like that; the wench deserves no better. I told you right away, there is something so mean about her."

This brutality angered the young man, he wanted to say something bitter in response, but he controlled himself in order to be useful to Joseph. He discussed with the Baron what should be done about it, and they agreed that they should take the whole matter to the civil courts and give mutual dislike as the reason for the separation. Of course, Given their religious differences, neither of the two parties could hope to find consolation in a new union; but Josepha, although she looked with horror into a helpless future, saw no fate so difficult that it would not have seemed tolerable in comparison to the undignified treatment she endured in Faldner's house and the Baron, although he was overcome with remorse in many lonely hours, sought distraction in his business and consolation in the thought that no one had known his shame in having made a beggar of ambiguous character Faldner's wife.

35.

A few weeks after this incident, Fröben was walking across the Rhine bridge in Mainz, where he had retired to be near Joseph. He thought of the strange chain of fate, he thought of various ways out that might still make him and his beloved wife happy; then a carriage drove across the bridge, the strange construction of which attracted the young man's attention from afar. But soon his eyes were fixed only on the servant sitting on the box; this brown-yellow, cheerful face, which looked around curiously, seemed as familiar to him as the bright colors of the livery. As the carriage, which was only allowed to move at a walking pace on the bridge, came closer, the servant also noticed the young man and called out: "San Jago di Compostella! That's him himself!" He tore open the carriage window that separated him from the interior of the carriage and spoke eagerly into it. A window was immediately lowered on the side of the carriage, and out came the well-known face of Don Pedro di San Montanjo Ligez. The carriage stopped; the young man ran forward joyfully to open the door, and the old gentleman fell into his arms. "Where is she, where have you her, the daughter of my Laura? Oh, for the sake of the Blessed Virgin, have you her here? Tell me, young man! Where is she?"

The young man remained silent, embarrassed; he led the old man further along the bridge and then told him that she was not far from this city and that he would take him to her the next day.

The Spaniard had tears of joy in his eyes. "How I thank you for the news you gave me!" he said. "As soon as I got my leave, I got into the car with Diego and had them drive me six miles a day from W. to here, because I couldn't stand it any longer. And is she happy? Does she look like her mother, and what does she say about Laura Tortosi?" Fröben promised to answer all his questions in his room. After the Spaniard had rested a little and changed his clothes, he had Xeres brought to him, poured them, Diego handed him the cigars, as he had done before, and when Don Pedro was quite comfortably seated, the young man began his story. The Spaniard listened to him with increasing interest; to Diego's great annoyance, he put out his cigar for the first time in twenty years, and when the young man came to that outrageous scene between Faldner and the unfortunate woman, he could no longer contain himself; his old, southern blood boiled over; He pushed his hat down on his forehead, wrapped his left arm in his cloak, and cried with flashing eyes: "Give me my long sword, Diego, I'll kill him, as sure as I am a good Christian and a Spanish nobleman. I'll stab him, even if he had a crucifix on his chest, I'll kill him; without absolution and without all the sacraments, I'll send him to hell, that's what I'll do. Bring me my sword, Diego!"

But Fröben pulled the trembling, anger-exhausted old man down to him; he tried to make him understand that all this was unnecessary, for Josephe had already been freed from the power of the brutal man and was living separately from him. To calm him down even more, he brought the picture and unfolded it before Pedro's astonished gaze. The Don looked at it in delight. "Yes, it is her," he cried, forgetting everything else, "my poor, unhappy Laura!" And weeping, he embraced the young man, called him his dear son and thanked him in a broken voice for everything he had done for the unfortunate mother and her poor daughter.

The next morning, he set out with Fröben for the countess's estate. It was a touching sight to see the old man holding Joseph's beautiful, youthful figure in his arms, observing her features attentively, his stern features softening more and more, and then, moved, kissing her eyes and mouth. "Yes, you are Laura's daughter!" he cried. "Your father gave you nothing but his fair hair, but those are her lovely eyes, those are her mouth, those are the beautiful features of the Tortosi! Be my daughter, dear child; I have no relatives and am rich; through kinship, my heart, and twenty years of grief, you are closer to me than to anyone on earth!' Her glances, which fell over his shoulders at Fröben, did not exactly seem to confirm this latter statement, but she kissed his hand, moved, and called him her uncle, her second father.

The joy of the reunion lasted only a few days. Don Pedro declared very firmly that his business was calling him to Portugal, and at the same time he did not seem to see what could prevent Josephe from following him there; he had too strict principles about the articles of his church to have believed that Fröben could desire Josephe, the separated wife of another, as his wife. We do not know what the lovers discussed on this point; only this much is certain: Fröben suggested several times that she should return to the Protestant faith, but that she, with infinite pain but very firmly, rejected this suggestion. The young man is said to have often suggested to her, in despair over the approaching separation, that she should let Don Pedro go, that she should live on her own, stay in Germany, and that if he could not become her husband, he would be with her forever as a friend. But she rejected this too; She openly admitted to him that she felt too weak to carry out such a relationship with honor, and made prouder by her misfortune, she shrank back from the thought of an unworthy union with a man whom she respected as highly as she loved him. Alone with herself, she admitted that an even more noble thought guided her steps. "Should he," she said to herself, "lose the prime of life to an unfortunate creature who can only be his friend? Should he give up the high enjoyment of domestic pleasures, the happiness of having children and grandchildren around him, for me? No, he has already lost me once, and time will ease his pain now too; he will forget an unfortunate being who will forever think of him, love him, and pray for him."

So, Joseph's prophetic words, "Forever!", seemed to come true. Don Pedro left the Countess's estate with his new relative to go to sea through Holland. Fröben, who was perhaps only inspired by the thought of soon following Joseph to Portugal and finding her. He accompanied his beloved on her journey through Germany and Holland, and whenever she asked him not to make the days of separation even harder by accompanying her for longer, he begged with tears in his eyes: "Only as far as the sea and then forever!"

36.

In August of this year, an English ship, carrying cargo and passengers to Portugal, arrived at Ostend. It was a fine morning, the fog had lifted, and the weather seemed to be favorable for the voyage. It was nine o'clock in the morning when a cannon shot rang out from the English ship, signaling that the passengers should go to the coast. At the same time, a sloop rowed up and threw out its plank to take the passengers on board. Many people with luggage came from the land, walked over the plank, and soon the sloop was full, and the first cargo was brought on board. Before the sloop docked for the second time, four people were seen approaching the beach who differed from the other poorer passengers by their gait, posture, and clothing. A tall, elderly man walked proudly in front; he had on a wide-brimmed hat and his cloak wrapped so artfully and comfortably around his shoulders that a boatman who saw him coming exclaimed: "I'll let myself be eaten if it isn't a Spaniard!" Behind him came a younger gentleman who was leading a beautiful, slim lady. The young gentleman was very pale and seemed to be fighting back a great sorrow in order to calm the lady's even greater one by persuasion. Her beautiful face was red around the eyes and forehead from violent tears, her mouth painfully pressed, and her cheeks and lower part of the face very pale. She walked unsteadily, leaning on the young man's arm; a little hat with flowing ostrich feathers, a flowing dress of heavy black silk, and rich gold chains around her neck and bosom, did not seem to suit the journey, and one could therefore believe that she was accompanying the young man on board; behind both of them walked a servant in brightly colored clothes; He carried a large parasol under his arm and had a Spanish net pulled over his dark hair.

When they had come down to where the sand was still wet from the previous flood to the place where the plank was thrown out to the sloop, they stopped and the beautiful young couple looked at the ship, then they looked at each other and the lady laid her head on the man's shoulder so that the ostrich feathers played about his face and hid his silent tears from the eyes of the curious. The old gentleman stood not far away, wrapped himself in his cloak, glaring darkly at the sea, and his eye flashed, one did not know whether from a tear or the reflection of the shining waves. Now the sloop splashed onto the shore; the plank was thrown out and a thunderous shot from the ship startled the couple from their embrace. The old gentleman came up, offered the young man his hand, shook it vigorously and then quickly stepped over the plank, his servant followed after he had also offered the youth his hand warmly. Now the young people embraced each other once more; he turned away first and led the lady to the board. "Forever!" she whispered with a wistful smile. "Forever!" the young man answered, looking at her tremblingly, with tears in his eyes. Another handshake and she turned to climb up the board. She was already at the top; the chief boatswain, a broad Englishman, was waiting at the board, stretching out his broad hand to receive the beautiful lady, and already had some well-meaning reasons for consolation ready. Then she turned her dark eyes from the endless sea back to the young man. Her tall, magnificent figure floated boldly on the narrow board, her slender neck was bent back towards the land, the swaying feathers of her hat seemed to greet her across. He spread his arms; his features mingled the bliss of love with the pain of separation. Then she seemed no longer to be in control of herself; She jumped over the plank and down onto the land, and before the boatswain could throw his hands together in amazement, she was already hanging on the young man's neck, on his lips. "No, I cannot go across the sea," she cried, "I want to stay; I want to do everything you want; I want to throw off these chains of faith that prevent me from following my better feelings; you are my country, my family, my everything; I'm staying!"

"Josephe, my Josephe!" cried the young man, pressing her to his heart with tumultuous delight. "My,[199] mine forever? A god has guided your heart, oh, I would have perished under the torment of this separation!' They were still holding each other when the old man climbed overboard with hasty steps and down the plank and went to the group: 'Children,' he said, 'it would have been enough to say goodbye once; come, Josephe, it's no use anyway, they'll shoot a third time in a minute.'

"Let her shoot with bullets, Don Pedro," cried the young man, his face filled with joy. "She'll stay here, she'll stay with me!"

"What do I hear?" he replied very seriously. "I hope that it is not as the gentleman says, you will follow your relative, Josephe!"

"No!" she cried bravely, "when I stood up there on the edge of the sloop and looked out at the waves that were to separate me from him, I knew what I must do. My mother showed me the way. She once followed the man of her heart into the wide world, leaving father and mother for love. I know what I must do too. Here stands the man to whom my poor mother owes her last sweet hours, to whom I owe life, honour, everything, and I should leave him? Greet the graves of my ancestors in Valencia, Don Pedro, and tell them that there is another of the Tortosi tribe who values love more than life!"

Don Pedro softened. "Then follow your heart, perhaps it will advise you better than an old man; I know you are at least happy in the arms of this noble man, and his high spirits assure me that he values our honor no less highly than his own. But Don Fröbenio, what will you say to your proud relatives when you introduce this child of misery? God! Will you also have the courage to endure the mockery of the world?"

"Farewell, Don Pedro," said the young man with a brave face, offering one hand to the other in farewell and clasping his beloved with the other; "be of good cheer and do not despair of me. I will show her to the world, and if I am asked: Who was she? I will answer with joyful pride: It was the beggar woman from the Pont des Arts ."

JEW SUSS.

1.

The carnival had never been celebrated in Stuttgart with such splendour and pomp as in 1737. When a stranger entered the enormous halls that had been built for this purpose and magnificently decorated, when he looked over the thousands of shining and cheerful masks, heard the laughter and singing of the crowd drowning out the numerous fanfares of the music choirs, he would not believe he was in Württemberg, in this strict, serious Württemberg, made strict by a zealous, often ascetic Protestantism that hated merrymaking of this kind as a relic of another religious party; serious, almost dark and gloomy because of the precarious situation, the misery and poverty into which the systematic artifices of an all-powerful minister had brought it.

The most splendid of these days of joy was probably the twelfth of February, on which the founder and inventor of these festivities and so many other things that were not exactly fun, Jew Süss , Cabinet Minister and Finance Director, celebrated his birthday. The Duke had sent him all kinds of gifts on the morning of that day; but the most pleasant thing for the Cabinet Minister was an edict bearing the date of this day of joy, an edict that absolved him forever of all responsibility for the past and future. Those innumerable creatures of every rank, creed and age, whom he had planted in the place of better men, besieged his stairs and anterooms to wish him luck and many a respectable, honest official was driven on that day to kiss the hand in the Jew's house for fear of making his family unhappy by defiance.

The same motifs filled the carnival halls in the evenings. For his followers and friends it was a celebration of joy that they planned to celebrate often; men who had secretly hated and had to worship publicly, wrapped themselves in their dominoes with gritted teeth and went with their wives and children to the splendid assembly of foolishness, convinced that their names would be entered in the register and that any omissions would be severely punished; but the people saw these days as dream hours when, in the intoxication of their senses, they could forget their oppressive misery; they did not calculate that the high entrance fees were only a new indirect tax that they were paying to the Jews.

The highlight of the evening was the moment when the double doors flew open, an expectant silence fell over the assembly, and finally a man of about forty, with striking, marked features, with bright, sparkling eyes that ran lively and lurking through the rows, entered the hall. He wore a white domino, a white hat with purple plumes, on which he had carelessly placed the black mask; there was nothing magnificent about him except an unusually large solitaire which held together at the neck the purple bayonet of silk veil that fell over the domino. He led a slender, delicately built lady who, dressed in an oriental costume laden with gold and stones, attracted all eyes.

"The financial director, the minister," whispered the crowd as he passed through the rows, greeting them with distinction, which were willingly opened for him; and when he reached the middle of the main hall, trumpets and drums greeted him, and a not inconsiderable number of the masks applauded him, while others were seen turning away as if from an indecent spectacle. But the interest with which they viewed the beautiful Oriental woman who had come with the minister seemed to be universal. His way of life was too well known for most not to have suspected one of his friends under the mask of the richly adorned lady; there seemed to be disagreement only as to which of them had received this distinction. One seemed too small for this figure, another too corpulent for this delicate waist, the third too clumsy to glide so lightly and almost as if floating over the ground, and a fourth, at whom one finally wanted to stand still, could not have this shining black hair that fell in rich curls around the proud neck, nor this magnificent, dark eye that one could see shining out from the mask.

The crowd, unless its curiosity is at once satisfied, does not pause long over anyone object on occasions so brilliant and lively as this carnival. "When she takes off her mask, we shall see!" they said, without paying any longer attention to the lady than was necessary to observe her beginning the minuet. But three young men, who were standing idly behind the rows of dancers, seemed still to be watching this apparition incessantly.

"Who could she be?" cried one impatiently. "I would gladly buy fifty tickets from the desperate Jew if he would tell me where this girl came from, whom he led into the hall like a princess."

"Brother!" replied the second, not taking his eyes off the Oriental woman as he spoke: "Brother, parole d'honneur ! I cannot reconcile these contradictions, even if I had studied logic and the ' cogito, ergo sum ' with Descartes himself; such an unusually fine figure, this posture, this movement measured according to the newest and most noble rules, this way of moving the wrist in a round and playful manner, such as I have only seen in the most important circles in Vienna and Paris, this decency with which she carries her neck -"

"God damn me, you're right, brother!" interrupted the third. "All this and - coming to the ball with Suss! No, I've never seen such a contrast in my life!"

"She cannot be one of our acquaintances," continued the first, "or one of our circles; for even if it is true what is whispered, that many a wretched father has sent his daughter to the Jew with a petition, no one lets his shame be so loud as to send his own child to the ball with this Mazette!"

"Please, for heaven's sake, brother, not so loudly, he has spies everywhere, and we don't like him anyway; think of your family, do you want to make yourself unhappy? But it is true, she cannot be a girl from a better class, and yet her nature is too respectable for a bourgeois daughter. But wait, who is the Saracen who is coming towards us there? The color of his turban is the same as that of the Jew's charmer!"

The young men turned around and saw a slim, well-built man, who, dressed as a Saracen, distinguished himself from more common masks by the simple splendor of his costume as well as by his gait and bearing. He too seemed to have caught sight of the young men, for he approached them slowly and hesitated to pass them.

"What is your watchword?" asked one of the young men, who thought he recognized a friend in the mask. "Is your only battle cry your Allah , or do you know some other saying?"

" Gaudeamus igitur, juvenes dum sumus ," replied the Saracen, standing still.

"It's him, it's him," cried two of these young gentlemen, shaking the Saracen's hand. "It's a good thing we gave the password, otherwise I would have had no way of identifying you, for I was so sure that you were here as a farmer that I bet the captain a bottle that you must be a farmer!"

"Let us go to the buffet," said the second, "I have someone here to introduce you, Brother Gustav, who is looking forward to meeting you, and you know that it is difficult to recognize one another in masks."

"Friend," replied Gustav, "I will not take off the mask, I have reasons; however pleasant it would be for me to make the acquaintance of this gentleman, I must save it until tomorrow."

"And what if it were Pinassa, of whom you have so often asked?" he answered.

"Pinassa? The man you fought with? No, that changes the matter. I want to see him and greet him; but I will only take off my mask for two moments and in the furthest corner of the dining room."

"We are satisfied, brother Saracen," answered the captain. "But let us first get to the second bottle, and then you shall confess the reasons why you will not let your face shine before your friends!"

2.

There were only a few people in the dining room they chose, because only selected wines, fine fruits and warm drinks were sold there, while the larger drinking rooms, where local wine, beer and coarser food were available, attracted the larger crowds. In a corner of the, In the other room there was an empty table where the Saracen, if he turned his back to the rest of the hall, could remove his mask without danger of being recognized. They chose this place, and when the full Romans stood before them, the two young warriors removed their masks and the captain began: "Brother, I have the honor of introducing you here to the incomparable Cavalier Pinassa, the most famous swordsman of his time; for he succeeded, with an invincible third-fourth-third, in making me - remember, me, the senior of the Amicist Order - hors de combat in Leipzig's unforgettable Rosenthal . Like me, he abandoned the muses, sang: 'If Minerva will not have me, then let Bellona advise', and exchanged the old sword and its enormous guard, on which he was accustomed to eat his breakfast, for the parade sword of a lieutenant of the Duke of Württemberg."

"The exchange is not bad, Mr. von Pinassa, and my country can congratulate itself on it," said the Saracen, bowing to the new lieutenant. "If you were to enter our service, this would be the most pleasant career. The civilian has little prospect at this time unless he is willing to buy an office from the Jew for five thousand guilders or for his conscience and honest name. But these thin wooden walls have ears - keep quiet about it, it cannot be helped. How different your circumstances are! The Duke is a brave man, to whom I would grant a state of two hundred thousand soldiers; for us - he is too big. War is his pleasure, a regiment in the splendor of arms his joy; unfortunately, the rest of us rarely have an idle hour, and that is why these Jews and Jewish Christians hold the sceptre. He is considered a great general, he has performed fine feats of arms with Prince Eugene, and a slim young man with a scar on his forehead and courage in his eyes, like you, Mr. von Pinassa, is always welcome in his army."

What a Saracen can say about Jews and Christians! said the captain. But open your visor and show your colours, my comrade shall now also know who he is talking to that is the prudent, legal, excellent Mr. Juris utriusque Doctor Lanbek, natural son of the famous regional consultant Lanbek, for whom he is substituted as actuary; an excellent boy, parole d'honneur , if he has not recently prostituted by strange melancholy , even better if the Lord had also implanted in him a taste for the fairer sex."

Lanbek took off his mask at these words and showed his new acquaintance a blushing face of great beauty. Yellow curls stole out from under his turban and flowed artlessly and unpowdered around his forehead. A boldly curved nose and dark, deep blue eyes gave his face an expression of enterprising strength and a deep seriousness that was in surprising contrast to his soft hair and its gentle color. But the severity of these features and these eyes was softened by a pleasant expression around his mouth as he answered: "I open my visor and show you a face that welcomes you warmly to us. I drink this glass to your health, but then you will excuse me if I leave."

"Pro poena you drink two," cried the captain with comic pathos, taking an enormous house key from his pocket and lowering it towards the Saracen as a sceptre. "Have you so little respect for your elder that you dare to drink in loco glasses without them being properly dictated to you by the preses? O tempora, o mores! Where have the discipline and manners of these foxes gone? Pinassa! In our time it was different!"

The young men laughed at this pitiful reminiscence of the former senior Amicist; but the captain looked Lanbek more closely in the eye and said: "Brother, don't take it amiss, but you've had something like a fever inside you for a long time, and tonight is the crisis; I'll bet my lost bottle, nothing will go away from that, but I'll bet ten new ones; be honest, Gustav - you were already here this evening as a farmer, and your old man knows nothing about the Saracen."

Gustav blushed, shook his friend's hand and waved yes to him.

"All of you!" cried the captain. "Boy, what are you doing? Who would have looked for this behind the quiet clerk? Changing your costume at the carnival! And so timid, so mysterious, so abrupt; are you going to attack the Jew?"

The man blushed even more and quickly took off his mask; before he could answer, Reelzingen said: Brother, you have put me on the right track. Where have you, you two, you and the Oriental woman that the finance director led, bought the material for your turbans? Gustav,

Gustav!" he added, threateningly pointing a finger. "You live opposite the Jew, I bet you know who the proud lady he leads is."

What do I know? muttered Lanbek under his mask.

"Not from this place until you say so," cried the captain; "and if you persist in your defiance, I will creep up to the Oriental woman and whisper in her ear that the Saracen has let me in on his secret."

"You will not do that if I earnestly ask you not to," replied the young man, apparently very seriously; "if I may trust my guess, it is Lea Oppenheimer, the minister's sister. And now adieu! If you should meet me in the hall, you will not know me, and Reelzingen, if my father asks -"

"Then I know nothing about you, of course," he replied. The Saracen rose and left. The friends looked at each other, and none of them seemed to know whether he had heard correctly or how to interpret all this. "Does the Jew have a sister?" asked Pinassa.

"Some time ago it was said that he had taken a sister in, but she was thought to be very young because she never shows herself anywhere," replied Reelzingen thoughtfully. "And the way he blushed, brother, you will see that Satan once again makes a sensible boy play a foolish trick."

3.

After leaving his friends, Lanbek wandered around the halls; his eyes wandered restlessly over the crowd, his face glowed beneath his mask, and he often had to struggle to catch his breath, so oppressive was the air in the hall and so heavy was the expectation, longing and fear on his heart. The crowd was pressed together more densely and stormily when he reached the middle of the second hall; he pushed through with difficulty for a while, but finally the stream that was pushing towards one side involuntarily swept him away, and before he knew it he was standing at a gaming table where *Süß* was playing cards with some of his financial advisors. Large piles of gold lay on the table, and the curious crowd watched. The most famous man in their country and whispered and murmured remarks about the enormous sums he gave away or won without changing his expression.

Gustav had never observed the mighty man so closely as now, when he became an involuntary observer, held in place by the crowd that stood around him like a wall. He admitted to himself that this man's face was naturally beautiful and noble, that even his forehead and his eyes had acquired something impressive through the habit of ruling; but hostile, repulsive wrinkles lay between his eyebrows where the clear forehead was about to join the beautifully formed nose, the little mustache on his upper lip could not conceal a malicious expression around his mouth; and the young man found the hoarse, forced laughter with which the Jewish minister accompanied gain or loss truly horrifying.

While the gentlemen, surrounded by the crowd, were playing and seemed to be waiting for something, a man dressed as a farmer from the Steinlach stepped out of the ranks of the curious. An old hat on his head, a rough blue jacket, a red waistcoat with large tin buttons, yellow leather trousers and black stockings made up his plain costume; but he wore a very fine, well-painted mask. He leaned on his five-foot-high knotted stick in the manner of a countryman, rested his chin on his hand and spoke in a well-imitated dialect of the Steinlach valley: "You have a lot of money lying around, sir! And did you earn it all yourself?"

The minister looked around and tried to smile at this freedom from wearing a mask. Perhaps he welcomed this opportunity to give himself a popular image, because he replied in a friendly manner: "Good evening, fellow countryman."

"I am not your countryman," replied the farmer with great calmness. "Mice do not usually behave like me." A suppressed laughter flew through the rows of spectators. The minister did not seem to notice, however, for he continued quite affably: "You are witty, my friend."

"God forbid that I should be your friend, Mr. Sweet," replied the farmer. "If I were your friend, I would not go in that shabby coat and hat with holes in it; you are making your friends rich."

"Well, then all of Württemberg must be my friend, because I will make it rich," said Süß, accompanying his speech with a hoarse, unpleasant laugh.

"You are a common goldsmith," replied the farmer. "How beautiful these ducats are; how many drops of poor people's sweat go into such a gold piece?"

“You’re a great guy!” cried Sweet, continuing to play calmly.

As the farmer was about to begin a new speech, a new figure attracted attention. It was a man whose costume was almost the same as the farmers, except that he had a long, pointed beard on his chin and was wearing a braided coat. The farmer looked at him in surprise for a while, then shook his hand and called out: "Hey Hans! Where do you come from and so smart and stately! Not at all like us!"

"That means," replied Hans, sniffing from a silver box, "that I have entered the service of a nobleman."

“Who is your master?” asked the farmer.

"A slave driver, but a noble one. Do you think he slaves common cattle, horses, dogs, and the like? No, he is a slave driver and a card manufacturer on top of that."

“A card maker?” cried the farmer.

"Yes, because you have to buy all the cards in the country from him, he stamps them; but he is also a tanner."

"Like that?"

"Now all the tanners in the country have to buy their tanned hides from him; but he is also a stamping machine."

"What! An embossing stamp?"

Yes, he makes all the money in the country.

"That's a lie," said the farmer, "you mean to say that he turns everything in the country into money; but that doesn't make him a mint. There is only *one* mint in Württemberg that has stamped his name on the country."

The crowd had hitherto only murmured its applause, but at the last allusion to the coin they burst into loud laughter; the brow of the mighty man darkened somewhat, but he still played calmly.

"But why did you let your beard grow so pointy?" the farmer asked. "It looks quite Jewish."

"It's just the fashion," replied Hans, "since the Jews are masters in the country; soon I want to become completely Jewish."

As Hans spoke these last words, a loud voice from the thickest crowd called out: "Wait a few more weeks, Hans, then you can easily become a Catholic."

Whoever has ever witnessed the terrible sight of a barrel of gunpowder bursting into flames in a crowded street, whether by carelessness or deliberation, has scarcely seen a scene so strange as that which these few mysterious words produced. The minister, pale as a corpse, jumps up from his chair, throws the cards on the table with a furious look: "Who says this? Seize him in the name of the Duke!" he cries, and rushes upon the crowd as if impelled by some invisible power; his companions, no less astonished, but more prudent, seize his arm and draw him back, trying to pacify him - his dark eye tries to pierce through the crowd to catch the object of his rage, the masks murmur indignantly and crowd together; but as the dreaded man stretches out his hand to the peasant and cries: "Then you shall answer for him to me," he is suddenly surrounded by a threatening crowd. "Freedom of the mask, Jew!" one hears in dull, dangerous tones, the farmer and his journeyman are separated from him in an instant, disappear, and as quickly as he was surrounded before, he is deserted again, for the crowd, driven by secret fear, scatters in all directions.

The crowd swept Gustav Lanbek away; his thoughts became confused; he was still unable to imagine clearly what could have caused this strange scene. He stood there for a few moments, lost in his thoughts, when suddenly he felt his hand grasped by another; he looked around, the Oriental woman was standing in front of him.

4.

"Where did the rose on your hat come from, Mask?" asked the Oriental woman in a trembling voice.

“From the Sea of Tiberias,” was the Saracen’s reply.

"Quick! Follow me!" cried the lady and slipped through the crowd. He followed, pushing through the crowd with difficulty, and only her turban showed him now and then the Away; his heartbeat louder, his ear still caught the last sounds of that sweet voice, and his eyes saw no other object than her. In a darker corner of the second room, she stopped and turned around. "Gustav, I implore you, what has happened to my brother? People are whispering his name everywhere; I don't know what they are saying, but I think it is nothing good; has he had a quarrel? Oh, I know very well that these people hate our people."

The young man was in a painful embarrassment. Should he suddenly destroy the innocent delusion of this lovable creature? Should he tell her that the curse of the Württembergers rested on her brother, that they prayed for all people and excluded him alone from prayer, that it had become customary to pray: "Lord, deliver us from evil and from the Jew Süss." - "Lea," he answered very embarrassedly, "your brother was disturbed by some masks in his play and had an argument that perhaps attracted attention in this very place. Do not be afraid."

"What a foolish girl I am!" she said. "I have such bad dreams, and then I am so sad and depressed during the day. And I am so irritable that everything frightens me, that I always think of my brother and believe that something bad has happened to him."

"Lea," whispered the young man, to dispel these thoughts, "do you remember what you promised if we met at the carnival? Wouldn't you give me just one hour of privacy where we could have a good chat?"

"I will," she said after some hesitation. "Sara, my nurse, is standing at the exit and will accompany me. But where?"

"That is taken care of," he replied, "follow me, do not lose sight of me; at the entrance on the right."

The inventiveness of the Jewish minister, when he arranged the carnival in Stuttgart and had these halls quickly erected out of wood, had ensured that, as in large houses and castles, smaller rooms would be added to these halls, where small groups could eat an evening meal without having to leave their incognito in the general dining room. The clerk had managed to get the key to one of these rooms through a third hand and sufficient payment; a small collation was waiting there, and Lea was pleased about this kindness of the young Christian, who had done his best to make the sense of a to satisfy the needs of a lady with experience in cooking, although the little room, which contained only a table and a few chairs made of light wood, offered little comfort.

"How glad I am to be able to take off this annoying mask at last!" she said as she entered with her nurse; she looked around for a mirror, and when she saw only empty wooden walls, she added with a smile: "You must serve me instead of a mirror, Gustav, and tell me whether this crowd has not spoiled my hair?"

The young man gazed at the beautiful girl with delight and with shining eyes. Her face could be called the perfection of oriental features. This symmetry in the finely cut features, these wonderful dark eyes, shaded by long, silky eyelashes, these boldly arched, shining black eyebrows and the dark curls that fell in such pleasant contrast around the white forehead and the beautiful neck, and which emphasized still more the point of union of these lovely features, delicate red lips and the most delicate white teeth; the turban that wound itself through her curls, the rich pearls that played around her neck, the charming and yet so modest costume of a Turkish lady - all of these, combined with these features, produced such an illusion that the young man thought he saw one of those splendid apparitions such as Tasso describes, as the excited imagination of travelers painted on their return home.

"Truly," he cried, "you resemble the sorceress Armida, and so I imagine the daughters of your tribe when you still lived in Canaan. So was Rebekah and the daughter of Jephthah."

"How often have I said this," remarked Sara, "when I looked at my child, my Lea, in her splendor; the pom-poms and hoop skirts, the high heels and all the other fashionable articles do not suit her at all as well as this costume."

"You are right, good Sarah," replied the young man, "but sit down here at the table; you have lived too long among Christians to shrink from this punch and this cake; amuse yourself with these things."

Sara, who knew the mind and manner of her neighbor, did not resist for long and took pity on the confectioners' products; but the young man sat down a few steps in front of her next to the beautiful Lea. "And now, honestly, girl," he said, "you are troubled, you hardly had anything yesterday, suppressed tears and today again there is a cloud on this forehead that I would so gladly dispel. Or do you not believe, unbelieving child, that I am your friend and would gladly do everything to cheer you up?"

"I know it, oh, I see it all the time, and I see it again today," she said, struggling to fight back her tears, "and it makes me happy. When you greeted me for the first time at our garden fence, when you later, it was the beginning of October, spoke to me over the fence, and afterwards and always were so friendly and confiding, not at all like other Christians towards us, then I knew that you meant well by me and - it is my only, my quiet happiness!" She said it, and a few tears stole from her beautiful eyes as she tried to look at him kindly and smilingly.

But still? asked Gustav.

"But I am still not happy, not completely happy. In Frankfurt I had my playmates, had my own world, and wanted nothing to do with the rest. I did not think about our circumstances, it did not hurt me that the Christians did not respect us, I sat in my little room among friends and wanted nothing to do with what was outside. My brother had me brought to him in Stuttgart. I was told that he had become a great man, that he ruled a country, that his house was splendid and full of joy, and that the Christians lived with him as we lived among ourselves. I confess that it pleased me when my friends painted such a bright picture of my future; what girl would not have been happy in my place?"

Tears broke again, and the young man, full of pity for her grief, felt that it would be better to let her tears flow for a few moments. There is a feeling in the human breast that makes one melancholier than any other grief; I would call it pity for ourselves; it overwhelms us when, standing at the grave of shattered hopes, we go back to the days when those hopes still flourished, when we recall the cheerful thoughts with which we looked forward to a bright future; truly, this bitter contrast has dissolved stronger hearts into melancholy than the heart of the beautiful Jewess.

"I have found everything different," Lea continued after a while. "I am lonelier in my brother's house than I was in my childhood. I am not allowed to come when he gives balls and big parties. The music sounds in my lonely room, I am sent cakes and sweet wines like a child who is not yet old enough to go out in company. And when I ask my brother to let me take part, at least in his house, he either turns me down coldly, or, if he is in a strange mood, he frightens me with his answer."

“What did he answer?” asked the young man eagerly.

"He then looks at me for a long time and sighs, his eyes become duller, his features gloomy and melancholy, and he answers: I must not perish too; I should pray unceasingly to the God of our fathers that he may keep me pious and pure, so that my soul may become a pure sacrifice for his soul."

"Foolish superstition!" cried the young man angrily. "Therefore, poor child, you must renounce all the joys of life so that he -"

"Has he sinned so badly?" asked Lea, as her friend quickly broke off, as if he had spoken rashly. "What am I to atone for? Such words thrown out of hand make me so unhappy: I feel as if some misfortune is hanging over my brother, and not everything he does is right. No one can tell me about it, and I cannot even interpret Sarah's words, for when I ask her about it, she evades the question or mysteriously calls him the avenger of our people."

"She is not wise," replied the young man, embarrassed. "Your brother, as is the case everywhere, has a powerful opponent; some of his financial operations are criticized. But you may sleep easy about him," he added, laughing bitterly. "The Duke has today given him a charter which protects him from all danger and responsibility."

"Oh, how I thank the good Duke for this!" she said cheerfully, brushing the dark curls from her white forehead. "So, he has no one to fear? The Christians cannot persecute him? You don't answer? Just confess, Gustav, that you are angry with my poor brother?"

"Your poor brother? If he were poor, I could perhaps honor him for his intelligence! But what does your brother have to do with us," continued Lanbek, smiling gloomily; "I love you, even if you had all the evil angels for brothers; but promise me one thing , Lea, and give me your hand on it."

She looked at him expectantly and tenderly, placing her hand in his.

"Never again," he continued, "ask your brother to admit you to his circles. Whatever his reasons may be, it is well that you are not there. I could assure you of this much," he added, his eyes flashing, "if I knew that you had been there even once, I would never speak another word to you!"

Embarrassed and with tears in her eyes, she was just about to ask for an explanation of this new mystery when a loud quarrel in the next room disturbed the lovers. Several men seemed to be arguing with the police, the door of the cabinet had been blown open, and this infringement on the rights of the carnival quickly and fiercely became the subject of argument.

"My God! That is my father's voice," cried young Lanbek. "Sneak into the hall with Sara, girl; take the key to this door with you, perhaps we can see each other again later." He quickly pressed a kiss on the surprised Lea's forehead, put on his mask, and before she could even think about this sudden change, the clerk had already rushed out of the door. In the corridor that he now entered; a dense crowd of people was already gathered around the open door of the next room. He heard his father's deep, weighty voice more clearly; he pushed and pushed his way through like a madman and finally came into the room. Five old gentlemen, who were well known to him as honorable men and friends of his father, stood around the old regional consultant Lanbek; some were quarreling, others were trying to calm him down. It was a dangerous thing in those days to get into a fight with the police; It was under the special protection of the Jewish minister, and there were several instances in which honest, quiet citizens and officials, perhaps just because they had contradicted a servant of this secret police or prevented violence, had been thrown into prison for several weeks and then released with the bare excuse that it had happened by mistake. But old Lanbek did not seem to fear these people; he insisted that the bailiffs leave the room immediately, and perhaps there would have been an even worse altercation than an exchange of words if a completely different matter had not attracted the attention of the leader of the bailiffs at that moment. Young Lanbek had pushed his way almost to his father's side, ready to intervene if it came to violence. should come to give the old gentleman strong support. He had just tied his mask tighter so that it would not be lost in the scuffle, when the police officer saw him and, pointing to him, called out in a loud voice: "In the name of the Duke, seize this one, the Turk over there, he is the right one!"

The surprise and six arms that suddenly wrapped themselves around him left him defenseless. So close to his father, who could have saved him, he did not dare to make a sound, because he feared his father's anger even more than the Jew's violence.

The old gentlemen were speechless with astonishment at this incident. The leader of the henchmen, having achieved his purpose, became more polite and apologized, whereupon they thanked him coldly and measuredly. The young man let himself be led there without will. The crowd that had gathered in front of the door parted, but some looked curiously into his eyes to guess who it could be who had been torn from the midst of public merriment. As he was led further, Gustav heard a faint cry; he looked around, and in the dim light of the lamps he thought he had seen the turban of the beautiful Oriental woman. Painfully moved, he walked on, and only when the cold winter night blew sharply towards him did he awaken from his stupor and consider, not without concern, the consequences that his capture might have.

5.

The police officers had taken the Saracen, probably out of consideration for his fine and rich clothing, to the officers' quarters of the main guard. The officer in charge, with a sullen bow, showed him to sleep on a bench in the farthest corner of the room, and, tired from his long wanderings at the ball, the young man did not find this couch too hard for him to fall asleep quickly.

Drums woke him the next morning; sleepily he looked around the desolate room, first at his hard bed, then at his clothes, and only after a while could he remember where he was and how he had got there. He went to the window; everything was still quiet on the square in front of the main guardhouse, and only the company that had just outside his window to relieve himself broke the silence of the dreary February morning. While the drums in the street were silent, he heard the eight o'clock strike from the collegiate church, and the sound of this bell brought back to him all the unpleasantness and anxiety of his situation. "Soon he will ask for you," he thought, "and how unpleasantly surprised he will be when he hears that I did not come home last night!" -

In the house of the old regional consultant Lanbek everything went on in such an orderly fashion that this event must have seemed very disturbing. At this hour the old gentleman had been accustomed to having his breakfast for many years; at the first stroke of the clock his son would appear, along with the servant who brought the coffee; they would discuss the news of the day, the progress of business, and at that time the all-powerful minister did not lack material for such conversations. The conversation always ended with breakfast; the clerk kissed the old man's hand and then, every day like the next, went to his office at a quarter to nine. Gustav recalled this long-standing custom of the house at this moment. "Now Johann will bring the cups," he said to himself, "now he will look expectantly at the door because I have not yet entered, now he will have me called; that I should have caused the good old gentleman such trouble!' He threw away his turban indignantly, rested his forehead on his hand, and resolved to ask the officer, as soon as he appeared again, the reason for his arrest.

The drums sounded again, the relieved men moved on, he heard the guns being assembled, and soon an officer entered the dimly lit room. He cast a quick glance at his prisoner in the corner, laid his hat and sword on the table, and sat down. Lanbek, who did not want to speak to him first, moved to indicate that he was no longer asleep. " Bonjour , sir," said the officer when he saw him, "would you like to share my lunch with me?"

The voice seemed familiar to Gustav; he stood up, approached with a polite greeting, and with an exclamation of astonishment the two young men stood facing each other. " Parole d'honneur , brother!" cried the Captain of Reelzingen, " I was not looking *for you* here! How did you end up in custody? God knows, Blankenberg was not wrong when he suggested that you would risk something contra rationem .

"I would like to ask you, Captain," replied the young man, "why I am sitting here? No one has told me the reason why I am being taken prisoner; you are on guard, Reelzingen; please, you must know -"

" Dieu me garde! I?" cried the captain, smiling. "Do you think he has honored me with his special appreciation and taken me into his confidence? No, brother! When I relieved him, the lieutenant from yesterday said to me: 'There is someone sitting upstairs whom they brought here from the carnival on express orders.' He usually does it that way."

"Who does it like that?" asked Lanbek, turning pale.

"Who?" he replied in a soft whisper, "your future brother-in-law , the Jew."

"What?" he continued, blushing, "you think he himself? I had hoped that there had perhaps been a mix-up! You must have heard of the incident with the Jew that occurred soon after I left you. They shouted something about becoming Catholic, and the finance minister exploded -"

"What are you saying?" interrupted the captain with a serious expression, coming closer to his friend and taking his hand. "So that was it? We were told differently; how did it happen? What did they shout?"

The clerk was not a little surprised by the seriousness he saw in the face of his otherwise cheerful and carefree friend; he told the story as he had witnessed it and saw how his friend's curiosity grew more and more, how his eyes became fierier but when he described how Süß had become angry after that mysterious exclamation and jumped up, he felt the captain's hand twitch in his in a strange way. "What moves you so much?" asked Gustav, surprised. "How can you take such an interest in such carnival jokes that ultimately lead to some kind of foolishness? If I didn't know that you were a Protestant, I would think my report had offended you."

"Brother," replied the captain, trying to conceal his seriousness behind an indifferent smile, "you know me, I am interested in everything in the world, and I am amazingly curious; besides, some things are more serious than one thinks, and there is often meaning in jest."

"How do you understand that?" said the actuary, surprised. "What makes you so thoughtful? Are you in debt again? Can I perhaps help you with something?"

"Brother," replied the soldier, "you must have been madly in love these last few weeks, otherwise your clear eyes would not have missed many things that even my light-hearted mind could not have missed. Tell me, what does Papa say about such times? Do you never see Colonel von Röder at his house? Weren't the prelates in your house on Friday evening?"

"You speak in riddles, Captain!" answered the young man in astonishment. "What does my father want with a colonel of the life squadron and with prelates?"

"Friend, make it short," said Reelzingen. "Do not think me frivolous in such matters; I do not wish to force myself into your confidence, but I can tell you that I already know quite a lot, and - parole d'honneur! " he added, "I think of it as befits a nobleman and my sword-knot."

"What do I care about your old letter of nobility and your new sword-knot?" replied the clerk; "and how come you are making such a fuss about me? I tell you that I don't understand a single syllable of all that you are babbling about in such mysterious terms, and I give you my word on it, and that's enough of that, Mr. von Reelzingen!"

" O mon Dieu! " he cried, smiling. "Brother, we are no longer in Leipzig. This room is not the divine town hall, but a guard room. We are no longer muses. You are the ducal clerk, and I am a soldier. But we are still friends in times of need and death, and so be sensible and do not get angry like you did before. I believe you when you say that you know nothing, but it would have been good of your father to have prevented you. Besides, your love affair with the Jewess is now absolutely not the time. We all beg you to leave your charmer, with whom you can never have a sensible and honorable liaison -"

"What do you know about this relationship?" the young man interrupted him, gloomy and bitter. "I think that before I ask your advice on this matter, you could reasonably wait with your warning."

The fiery young soldier, in order to help his friend, was just about to reply in the same language when there was a knock at the door. The captain opened it and one of his sergeants beckoned him to come out. Gustav heard them exchange a few words and soon saw his friend return with a perturbed expression. "You are receiving a strange visitor," he whispered to him, "he will come in himself soon and I must not be present."

"Who? My father?" asked Gustav, dismayed.

"He's coming," said the captain, hastily taking his hat and sword from the table, " *the Jew Suss* !"

6.

At the door of the officers' room, his servants had taken the minister's Spanish cloak, and he now entered, handsomely adorned and elegantly dressed, as became a favorite of fortune and a duke in those days. He wore a red coat trimmed with gold tassels and tassels; the gold-embroidered lapels of his coat went back to the elbow, and the gold brocade waistcoat reached down to the knee. A short, broad sword with a richly decorated handle hung at his side, a powerful cane supported his hand, and on the rich, light-brown curls that fell deep down to his neck sat a little hat of fine black oilcloth, trimmed with gold and white feathers. The features of this remarkable man, seen up close, were a little too bold to be called beautiful and graceful, but they were nobler than his profession and unusual; his dark brown eyes, which looked around freely and proudly, could even be considered beautiful; The whole appearance was impressive, and it would even have had something dignified and sublime about it, had it not been for a malicious, hostile expression around the proudly pursed lips, which spoiled this impression and filled many who met him with uncanny horror.

The captain stood firm and erect at the door, his hat in one hand and the hilt of his sword in the other, when Minister Süß entered. He took off his hat, leaned on his stick, examined the soldier with a sharp look and then said briefly and in a low voice: "What is his name?"

Hans von Reelzingen, captain of the second grenadier battalion, third company.

“You have studied?” the Jew continued, somewhat more politely.

"The jurisprudence in Leipzig," answered the captain with military brevity.

»How long has the captain been serving?«

"One year and two months; first at –"

"Very well," interrupted the minister with a gracious gesture of his hand, "we can resign."

Captain Reelzingen hid his annoyance at the upstart's proud demeanor with a deep bow and left. The clerk, however, although he had no fear of man, felt his heart pounding as he was now alone with the man before whom a whole country trembled with superstitious fear. He blushed involuntarily as the latter looked at him long and searchingly, giving him the opportunity to examine his features and now and then to find something that reminded him of the beautiful Lea. The minister finally sat down in the armchair that the officers of the garrison had donated for the comfort of this room and condescendingly beckoned the Saracen to sit down on a bench that stood nearby.

"Young man," he said, "if you value your own peace and well-being, answer me frankly and honestly what I am about to ask you; for you may well imagine that it will not be difficult for me to convict you of every lie you dare to tell."

"I am the Duchy of Württemberg's secretary," replied the young man, "and the oath I took as a Christian and citizen -"

" Laissez cela ," interrupted the Jew, "you would not be the first to break your oath. Who were, I ask, the two masks who were talking at my table yesterday for the amusement of the audience? You know, you were standing next to me first."

"I am not aware of that, Your Excellency," said Gustav in a firm voice.

"Not known?" cried the minister. "Consider well what you said. I stand here as your judge. Did you not recognize anyone by their voice?"

None.

"None?" he continued, more vehemently. "And you don't know your father by his voice?"

" *My father!* " cried the young man, turning pale; but after a while he added more cautiously: "You are mistaken, Mr. Financial Director, or rather, you have been misinformed; my father is a quiet, composed man, and his character, his position, and his years forbid him from entertaining the public at a masked ball."

"*You should* forbid him," replied the other, his eyes flashing, "and I will find a way to forbid him. I know very well that I am a thorn in the side of these gentlemen from the countryside, and for the sole reason that they cannot do arithmetic. If they understood their multiplication tables as well as I do, they would see what is good for the country. But it is not yet the end of the world, and I will show these rebels who *they* are and who *I* am!"

“Mr. Financial Director!” cried the young man, a blush of displeasure on his cheeks.

“Mr. Actuary?” replied Süß with a mocking smile.

"My father is a man of honour," continued Gustav, not intimidated by the proud countenance of the mighty man. "You speak of rebels? How can you say that my father has not always served the Duke faithfully? How dare you call him a rebel?"

"Dare?" laughed Süß. "There is no question of daring here, Mr. Actuary, but anyone who serves only the country and not the Duke is a rebel; he is the Duke's servant, but he serves him badly; but that will not last much longer. You can tell the district consultant, your father, that I know very well what the two masks wanted, and that they had arranged it with the third one; I could have had him arrested last night as well as you, and if I *didn't*, he only owes this mercy to you!"

"Me?" answered the young man in astonishment. "Me? And is this perhaps also a mercy, that I was allowed to spend this night in this room without having committed a crime?"

"No!" he continued, smiling kindly, "this was only arranged to cool off before your rendezvous." He gloated for a few moments at the youth's embarrassment and then continued: "The good child, how she begged me and begged me on her knees to save you! She believed nothing else than “You're imprisoned for some capital crime. What? And you have nothing to say to me, Mr. Lanbek?"

"You did not know me," replied Gustav, "and I can now understand why you treated me so harshly; but Lea's character could have assured you that there was nothing criminal in this relationship."

"Really? Mort de ma vie! " cried the minister. "Nothing punishable? Do you think that if I suspected something punishable in this regard, you would have atoned for it with a night on guard duty? By the bones of my fathers! If I - at Neuffen or Asperg there are cellars and casemates where neither moon nor sun shines - I would have left the Saracen gentleman sitting there until he had reached his Swabian age. Or do you think, in your Christian arrogance, that an Israelite does not value the honor of his family as highly as a Nazarene?"

The young man was frightened by this threat, for he considered that it would have been easy for the Almighty to make him disappear from the earth without a trace, but his courageous spirit rebelled against the arrogance of this man who made his private affair public and threatened to use the fortresses of the country to protect his own rights. "Your Excellency," he said, looking at him, before which the minister cast his eyes down, "I do not know what you think of your own honor, but it does not seem very honorable to me to utter such threats. My father is indeed only a small man compared to such a powerful and high lord; but the regional consultant Lanbek knows where to find justice in Germany. Vienna is not so far from Stuttgart, and the Emperor did not sign your letter of mercy of yesterday; but as for your sister's honor, I can assure you that it is no less dear to me than my own."

"You have good qualities for a regional consultant," said the Jew, smiling calmly. "Incidentally, in confidence, you must not insist too much on the Emperor; no one in Vienna will start a quarrel with us over a Württemberg clerk. But I like you, my dear; I have heard your work praised, and minds like yours can be used for something better than stapling documents and binding fascicules; you are an expeditionary councillor with six hundred guilders. Salary, and I am pleased to be the first to congratulate you on this."

The young man jumped up from his bench and wanted to speak, but surprise and terror closed his mouth. A hundred thoughts crossed his mind. It was not the joy of having leapt over four steps in an instant, through which one would otherwise have dragged oneself long and laboriously, that filled his soul; it was the terrible thought of being considered a favorite of this man in the eyes of the world, of being branded in the eyes of his father, in the eyes of all good men.

"Your Excellency!" he said awkwardly. "I may not, I cannot accept this favor! Think about what people will say, so many older, deserving men -"

"What! I have made room for you," answered the Jew in a commanding tone, "I have appointed you to the council and you are it. No thanks, no great delicacy, I do not like that. Well," he continued kindly, almost tenderly, "and how are you with my Lea? You have completely enchanted the quiet, stupid child. Do not be afraid of me, young sir, I am not the kind of man who is so concerned with wealth; your family is one of the oldest and most respected bourgeois families, and in this case that is as much or more important to me than wealth. Your father will not give you much, but you shall be satisfied with me; I will equip my Lea like a prince."

The rock cellars of Neuffen and the deep casemates of Asperg would have been more welcome to the young man at that moment than this assurance; he thought of his proud father, of his distinguished family, and so great was the fear of disgrace, so deeply rooted were the prejudices against those unfortunate children of Abraham, that they even overcame his tender feelings for the beautiful daughter of Israel at that terrible moment. "Mr. Minister!" he said hesitantly, "Lea cannot have a warmer friend than me; but I fear that you are misinterpreting this feeling, confusing it with another, which - I do not want you to misunderstand me, and Lea will never have told you that I ever spoke of it -"

The proud man blushed, pursed his lips, almost closed his eyes, and a vein began to appear on his forehead to swell up. "What is that?" he said sternly. "How should I interpret this expression?"

"Mr. Minister," replied Gustav more composedly, "consider the difference in religion."

"Did you think of this, sir, when you put these love affairs into my sister's head? But I can console you, Lea will not hinder you in this respect. Are you silent?" he continued more vehemently, "shall I speak to your father about it, young man? Was my sister good enough to fill your idle hours, but you do not want her as your wife? Woe betide you if you think so! I would ruin you and your whole family! Your father was guilty of a serious crime yesterday, it is in my power to call him to account; I now place your father's fate in your hands; either you make up for your imprudence towards my house and marry my sister, or I will publicly declare you a villain and have the consultant put in chains. I will give you four weeks to think about it; my house is open to you, you can visit your bride as often as you like; four weeks, do you understand me? Now you are free, and tomorrow, Mr. Expeditionary Councilor, you will take up your office."

After these words he bowed briefly and left the room with proud steps; he ordered the captain, whom he met in the anteroom, to bring clothes for the expedition councillor and to announce his freedom to him.

Reelzingen entered his room, amazed by the whole incident, especially by the minister's last words. He found his friend pale and distraught, his arms crossed over his chest, his head drooping limply on his breast. "Now, for heaven's sake, tell me," began the captain, stopping in front of Gustav, "what did he want with you? Why did he have you arrested? What does his visit mean?"

"He came to congratulate me," he answered with a strange smile.

"To congratulate you? For what? For spending a night on guard duty?"

"No, because I became expedition councilor that night."

"You?" cried the captain, laughing. "Thank God you are so cheerful and can joke; when I came in and saw you, I didn't think you were so funny; but seriously, friend, what did the Jew want?"

"I told you so, and I mean it; he made me a councillor. Isn't that a nice advancement?"

The captain looked at him for a long time with doubtful eyes; finally, he said, moved: "No, you cannot become a villain too, Gustav; God knows how this may be connected! But look, if I had not known you so long and so well - believe me, the world will judge you harshly; but no, you smile, admit it is all a joke. Expeditionary Councilor! You might as well marry his sister."

"Well, that's what will happen," said Lanbek with a gloomy smile; "in four weeks, my brother-in-law says, the wedding will be."

"Death and hell!" exclaimed the captain, "don't make me mad with these answers. Truly, such things are not to be trifled with."

"Who says I'm joking?" replied Lanbek, slowly getting up. "It's all as I said, on my honour!"

A tear welled up in the captain's eyes when he heard the friend he had loved speak; thus, but he yielded to these softer feelings for only a moment, then he stamped heavily on the ground, put on his hat, and cried: "Then be the day cursed when I first saw you and called you brother. Go, help your Jew to completely strip the poor country of its skin, and get a piece of yourself and make yourself rich. Oh, Lanbek, Lanbek! But I would trade my sword, yes, a year of my life, to buy the guard from one of my comrades; I myself will command the execution when you and the Jew are led to the gallows."

"I will not boast so highly," replied Gustav, calmly and seriously, "but you can follow my corpse when they bury me next to the churchyard wall at midnight tomorrow."

The captain looked at him in shock; he must have read deep seriousness on the young man's forehead, for he repeated this look and met Gustav's eyes. "Will you listen to me for five minutes, Reelzingen?" he asked. "Then you will be amazed at the unselfishness of this minister. Usually, the price of an office was two thousand and an expedition council. His three thousand guilders were worth between brothers; but I, the lucky one, get it for nothing, purely for nothing ! For the happiness of my life, the peace of my family, the serene peace of my father - that these are lost in the bargain is of little account. But listen."

The captain heard these words in astonishment; he sat down attentively next to Gustav. The more his faith in his friend grew during his story, the more anxiously he became for him and his family. He took him in his arms and tried to comfort him, although he himself did not believe in these comforts. "The Jew is a fine player," he said, "he has stolen your best tarot cards from you and the game seems to be in his hands; but - he may have miscalculated; we will see how good he is when we play Spadi."

7.

We take our readers from the officers' room of the main guard in Stuttgart to the house of the regional consultant Lanbek. In a wide, spacious room, the furniture of which is not overly lavish and splendid, but solid and stately, we find an elderly man of more than average height. His face and figure show that when he was in his fifties he must have been well-fed; now, ten years later, wrinkles had formed around his mouth and forehead, and his wide dressing gown of fine green cloth, trimmed with fur, was made to accommodate a large body and now had wide folds around his body; but his ruddy cheeks, his clear grey eyes, and the firm step with which he walked up and down the room gave one the impression, even before one heard his full, sonorous voice, that the old consultant was still fresh and vigorous in mind and body.

In the recess of the wide window sat two beautiful girls aged between eighteen and twenty, who looked anxiously and anxiously at the old man whenever he turned his back on them, and who probably whispered to each other as long as he could not see them. One of them was trying to straighten her father's enormous, long wig and despite the sorrow that spoke from her eyes, she seemed to find joy in the beautiful contrast that the black curls of this hair made with her delicate, white hands. The dark blue eyes of the other young lady seemed more occupied with the street than with the delicate work she was sewing, but her features were too grave to be attributed to idle curiosity.

They had been silent for several minutes, for the girls had been brought up too strictly to bother their father, who was lost in thought, with questions; suddenly the young seamstress jumped up, let her beautiful work fall to the floor, bent her slender neck closer to the window and looked intently at the street. The father saw these movements, stopped walking, looked attentively at his daughter and asked only with glances; Käthchen, the younger sister, quickly finished another forelock of the wig, then carefully placed the magnificent work on a chest of drawers and arrived just in time to call out with Hedwig: "It's him, he looked up, father; he's walking very quickly; look what a strange coat he's wearing!"

"That is Blankenberg's hunting dress," said Hedwig softly to her sister.

"Come on, what do you know about Blankenberg's wardrobe?" replied the younger one, smiling meaningfully.

"He has often visited Gustav in this dress," she answered, a dark blush spreading across her cheeks.

Gustav's arrival prevented his younger sister from tormenting Hedwig any longer, as was her habit. The father looked even more serious than before. He had sat down in his armchair and was staring sternly at the door. The sisters' hearts were pounding anxiously and fearfully as the door opened and their brother entered. After the first "good morning," there was an awkward pause for all three parties. Finally, the son modestly approached his father. "You must have missed me this morning, father?" he asked. "It is certainly a rare occurrence in our house, and you may have been worried about me."

"Not that," answered the old man very seriously; "you are old enough not to get lost; but two things have struck me, namely, that you were only seen for an hour at the carnival, and that you extend this night and its festivities so irregularly until nine o'clock in the morning; you should have been in your office half an hour ago."

"I am excused from being there today," said Gustav, smiling; "I have been raving so terribly since one o'clock this morning and lived so disorderly that it is no wonder that one comes home so late; guess, girls, where I have been!'

The sisters looked at him with displeasure, for they rightly feared that this frivolous tone would displease the old man. "How can we know?" replied Hedwig. "I have never asked where you and your friends are; but today, brother, you are a mystery to me."

"And I have been in a pleasure palace," continued the young man, "where neither you nor Papa have ever been; you will never guess it—on guard duty."

“On duty!” the nurses cried in horror.

"This is very unpleasant for me, Gustav," added the district consultant; "as far as I know, you are the first Lanbek to be put on guard duty."

"It is doubly unpleasant for me," answered his son, looking steadily at his father, "because it seems to be a confusion of names; for as far as I know, I am not the Lanbek who performed the scene at the Jew's table."

The old man looked at him, pale and shocked. "Go into the next room, girls!" he called, and when the sisters had withdrawn in amazement, but quickly and obediently, he took his son's hand, pulled him down onto a chair next to him and asked hastily but in a low voice: "What is that? How do you know? Who told you about it?"

"He himself," answered the son.

"The Jew?" asked the old man. "How is this possible?"

"He was on watch with me; I see how astonished you are, father, but prepare yourself for even more wonderful things." The young man thought it best to reveal as much as possible to his father; so, he told him how angry the minister was with the consultant and his party, how his son had contradicted him, and how the minister, instead of becoming angrier, had suddenly appointed him counsellor of the expedition. He did not mention Leas at all, the captain had advised him to do so, and he resolved to keep quiet about it until he had taken his measures, or the discovery of the unfortunate affair was inevitable.

"I see what I see," said the consultant after some thought. "Do you think that if he had not feared us, he would have spared me and seized you instead, to shame me, as it were, by his grace? He feared me, and he has every reason to be. I am too popular for him, and you too are gradually becoming too well-known to him among the local citizens, because you are now conducting the poor cases instead of me. The expedition council is - a trap that he wanted to lay for both of us, the clever fox."

"How do you understand this, Papa?" asked Gustav, feeling lighter now that he had an inkling of how his father would take the matter.

"Look, friend," said the old man more confidently than he ever did, "you will be the victim of this intrigue; but as sure as I am your father, you will not be one for long. But this Jew thinks this way: if I refuse to let you take this position because it could bring you into bad esteem, he will make it a point of honour, complain to the Lord and seize the only opportunity that presents itself to force me to give up my office too. He knows me, he knows that he can no more depose me than the Duke can, he also knows who old Lanbek is, namely - his enemy. If we accept the position, he continued, we will become suspicious to all who want the better. The father, a consultant to the region, one would think, the son - expedition councillor; the old man did not buy him the position and as is well known, Süss does not give anything without a great deal of money or secret influence, consequently - we have gone over to the powerful man. That, he believes, is how people will judge, and he has done it very wisely, but he does not know me completely; I still know, thank God! a way to keep the trust of our betters and you - will be and remain expedition councilor; if circumstances change, you will become an actuary again and people will then recognize your innocence."

"But father!" said the young man hesitantly. "Your reputation is rock solid, but mine? How long will it be before things change!"

"Son!" replied the old man, not without emotion. "You see how this beautiful country is shattered to its core; do you think it can go on like this forever? Believe me, before spring comes to the country, things must change; it can never get worse, but better. Therefore, believe me and trust in God!"

8

While old Lanbek was still speaking and trying to encourage his son, the doorbell rang loudly, and soon an officer entered the room, whom the consultant hastened to greet in a friendly manner. When one saw the man's dark red face, his free, courageous features, and his small but keen eye, one could believe the story of the bold determination and almost fabulous bravery that he was supposed to have shown under Duke Alexander and Prince Eugene.

"My son, the former actuary Lanbek," said the old man, "Colonel von Röder, whom you will know at least by name."

"How could I not?" replied Gustavus, bowing; "when our troops speak of Malplaquet and Peterwardein, one always hears this name ranked among the first and most brilliant."

"Too much honor for an old man who has only done his duty," answered the colonel. "But consultant, what do you say to the Jew now interfering in our business? I have only come to you to ask: should I or should I not?"

"How am I supposed to understand that?" asked the consultant in astonishment. "Röder, don't do anything hasty!"

"That's just it!" cried the other, stamping on the ground. "My honour and the honour of the whole corps have been insulted! I should rightly have one of my most talented officers dismissed for the sake of this dog, and if I do so, I myself will be out of service tomorrow."

"But speak up, Colonel," said the old man, motioning to his son to sit down. "Sit down, you are still in the heat of the moment."

"My regiment was on duty yesterday and today," he continued eagerly; "and last night a man was brought from the redoubt to our guard, with the express order from the Jew to guard him well, but not to give any further reports; this morning Captain Reelzingen came up, found a prisoner in the officers' room, about whom there was no report, and just imagine - after half an hour the minister himself came, sent the Captain leaves the room, secretly interrogates the prisoner on our watch, then releases him and orders the captain once again not to make a report and takes his word of honour - he takes the word of an officer on the watch not to mention the prisoner's name; so it has come to this, that every clerk or even a Jew who comes along is ordering us? According to the law of war, I must have the captain arrested; my honour demands that I do not tolerate it, for I was on duty, and I must take action, even if it costs me my job."

The two Lanbeks had exchanged meaningful glances during the Colonel's heated speech. "The Jew is more cunning than we thought," said the father when he had finished. "So, the Colonel was also targeted, the trap was set for him too! Who do you think the prisoner was? There, look at him, my own son was on guard duty last night!"

The colonel recoiled in astonishment, and his anger at the infringement on his military rights was so great that he could not refrain from casting an angry, dark look at the young man. But when old Lanbek went on and told him how he himself had actually been the cause of this incident, and how everything else had turned out so strangely, when he explained the minister's malicious plan in more detail, Herr von Röder jumped up from his chair. "Well, old man!" he said to the consultant in an emotional voice, "that he persecutes and hates me means nothing in the end, and that is only the fault of General Römchingen, who never liked me; but he must break his neck over you, or I will not be saved! Mr. Actuary! You must accept the position, that is no longer a question! Because your father must not resign from his post now, or the constitution and religion will be at stake. But I will go to the Duke and speak, even if it costs me my life."

"You will not do that, Colonel!" said the old man emphatically and seriously. "Read this letter that was sent to us from Würzburg and then tell me whether you still dare to go and speak to the Duke." The Colonel took a letter from his hand and began to read; but the further he read, the more dismayed his features became, until he looked astonished but looked at the old man with angry eyes and let his arms fall.

"Father!" said the young man, who looked in shock first at the old man and then at the colonel, "Father, you are making me a witness to a scene at which I would perhaps have been better off not being present. But I am being forced to take on a role that does not suit me. I have been appointed expeditionary counsellor and I do not know why; I cannot refuse the position, although it makes me a villain in the eyes of the world, and I do not know why; things are going on in the state and in my father's house that are being concealed from me, and I do not know why. Colonel von Röder, you are persuading me not to refuse a position that insults my father's name; I believe I can ask you for reasons why I should not do it?"

"God knows he's right!" cried Röder, looking thoughtfully at the young man. "I don't know, old man, why you didn't give him the key long ago. If you don't want to open his eyes, I'll do him that favor, because I know how oppressive it is to half guess and half suspect an important secret."

"So be it," said the father, "sit down again; if I have not yet familiarized you, my son, with such matters, it is only out of fear of being thought an overly proud father, for we had promised ourselves that we would only entrust ourselves to tried and tested men. I must not tell you what has become of Württemberg in the three years since Alexander reigned. One cannot say of Lanbek that he has murmured against his master; he is a brave man and after Prince Eugene perhaps the first general of our time, but the field regiment is useful in the camp and in the face of the enemy, not so much in the chancellery. He views the government of the little country, as he says, a little too heroically, that is to say, he overlooks it and lets others take care of it."

"This little country!" cried the colonel bitterly. "This beautiful Württemberg! There is an old saying that, even if one tries very hard, this country cannot be ruined; but nous verrons ! If it continues like this, if one deliberately ruins it by selling offices, by mocking the better people, by elevating the most ignoble fellows, corrupted when one drains his strength to the core –

"In short, my friend," the old man continued, "it cannot go on like this. Things cannot get better gradually, because we already have five scoundrels in our region who even God be with us would not allow to represent him, all offices have been sold or can be bought by Süß's creatures, so things can only get worse. But there are two parties that say: 'It must be different.' One party is Süß, the ignoble Jew, General Römchingen, the finest of these fellows, Hallwachs, your new colleague, Metz and a few others from the region. We know what they want, and it is nothing less than the complete abolition of the Estates and the Diet."

"And, God bless you," said Herr von Röder, "you have caught the Duke's noble side; he is happy with everything. The country is angry with the Estates, they tell him, people are grumbling about the countryside, and now he has decided to dissolve the institute like a corps of invalids, to generously donate the annual costs of the Estates to the country and to rule alone."

"What? Do I understand correctly?" cried young Lanbek. "So, they want to rob us of our last protection against the evil will or the wrong opinion of a gentleman? The constitution is at stake? But that is not possible, Alexander has sworn to it and by what means does he dare to do this? Do you really think, Colonel, that the Württemberg soldier will suppress his own rights?"

"Here are the dogs," replied the colonel, pointing to the letter, "that they want to use in this hunt."

"Just be calm," said the regional consultant, "listen to me completely. The Duke is horribly deceived; he firmly believes that it will only cost him a word and the estates will no longer exist and all hearts will fly to him. That is what the Jew and Römchingen told him; but they know us better and know that force is part of such a step. Here is a letter to the Archbishop of Würzburg, written by General Römchingen: they want to make some changes for the good of the country, but they cannot rely on the troops in the country, so the Bishop should ensure that the troops of the Franconian district are at our border on a certain day. Also to, He issued similar letters to some of the Imperial Estates in Upper Swabia.

“And in the name of the Duke?” asked the young man.

"No, they are only letting him know, but they have thrown another bait to the bishop. It is not without reason that they say that our old reformer Brenz has been rising from his grave for several nights and climbing the pulpit - they want to make us Catholic. Are you astonished? You don't want to believe it? I also believe that they do not want to do it out of religious feeling, but either it is to bind the bishop and the Upper Swabians closer together for the cause, or they think that they will be pleasing to the duke if they reform the faith in twenty-four hours, just as they want to reform the old law."

"It cannot, it must not be!" cried the young man. "To overthrow the foundations of our happiness and our contentment at one blow? It is not possible; the Duke cannot tolerate it."

"He knows not, nor thinks, that they are planning all this," said the Colonel; "his fame is too dear to him to be tarnished in this way; but if it is done without the blame falling on him, I fear he will not restore the old ways. For what purpose, then, do you think, did the Jew persuade the Duke to give the edict of yesterday, in which he is absolved of all responsibility for the past and future? This is to protect him in the hardly conceivable event that the Duke should become angry with the faithful and devoted councillors who lay absolute power at his feet and plant a crosier in the collegiate church."

“And you want to fight against them?” asked Gustav, worried and doubtful.

"Fight or perish together," said the old man. "You don't need to know who is allied with us now; it is enough for you to know that they are the most distinguished of the nobility and the bravest of the citizens. We wanted to implore the Emperor for protection, but the circumstances are unfavourable, the time is too short to reach him by all the detours, and besides, the Duke has had a great deal of influence since the last wars; we would be turned away. We have no choice but to -"

“We must,” cried the Colonel boldly and resolutely, “that We must play the role of prevenire; they have set themselves the goal of St. Joseph's Day, March 19th; but a few days beforehand we must capture the enemies of the country, lead the loyal troops to Stuttgart, call upon the country people to help us, and when we have succeeded, pay homage to the Duke once again and show him the terrible abyss on which he and we stood. And then - he is a brave soldier and a man of honor, then he will blush at the disgrace to which those wretches wanted to seduce him."

"But the Duke," asked the young man, "where is he to be and where is he to remain while you blow up this terrible counter-mine?"

"That is precisely what forces us to hurry," replied the colonel. "They have persuaded him to visit the fortresses of Kehl and Philippsburg next month and behind his back they want to reform. He wants to leave on the eleventh; the adjutants who are to accompany him have already been appointed, and, if I may say so, this journey is being talked about with such pomp and so much and so loudly that I fear the whole journey is a mask and the Duke will not cross the border."

"You now know our plans," said the old man to his son, "be wise and cautious. One word too many can give everything away. Therefore, as is our custom, put your hand in that of your father and this brave man and swear to us that you will keep silent."

"I swear," said Lanbek, in a firm voice, but pale and staring; and his father and the colonel drew him to their breasts and greeted him as one of their own.

9.

A heavy, gloomy fog lay over Stuttgart and gave the surrounding mountains and the city a sad, desolate appearance; just as a gloomy, anxious seriousness lay on the faces that one saw on the streets, and it was as if a misfortune that one could not forget, or a new stroke that one feared, had veiled all hearts like the otherwise lovely mountains and wrapped them in mourning. On the evening of one such day, young Lanbek crept through the damp paths of the garden. His face was pale, his eyes dull, his mouth tightly pressed together, he no longer carried his tall figure as lightly and erectly as before, and it seemed as if he had been in the. He had become as many years older in the last eight days. What he had foreseen had come to pass; no one who knew the Lanbeks even by reputation could understand or justify the young man's rapid rise. The favourites and creatures of the powerful Jew approached him with that annoying familiarity, with that crude joy, as thieves and gamblers show their wickedness to a new companion, and young Lanbek's feelings at such new, valuable acquaintances can best be compared with the unpleasant and melancholy feelings of a man whom misfortune has cast into a prison with the dregs of humanity and who must allow himself to be greeted by robbers and common women as their equal.

The gracious glances that the minister occasionally gave him in public, almost in mockery, marked him as a new favourite. Only now did he see how many good people had previously wished him well; for so many familiar faces that had previously smiled "good day" to old Lanbek's son now appeared gloomy, and even worthy citizens and those honest, honest winegrowers who had so often sought advice from him and the old man now averted their eyes and walked past without tipping their hats.

The thought of Leah increased his misery. He knew well how unhappy his old father, himself and his family would be if the desperate blow they were about to strike failed; and yet, great as the crime that that terrible man had committed, he was still horrified when he considered the consequences that his fall would entail. What would become of poor Leah if her brother were imprisoned for months? Could the Duke, so severe a lord, forgive such transgressions and schemes as those of the Jew, even if he had assured him of impunity by that edict?

And then the memory flashed through his mind again of the terrible threat that Suss had uttered against him when he had mentioned the young man's relationship with his sister. All his fear of his old father, of the shame that such a relationship would bring if it were even discussed, came over him. There were moments when he cursed his folly in having exchanged even a word with the beautiful Jewess, when he was determined to leave the garden, never to see her again, to tell his father everything before it came to late but when he then thought of the beautiful oval of her head, the pure, innocent and yet so interesting features and that eye that rested so willingly and with such indescribable expression on his own features, then it was - I know not whether it was vanity, foolishness, love, or even the influence of that wonderful magic that is said to have survived among the daughters of Israel from Rachel's days - something irresistible drew him towards that side where, since the twilight of the first March evening had grown darker, the beautiful Leah had been waiting for him.

"At last, at last!" said Lea, with tears in her eyes, as she offered her white hand through the pickets that separated the two gardens. "If spring had not come by now, I should have thought that three months had already passed. I am very annoyed; why should I go into the garden at this terrible time of year, when you can come in freely and openly through the front door? Just know, Neighbor, that I am very dissatisfied."

"Lea," he replied, drawing the beautiful hand to his lips, "don't mistake me, girl! I really couldn't come, child! I wasn't allowed to come to you, and I don't go to your brother's circles; and if I knew you were there even once, I wouldn't speak to you again." Despite the darkness, the young man still thought he saw a deep blush rise on Lea's cheeks. He looked at her doubtfully; she cast down her eyes and answered: "You are right, I'm not allowed to go to my brother's circles."

"So, you were there? Yes, you were there!" Lanbek exclaimed angrily. "But admit, I can already read everything in your eyes."

"Listen to me," she replied, pressing his hand with emotion, "the nurse told you what happened after the carnival, and how I begged and implored him to let you go. Since then, his behavior has changed completely; he is more friendly, treats me as if I had suddenly grown five years older, and sometimes even lets me go out with him. A few days ago, he ordered me to dress as nicely as possible, put a beautiful necklace in my hand, and in the evening he led me downstairs to his own rooms. There were only a few people there that I knew, most of the gentlemen and ladies were strangers to me. They played and danced, and from the beginning I liked it very much, but not afterwards, because –

»Because?« asked Lanbek excitedly.

"In short, I didn't like it, and I won't go there again."

"I wish you had never been there," said the young man.

"Oh, how could I have known that the company would not be suitable for me?" replied Lea sadly. "And besides, my brother said expressly that my fiancé would be pleased if I also went out among people."

"Who did he say would be happy?" cried Lanbek.

"Well, you," answered Lea; "in fact, Lanbek, I don't know how to understand you; you are so cold, so tense; just now, when we can talk openly and without hindrance, you are so anxious, almost mute; instead of coming into the house to see us, you secretly invite me into the garden; I don't know who there is to be so afraid of when you are in such a relationship?"

“In what proportion?” asked Lanbek.

"Well, how strangely you ask again! You asked my brother for my marriage, and he agreed to it if I wanted it, and the Duke would remove the obstacle between us on the grounds of religion by a rescript. I am only glad that you are not a Catholic, otherwise it would not be possible, but you Protestants have no head of the church and are really as much heretics as we Jews."

"Lea! For God's sake, do not be wicked!" cried the young man in horror. "Who told you these things? Oh God, how can I excuse you from this terrible error?"

"Oh, go on!" replied Lea. "It makes you angry that I dared to place my hated people next to you. But do not be afraid; my brother, people say, can do anything, he will certainly help us, for what he says pleases the Duke. But I have one request, Gustav: will you not introduce me to your family? You have two lovely sisters; I have seen them several times from the window; how happy I am to be so closely connected with them one day! Please, let me get to know them."

The unfortunate young man was unable to reply a single word; his thoughts and his heart seemed to stand still. He looked like one who had been suddenly frightened deprived of all senses, with wide, dry eyes at the girl who, if not at this moment, then perhaps soon, must be even more unhappy than he, and who was now, smiling, dreaming, carefree like a child at the foot of a terrible abyss, picking flowers for her wreath.

"What's wrong with you, Gustav?" she asked anxiously, as he was still silent. "Your hand is shaking in mine: are you ill? You are so changed." But - before he could answer, a deep voice spoke next to Lea: " Bon soir, Mr. Expedition Counselor; are you talking here in the dark with your bride? It is a cool evening; why don't you go upstairs to the warm room? You know that my house is always open to you."

"Who are you talking to, Gustav?" said old Lanbek, who approached at almost the same moment. "Your sisters say you are talking to a woman down here."

"It is the minister," answered Gustav, almost breathlessly.

"Obedient servant," said the old man dryly, "I do not have the pleasure of seeing your Excellency in this darkness, but I take the opportunity to offer my most humble thanks for the elevation of my son; I am also very much charmed that you keep such loyal neighbors with my Gustav."

"You are mistaken," replied Sweet, laughing hoarsely, "if you think I am trying to talk to the son over the fence in the dark. I only came to pick up my sister because the weather is a little cold, and the night air might harm her."

"With your sister?" said the old man sternly. "Boy, how am I supposed to understand that, speak!"

"Don't get so worked up, Mr. Regional Consultant!" replied the Jew. "Youth has no virtue, and he is only courting my Lea with all due respect."

"You scoundrel!" cried the old man, throwing his hand around his son's arm and drawing him away. "Go to your room; I want to have a word with you; and you , Miss Süßin, never dream of speaking a word to the son of an honest Christian, to my son, even if your brother were King of Jerusalem, it would still be no honor to my house." With staggering, uncertain steps he led his son away. Lea[240] cried loudly, but the minister laughed mockingly. " Parole d'honneur! " he cried. "That was a beautiful scene; by the way, don't forget, Mr. Expeditionary Counselor, that you only have fourteen days left to make your request; up to and from then on I will keep my word."

10.

The respect of young Lanbek, which bordered on fear, made him follow his father patiently and without complaint, and long-standing experience of the old man's character forbade him to apologize at this moment when appearances were so strikingly against him. The regional consultant threw himself into an armchair in his room and covered his face. Gustav stood anxiously and fearfully beside him and did not dare to speak; but the young man's two beautiful sisters flew over when they saw their father's weakness, asked tenderly what was wrong with him, tried to pull his hands down from his face and wet them with their tears. - "That is the boy," he cried after a while, his anger overcoming his physical weakness; "he is the one who covered your father's house, our old good name, you, you innocent children, with misery, disgrace and shame; Judas, the parricide - for today he has driven the nail into my coffin."

"Father! For God's sake! Gustav!" cried the girls trembling, looking shyly at their pale brother and clinging to old Lanbek.

"I know," said the unfortunate young man, "I know that appearances are against me—"

"Will you be silent?" the consultant burst out, his eyes glowing and his gesture threatening. "Appearance? Do you think you can blind my old eyes again like you did after the carnival? Isn't it true that it would be far more convenient if these two eyes had already closed completely, if they had buried old Lanbek so deeply that no news of the shame of his name could reach him. But you have miscalculated, you wretch! I will disinherit you; here stand my dear children, but you shall be cast out, robbed of my honest name, cursed -"

Father! his three children cried in one voice; the daughters rushed at him and for the first time dared Hedwig to lay her lips on her father's sacred lips, sealing his mouth with kisses as it was open to curse. The younger had involuntarily placed herself in front of Gustav, grasped his hand as if she wanted to defend him but the young man tore himself away vigorously; never more than at this moment did his face, his threatening eyes, resemble his father's features, and throwing out his constricted chest, he said: "I have borne everything that a son can possibly bear from his father, but I have other duties, I must protect my own honor, even if it is my own father who infringes on it. It would have been enough for you if I had assured you, by all that is sacred to me, that I am not what you think I am. If you no longer have faith in me, if you give me up, then there is nothing left. Farewell - I only want to disgrace you."

"You stay!" the old man called after him, more anxiously and trembling than in a command. "Do you think this is the way to reconcile an offended father? Are you in such a hurry to go ahead of me and take a path where I shall never meet you again? For I have lived honestly and according to my conscience, but I understood you and your intention well."

"But father," said his youngest daughter in a gentle voice, "we have always loved Gustav so much, and you yourself have often said how capable he is; what could he have done that was so terrible that you should treat him so harshly?"

"You don't understand, or yes, you can understand he loves the Jew's sister, and he was talking to her and his brother-in-law, Suss, at the garden fence. Now speak! Can you excuse yourself? Oh, fool that I am, who imagined that he had been raised up and employed to set a trap for me! His Jewish charmer has made him an expeditionary counsellor!"

"Father doesn't want to understand me," said the young man with tears in his eyes, "so I want to talk to you. I want to tell you honestly, dear sisters, how things are, and I don't think you will condemn me." The girls sat down sadly, the old man rested his furrowed forehead on his hand and listened attentively. Gustav, blushing at first and then often interrupted by sadness, told how he had met Lea, how good and childlike she had been, how much she enjoyed talking to him because she had no one else to talk to. He then repeated the conversation with the Jewish minister and his deceitful proposals; he assured him that he had never given any thought to a relationship with Lea, and that he would have told the minister himself that evening if his father had not intervened so suddenly.

"You have made a great mistake, Gustav," said Hedwig, his older sister, a quiet and sensible girl. "Since you could never even remotely think of a relationship with this girl, it was your duty as an honest man not to get involved with her. You also made a great mistake in not telling your father everything right away; but now you have made your whole family unhappy and a laughingstock; for do you think Süss will not keep his threat? Oh, he will take revenge on Papa, on you, on all of us."

"Go, beg your father for forgiveness!" said the beautiful Käthchen, crying. "You must not reproach him, Hedwig, he is unhappy enough.

Come, Gustav," she continued, taking his hand and leading him to her father, "beg him to forgive you. Yes, we shall be very unhappy, the wicked man will ruin us as he ruined the country, but then at least let there be peace among us . If we still have each other, we have a lot, if he takes everything else from us."

The old man looked at his son for a long time, but not unwillingly. "You have acted like a vain young man, and the attention that this Jewess gave you has blinded you. I feel for you that you have perhaps already paid for it for some time, but certainly this evening. Katharine is right; I will not bear you a grudge any longer; we must now arm ourselves against a terrible enemy. Do you think he will keep his word about the fourteen days' grace he has given you?"

"I believe and hope so," answered the young man.

"At that time more than just the fate of our house must be decided," continued the old man. "Römchingen and Süß - or we; whoever loses pays the price. But now, Gustav, promise me never again to visit the Jewess, neither in the garden nor anywhere else, and on this condition I will forgive your folly."

Gustav promised with trembling lips and then left the room to conceal his emotion. For a long time and with infinite sadness he thought about the unfortunate creature whose heart belonged to him and whom he was not allowed to love. Although he shared all the strict religious views of his time, he shuddered at the curse that pursued a homeless tribe of people down to the thousandth generation and seemed to drag to ruin anyone who approached even the noblest among them in the most natural way. Although he found no excuse for himself and his forbidden attraction to a girl who did not share his faith, he gained some consolation by subordinating his own fate to a higher providence.

His father and sisters talked about him and these incidents for a long time, and the memory of the young man's many fine virtues gradually reconciled the old man, so that he himself somewhat excused keeping the minister's suggestions secret. But late in the evening, when the two sisters were alone, Käthchen said: "It's true, Gustav was indeed absent. I saw her once at the window and once in the garden; I have never seen her so beautiful and graceful in my whole life. What are all the faces in Stuttgart, what is even the beautiful Marie, of whom so many wonders are, compared to this magnificent face! No, Hedwig, I could have fallen completely in love with her!"

"How dare you talk so foolishly!" replied Hedwig angrily. "She may be whatever she wants, but she is and will always remain just a Jew."

11.

It was not just their brother's unhappy love that frightened the beautiful daughters of the regional consultant Lanbek in the days that followed; no, it was the strange and oppressive relationship that seemed to prevail between father and son, which caused the four beautiful blue eyes to shed so many tears in secret. One could not say that they looked at each other darkly, asked each other questions grumpily, or answered coldly; but one could still see that they were both preoccupied with grief and worry, and the girls were repeatedly led astray in their guesses about the reason for this grief when they occasionally saw the old man and his son standing together in a window niche, looking more and more trustingly, but also more and more...more seriously than ever before. Finally, they were formally expelled from the large family room, which served as their winter residence, for three evenings a week, and, what they knew had never happened, Papa's little library room was specially heated for them for such evenings, and they were given permission to amuse themselves with the excellent lawyers and philosophers.

Of course, during such an exile neither father nor son considered that from the library on the upper floor one could go into the study, from there into the guest room, and from the guest room into the so-called lumber room, from which a square opening with a small lid led down into the living room to let air or heat into this room; nor did they consider that female curiosity would have broken through even stronger barriers than those that lay between that room and the library. For some evenings, however, an even more powerful feeling than curiosity had kept the girls in the library, namely fear. Hedwig claimed that she had often heard footsteps and terrible groans in that room, and the beautiful Käthchen was afraid to go there, because that room was only separated from the rooms of the dreaded Jew Süss by a thin wall of wood and brick.

One evening, however, when the girls had long since been sent away, Käthchen, who had crept down to the middle of the stairs, saw three men enter her father's house, which aroused her curiosity to the highest degree. The first, who slowly and puffingly crept up the lower stairs and stopped in the hallway for a few minutes to catch his breath, was none other than the Lutheran prelate Klinger. His snow-white wig, his prelate's chain, which rested just on his stomach, and his old, weathered features inspired the girl with immense awe; he was followed at a brisk pace by the colonel and stable master von Röder, a man who was considered very clever and brave, but at the same time very unholy in his morals, and she almost laughed out loud at the third; it was the cheerful Captain Reelzingen, who knew how to tell such funny stories and anecdotes and had almost made her laugh at many a ball. Today he had put his face in very respectable wrinkles and looked just like he had when he swore to her on parole d'honneur that he loved her vraiment. She watched him with a smile until his huge sword had disappeared into the door, and then hurried into the library, where she met the blonde Hedwig, who had her eyes tightly shut so as not to be frightened by a ghost if one happened to be walking up and down in the library. "Today we must look down!" explained Käthchen. "And come with me now; just imagine, the people are gathering here like at a carnival. Have you ever seen Prelate Klinger and Captain Reelzingen in one room before, and Colonel Röder too, and" - she added when her sister hesitated - "I would be very much mistaken if I had not seen Blankenberg as well when the door opened."

This last name decided; Käthchen took the light and went ahead with a pounding heart; Hedwig followed her, pressing as close as possible to her braver sister, and when the latter opened the fateful chamber door, she held on tightly to her dress. The opening was directly above the stove in the living room, which was one floor below, and when Käthchen opened the flap, even if she lay on her knees and bent her head low, she could not see more than four or five of the assembled men; Hedwig also bent down now and tried to look even deeper than her sister, but she stood up again sullenly and said: "I can see nothing but the prelate's broad back, a few wigs, and the colonel's uniform; are you sure that Blankenberg is here?"

"Sure!" replied Käthchen, smiling mischievously. "But let us listen to what they say, perhaps you will recognize your lover by his voice."

They sat down on the floor next to the opening and listened; the pleasant warmth that came from the stove and their curiosity made them forget for a while the bitter cold of the March night; finally, Hedwig sat up in annoyance. "Do you think we'll learn anything from this chatter, of which we only understand half? They're chattering again, as always, about the welfare of the country, about the Duke, about Suss, about everything; what does that have to do with us! Come! It's really dreadful and cold here. Girl, get up!"

But Käthchen motioned for her to be quiet; Colonel Röder could now be heard reading something in a clear and distinct voice; the deep silence around was only occasionally interrupted by a quickly fading murmur of displeasure said old Lanbek; Käthchen's cheerful features gradually gave way to amazement and fear; finally, when the men downstairs were again talking loudly but approvingly and clinking their glasses, a deep blush flew over the girl's face, her eyes shone as she carefully closed the hatch, took the lamp and started back with her sister.

"Did you understand something?" asked Hedwig. "You suddenly seemed so attentive; what did they say that was special?"

"I don't know everything, I can't tell you everything," replied Käthchen thoughtfully. "I feel as if I had dreamed it all. Listen - but be quiet! It could make us all unhappy. Those are dangerous people in father's room downstairs. I shudder when I think of what could come of it."

"Speak then, you silly child! I am two years older than you, and you shall have no secrets from me."

"Just imagine," Käthchen continued in a low voice, "Süss wants to make us Catholic and overthrow the country; then our father would lose his job and everyone else would lose their jobs!"

"Catholic!" Hedwig cried in horror. "Wouldn't we have to become nuns if we remained single? No, that's disgusting!"

"Ah, why not," replied Käthchen, smiling at her sister's misery, "there would have to be many nuns if all those who couldn't find husbands went to the convent; but don't worry, it won't come to that. In three days, said Röder, the Duke will be travelling, and while he is in Philippsburg, the men down there want to capture the Jew and all his assistants in the name of the region and then prove to the Duke how bad his ministers were."

"Oh God, oh God! This is not going to end well," said Hedwig, crying. "They will lose everything, because the Duke trusts everyone more than those from the countryside; I know what the head huntswoman once told me about my father. You will see, it will end badly!"

"And even if that is the case," answered Käthchen, "we are the daughters of a man who does what he does for the good of his country. That can console us." The brave girl took a Bible decorated with many beautiful engravings from the cupboard. She gave her weeping sister the New Testament so that she could distract herself with the engravings and rhymes. She opened the Old Testament herself. She hid her own concern for her father under a little song that she sang softly to herself, while her beautiful little fingers busily ran through the yellowed pages from one picture to the next.

12.

There are moments in the life of individual states when the attentive observer will say even a century later that a crisis had to occur here, precisely here; one or two years later the same circumstances would not have had the same effect. It is then no longer possible for the finite mind to think away such a turn of events and to link together from the infinite series of possible consequences those which form a whole that is just as necessarily linked as a past century with all its historical truths. Here the finger of God is revealed, as one usually says when one comes across such important moments in the life of a state. But there have always been men who, whether guided by their own genius or by the study of history, have sensed and calculated such moments, and they had the most surprising effect when they were not content with having foreseen such crises, but when they had enough courage to intervene themselves at the right time, enough strength to play a role. History has long since decided on the short reign of Charles Alexander's ministers. She curses no mortal, otherwise she would have to transform the tears and sighs of Württemberg into harsh words against the perpetrators of its misfortune in 1737; but she remembers with affection a few men who did not allow themselves to be swept away by the current of general corruption, who sensed that things must turn out differently, who did not tremble at the thought of bringing about a change in things, and who led the cause of their country with calm and composure even when a higher power had undertaken to bring about an unexpectedly rapid change in things by closing two fiery eyes and ordering a brave heart to stand still.

Who would be able to tell from this cheerful Stuttgart and its peaceful streets that it was once the scene of such pressing concerns? How reassured about the course of events are the grandchildren of those who, in that fateful March, hour for the fate of their families, for the ancient rights of their country, even for their faith!

Anyone who saw the arrogant Süss driving through the "rich suburbs" in his carriage, drawn by six horses, smiling proudly at the pale, hostile faces he encountered everywhere; anyone who saw the terrible Hallwachs, his dear friend and adviser, standing beside him and considering how many destructive plans this man had devised, how many unheard-of monopolies he had introduced and how he was always trying to invent new ones; anyone who knew the unlimited trust the Duke placed in these people, would have despaired of the possibility of rescue.

In addition, there were the strange and contradictory rumors that were circulating. Some said that the Duke had traveled to Philippsburg and Kehl but had not given the regiment to the Privy Councillor, but rather the seal to the Jew Süß; others contradicted this and claimed that the Duke had been seen at a window of Ludwigsburg Castle, that his horses were still there and that he had not left. In a village on the Austrian border in the Oberland, the Catholics are said to have suddenly attacked the Protestant inhabitants, and when the latter claimed the battlefield, a company of district troops crossed the border into the village. The strangest sounding rumor, which was also confirmed, was that the Chief Financial Counsellor Hallwachs had ordered a valuable vestment from the court embroiderer and ordered him to have it ready by March 18th and if he had to work with fifty journeymen; if he did not finish it, he would be put to work. A Lutheran clergyman, who was mentioned by name, is said to have given the children in school little crosses carved from wood, with the words: "Only when you hold these in your hands can you pray properly." Finally, it was said as something authentic that the Jew said to the Duke over the table: "Your estates, Your Highness, are real obstacles; but they have been standing there for so long that they are tired and weary." Charles Alexander replied with a smile: "C'est vrai; allons donc leur donner des chaises, et une fois assis, ils ne se leveront plus. "Even those men who were determined to forestall the impending doom heard these rumours. But they were cold and calm about it; they knew that Württemberg was about to undergo such a change that it would either be relieved or would be plunged into such deep misfortune that the lamentations of the individual would be silenced. It is said that they had prepared everything that was necessary to confront a powerful and malicious enemy with the help of the country people, and that if their undertaking should succeed, it would only be thanks to the few bright names of a few men from the countryside; for in Württemberg people were accustomed to chaining the interests of the country to these.

It was late in the evening of March 11th when the regional consultant Lanbek was sitting with his son and Captain Reelzingen in his living room drinking wine. The two Lanbeks were serious and gloomy, but the captain could not hide his cheerfulness, for he divided his attention and his conversation between the window niche, where Gustav's two sisters were sitting, and between the two men at his side. Hedwig looked pale and silent at her needles, but Käthchen's face was more red than usual and every now and then she showed her white teeth and the beautiful dimples in her cheeks, for the captain once again had wonderful jokes and stories to tell.

"How is your horse, captain?" asked old Lanbek.

"My chestnut is a better infantryman than I am," he replied. "If I ride the first six hours at a trot and uphill at a walk, I can easily ride the next six at a gallop. He has only one fault, and that is that he has not yet been paid, and this vice often causes me great distress."

"You can," continued the old man, "if you ride at a brisk trot from the Galgensteige, pass Ludwigsburg between eleven and twelve; you must be in Heilbronn by four o'clock and let the horses rest there; between eight and ten o'clock tomorrow you will be in Oehringen."

"But father," Gustav interrupted, "would it not be more advisable to ride towards Heidelberg? I would bet that we are no longer safe towards Oehringen. Consider that the Teutonic Order extends deep into that region, that they in Mergentheim are certainly informed by the Bishop in Würzburg, that -"

That continued the father, you will be much more conspicuous on the road to Heidelberg and that, if you cannot find the area any cleaner, you will have a last refuge with my old gentleman and patron, the Duke in Neustadt, who will certainly not release you in the first few days. If Karl Alexander is satisfied with what we have done here, you can always return; if not, you will go on to Frankfurt, as I have already said."

"God! That I should leave you behind in such a crisis!" cried Gustav with tears. "That I am perhaps to blame for your misfortune; that everything could go badly if Süss finds out about my flight and takes revenge on you, father! No, I cannot, I must not go!"

"No, father," Hedwig interrupted, rushing forward even paler than before and taking her father's hand, "he must not leave us; oh, you have terrible plans, I know it well; you want to form a conspiracy against these powerful people. Leave it alone, father; Suss and the others will forgive you; oh, fear is killing me!"

"Go, girl," said Käthchen, who had also come forward; "what men do and what our father does is none of our business. But why should Gustav go away so quickly now? He could be so useful to us all."

"Because I don't want a Jew as a daughter," said the old man sternly, "that's why he must go. Because I intercepted a letter from his charmers and sent it to the Jew with a protest, and because he is now raging and wants to have your brother as a brother-in-law by force or put him on Neuffen, that's why he must and should get out of his way now. But I didn't want to hurt you at this hour, Gustav; we part as friends, and everything else should be forgotten, who knows when and where we will meet again!"

As the old man spoke the last words and held out his hand to his son, there was a quick and violent knock on the door, and before anyone could answer, a figure wrapped in a cloak suddenly entered. "What is this about?" old Lanbek exclaimed. "Who is forcing your way into my house at night? Who are you?"

"Blankenberg!" cried Hedwig, as he threw off his cloak, and she quickly and blushingly took a few steps forward.

"Pardon me, Mr. Consultant," said the young man hastily, "I must excuse myself in need. Gustav, you must leave immediately; Lieutenant Pinassa has just written to me that he has sent you tonight on the orders of General Römchingen between eleven and twelve o'clock. The honest boy would not like to meet you in the nest."

"Thanks, thanks," replied the old man, shaking Blankenberg's hand. "Drink up, children, and make your farewell quick; here, my dear Reelzingen," he continued, pressing a large bag into the surprised captain's hand; "one cannot know whether your paths will not part. You are so generous as to accompany my son."

"And you want to reward this with money?" the captain interrupted him angrily. " Parole d'honneur , sir! I accompany my brother because we are old Amicists and not because of your spears. So, I should -"

"Reelzingen," said Käthchen in her sweet voice, "you don't understand any jokes; they are all copper coins, and I gave the bag to father to send you in April."

"I understand," whispered the captain, blushing and kissing the beautiful girl's hand. "I will bring you something beautiful from Frankfurt in return."

"Just bring me back our Gustav safe and sound," she answered, unable to hold back her tears any longer, "and," she added, smiling through her tears, "don't play any foolish tricks on me that might give you away."

"The horses are in front of the lake gate," said the old man to Reelzingen and his son. "You must not go through the gate yourself, for the first round is already over. Accompany my son, Mr. von Blankenberg, through the gardens and bring me news of how they got away."

Young Lanbek embraced his father and siblings, his sisters followed him and his friends, crying, to the garden gate, and when Hedwig later bitterly rebuked her younger sister for allowing the captain to kiss her on the mouth, she replied: "It was you who was at fault, not me, for omitting it; we owed such courtesy to a man who does so much for our brother."

"Well," replied Hedwig, blushing, "Blankenberg actually saved him too."

13.

The two young men rode silently through the dark night. There was no star in the sky and the wind howled around the mountains. "Hu! Do you see that?" whispered Reelzingen as they rode past the iron gallows that Duke Friedrich had once (1597) built for the alchemist Honauer from the metal that he had promised to turn into gold. "Look at this enormous number of ravens, it's as if they smelled new prey."

His friend looked up in silence, but suddenly cast his eyes down again, for he thought he saw Lea's fine, lovely figure sitting mournfully beneath the gallows. "This iron pillar of shame is strong enough," continued the captain, "to support all the villains in the land; but if they were to hang the gold they have pocketed on it, even this gallows would crumble like a rotten stick! How these ravens sing horrible melodies! But how? - Dieu nous garde, comrade! Spur your horse, for there is truly a ghost sitting on the gallows!"

It was as if the horses themselves feared this place of terror, for at this call they raced up the mountain with great speed and did not rest until the screeching of the ravens could no longer be heard.

There is a small bridge between Stuttgart and Ludwigsburg, of which people have many gruesome tales to tell; one thing is certain: inexplicable things have happened there, and many a man says his prayers when he rides alone over this spot at night. Legend has it that the son of the consultant and his friend, the cheerful captain, reached the bridge safely and in a short time; but there their horses would not move and snorted and trembled. The young people spurred and used their whips when an old, trembling voice called out: "Give an old man alms!"

"Who will pull the bag in the night and fog? Back, old man, away from the bridge, our horses shy away from you, back, I say, or you shall feel my whip!"

"Not so fast, young blood! Not so fast!" said the old man, whose dark figure they now saw on the bridge railing. sitting there. "Make haste slowly! Come early enough and give an old man alms!"

"Now I've run out of patience," cried the captain, brandishing his whip in the air. "I count three, and if you don't go away, I'll hit you."

The old man coughed and giggled, Gustav felt as if his dark figure was growing to infinity and a long arm stretched out a large hat, and for the third time, but threateningly and in a terrible voice, the man from the bridge croaked: "Give an old man alms! It will bring you luck, and don't ride so fast; you mustn't be there before twelve o'clock."

Reelzingen let his arm fall, weak and trembling; he later confessed that a cold hand had touched him. But Gustav, with a pounding heart, pulled out his purse and threw a silver coin into his big hat. "What time is it, old man?" he asked.

"I don't know the hour but twelve o'clock," said the figure, who was crouching on the railing again, in a dull voice. "Thank you, you'll have luck; ride on!" He said it and fell backwards with a dull fall into the swamp over which the bridge led. Horrified, Reelzingen spurred his horse so that it reared up high and then jumped over the bridge in two leaps. But Gustav, frightened, stopped his horse, dismounted and looked over the railing of the bridge. Nothing moved. "Old man!" he called down, "have you been hurt? Can I help you?" No answer, and everything below was as quiet as in the grave. Now young Lanbek was also seized by an inexplicable fear; as he mounted, he felt his horse trembling; he did not dare to look back at the horrible place as he chased after his friend.

"This is the second time I've met him," whispered Reelzingen, breathing deeply, when Lanbek was back at his side.

“Who?” he asked, concerned.

"The devil," answered the captain.

Lanbek gave him no answer to the strange speech, and they continued to race through the night. In Zuffenhausen it was a quarter to twelve as they rode through; in most of the houses the candles were still burning and here and there one could hear spiritual songs coming from the rooms. The night watchman was just blowing the horn and calling the hour; the captain stopped and asked him what the late songs and prayers meant.

"Ah, Lord! This is a terrible night," he answered. "A man knocked on many houses and ordered the people to pray all night until twelve o'clock."

“Who is the man?” asked Lanbek in astonishment.

"Old people, sir, who have seen him, assure you that it was our old pastor; God rest his soul, he has been dead for twenty years; but what he asked for was nothing unchristian, so they pray and sing in the candlelit chambers and spin stories."

"This night may drive me mad," cried the captain, as they rode away. "Gustav, I believe he is walking the earth in the flesh tonight; I think this would be just the time to summon the old fellow if one wants to become a colonel quickly, or to have two hundred thousand Spanish quadruples."

"Fool!" answered the friend. "The one you mean has nothing in common with prayer."

It was as if their horses were only lifting their legs for show, for every quarter of an hour they covered seemed to add up to a new one. Ludwigsburg still did not appear, and the night was so dark that they could not tell from the scenery whether they had taken the wrong turn or whether they were already close to the city. Finally, after they had ridden for about half an hour, they saw lights shimmering at a distance of about a thousand paces, but at the same time found their way blocked by four horses that were harnessed to a carriage and standing across the road.

"Lead your horses away, driver!" cried the captain, "or my whip will soon drive them away; why do you block the way?"

"Easy, gentlemen, it shall be done immediately," answered a man who got down from the carriage. But the time it took him to pick up the fallen reins and arrange them took too long for the quick soldier, he tried to jump over the slack ropes of the leading team and asked his friend to do the same; but as is usually the case in such cases of blind haste, at the same moment the man at the carriage pulled on the reins and the captain's horse got one foot caught in the tightly erected ropes.

Lanbek jumped off to help his friend, the coachman ran over regretfully, and the unpaid horse's foot was just free when several riders were heard racing towards him from the town. The first one might have had a head start of five hundred paces, but he was not a good horse, for the captain could clearly tell that they were going at a short parade gallop, and the steps of the horses behind him were less powerful, but more fleeting. "Stand - allons! - Stand!" shouted the first rider; but at the same moment the two young men also heard a familiar voice calling with the wildest expression: "Halt, Jew! or I'll shoot you right through the body!"

Among the people of Württemberg one sometimes still hears a rhyme that describes this strange moment, it goes:

Then Mr. von Röder said: Either stop or die!

And it was the old colonel who, at that moment, galloped ahead of his companions, a pistol in his hand, and angrily seized the first rider by the arm, shouting: "Where are you going, Jew? Why so quickly on horseback, when I called after you to wait?"

"Restrain yourself, Colonel," replied the first in a proud tone, but one in which a certain fear trembled; "I am going to Stuttgart to tell the Duchess Serene Highness what measures are to be taken at this moment -"

"That is my way too, sir," replied the colonel in a terrible voice, "and do not leave my side for a moment, or I will shoot you with my pistol. Make way, who is standing in the way?"

“Captain von Reelzingen of the third company and expeditionary counselor Lanbek.”

"Good evening, gentlemen," Röder continued. "Do you have loaded pistols, Captain?"

"Yes, Colonel," was the soldier's reply, as he unhooked them from their holsters.

I command you, whatever your mission may be, to ride on the left side of Minister Süß. By your service and your honor as a nobleman. As soon as he makes a move to escape, a bullet follows him. I take responsibility for that."

"Mr. Expeditionary Counselor," cried Süß, "I take you as a witness that shameful violence is being done to me here. Colonel Röder, I warn you once again; this scene shall be avenged!"

"But Herr von Röder," whispered Gustav, "for heaven's sake, do not rush into anything; consider what may result from this. Consider," he added louder, "the terrible wrath of the Duke."

"The Duke is dead," said Röder loudly enough for everyone to hear.

"Karl Alexander dead?" cried the captain, all the events of that night suddenly flooding back to him in terrible memories.

"Is there any reliable news? God! What a case!" said Gustav anxiously. "Was he in Kehl?"

"He died quickly and suddenly in Ludwigsburg a quarter of an hour ago. It is therefore our duty to quickly bring this gentleman, who was very busy with the government, to the orphaned helm of state."

"What, in Ludwigsburg, you say," cried Lanbek, "and died quickly? Oh, eternal caution!"

"In this Ludwigsburg here," said Röder wistfully, "and died in bed of a stroke. Peace be with his ashes! He was a brave man. But now, friends, let the news not get to Stuttgart before us!"

"Gentlemen," cried Süß, in a voice that almost stifled anger and fear, "I am still a minister, and I remind you of the Duke's edict, which absolves me of all responsibility; I tell you, it could go badly for all of you if you associate with Herr von Röder. In the name of the Duke and his heir, I order you to leave me alone."

"Now your kingdom is over, Jew!" cried the captain, laughing wildly, ripping the bridle from his hand and hitting his horse on the back with his long whip; the colonel rode on the right flank, his pistol in his hand; the procession set off into a gallop, and Gustav followed, half dreaming, through the singing village, past the old man, who laughed hoarsely again sat on the bridge and past the gallows, where the ravens were cawing and flapping their wings. Only here, when he cast a shy glance at the place of execution, did he remember Lea and her unfortunate fate with a fearful premonition.

14.

When the people of Stuttgart awoke the morning after this fateful night, they were surprised by two almost unbelievable pieces of news. Instead of travelling abroad, the Duke had died quickly that night in Ludwigsburg. He had been a healthy, strong man, to whom many who had seen him would have given another twenty or thirty years. The lamentations about his death were almost silenced by the joy over another piece of news: the Jew Süß had been with several of the highest courtiers in the Ludwigsburg castle when the Duke died so suddenly; immediately after seeing the body, he had jumped onto his horse and ridden like a madman towards Stuttgart; but Herr von Röder, a man who was not to be trifled with, had caught up with him and led him to Stuttgart under guard. People laughed at the Jew's strange delusion; When he came out of the Duchess's house, whom he had waited on the night before to offer his condolences and asked for an escort home because he had to fetch important documents, a lieutenant and six men followed him. At the end of the corridor a captain paid him the compliment and followed with twelve men; the captain said with a smile that "it was too much of an honor," but when he turned the corner at Lanbek's house and noticed four sentries in front of his palace, when he saw bayonets flashing at the top of the stairs and Lea rushing towards him, pale, distraught and crying, he realized what hour had struck and called: "Ciel, je suis perdu!"

Although the will of the late Duke had appointed an administration in the event of his death that would have been more acceptable to his ministers, Duke Rudolf of Neustadt, despite his advanced age, took over the administration as the next agnate, and the country felt relieved and satisfied. He left everyone, except for admittedly bad people, in the dignity in which they had stood under the previous government, and this was really a kind of act of grace, considering that previously two thirds of all offices[258] in the country. Only one person was not satisfied with the office which the Duke Administrator had confirmed to him in the most gracious terms; it was young Lanbek. Not only was he reappointed as expedition councillor, but when old Röder, in the fire of friendship for the regional consultant, described his son as a clever mind and excellent lawyer, the Duke even elected him to the commission which was to conduct the trial against the Jew Süß. Old Lanbek felt no little honoured by this and repeatedly called his son the pride and pillar of his age; but Gustav made this choice unspeakably unfortunate. Not that he, like every other citizen, did not condemn the man who had plunged the country into such deep misery; not that it was against his conscience to bring to light crimes which had been so artfully concealed; but Lea, it was her brother whom he was to judge, and it was the thought that made this job abhorrent to him. Small souls like to satiate themselves with revenge, and many a man would have taken great joy in visiting a man who had so recently been so high in the deepest casemate of the fortress, and in an imperious voice to chase him from his bed and to torture and torment him. This man had also offended Gustav personally, he had treated him with the most outrageous arrogance, even threatening him with the same prison in which he himself now languished, fearful for his future freedom, perhaps even for his life. But the young man's heart was too big to beat with joy when he entered for the first time as judge the dungeon of the man who now, stripped of all earthly glory, clad in ragged clothes, pale, wild, slowly rose from his rattling chains. This face still reminded him of the features of an unfortunate, beloved being; and he could hardly keep from crying when, after the interrogation was over, the prisoner said: "Mr. Lanbek, there is an unfortunate, innocent girl whom we both know; when they sealed my house, the rude people threw her out into the street - she was a Jew and therefore deserved no pity. - I, sir, have not a penny left with which to support her; I do not know where she is - if you should hear anything from her - she has nothing but the dress she was wearing when they from the threshold – give her alms out of mercy."

The young man gave free rein to his tears as he descended the hill from Hohenneuffen alone; he later learned that the Jew had lied to him, that although over five hundred thousand guilders in gold and jewels were found in his house, he had nearly a hundred thousand in safe hands in Frankfurt, and Gustav could easily understand that Süss had only wanted to soften him by these images of misery; but he could not remove the thought that Lea was abandoned and unhappy, and this thought became more and more distressing when, despite his searches, he could not find any trace of her.

Spring, summer and autumn had passed, and the trial was still going on. Things had been discussed that even the coldest judges would dread; but although young Lanbek presented to the commission with noble indignation that four other men were no less guilty than Süß, it seemed that they only wanted to take serious action against him, because the general hatred declared him to be the most guilty.

It was on a gloomy October evening - the old consultant had been away for a few days and his son was working in the library on a new interrogation - when his younger sister, now the happy bride of Captain Reelzingen, came in more seriously than usual. At first she spoke indifferently, but only with difficulty seemed able to suppress a tear, which finally really shone in her gentle eyes when she asked if he would not be angry with her if she brought a known person to him? He looked at her in amazement and surprise, but before he could give an answer, Käthchen hurried out of the room, crying, and soon came back in with a veiled girl. Even before the dim candle showed its clear outline, even before she threw back the veil, his prescient heart told him who he was facing; He jumped up, blushing, but the unfortunate woman had already thrown herself down before him, thrown back her veil, and it was Lea who raised her once so beloved eyes to him, dark and pleading, and stretched out her pale, thin hands, clasped together, pleadingly. "Mercy!" she cried. "Just don't let him die; they say he must die; his only hope still rests on you. Where shall I find words to soften your generous heart? What language shall I think of to speak to an ear that once understood me so well?' Tears prevented her from speaking any further, and Käthchen wept bitterly too. Full of pain and surprise, Gustav took her cold hands and raised them up; he looked at her - how painful the sight of her was to him! Her cheeks were pale and sunken, her beautiful eyes were deep-set, and her mouth, which otherwise seemed only made for smiling, showed that it had long since forgotten that sweet smile. The black hair that hung around her white forehead and her pale face completed the ghostly appearance of her.

"Lea! Unhappy Lea!" cried the young man. "How long have you remained hidden and robbed your friends of the last consolation of knowing whether you lacked nothing, whether your friends could do something for you?"

"Ah! That is not what I asked your generous sister to bring me here," she said, smiling painfully. "Why should I not be well? I have long since buried all my hopes and dreams; I planted memories like flowers on the grave and water these flowers with my tears. No! You have always been so generous to the unfortunate; just give me the consolation that my brother must not die. Ah! it is so bitter to die, and what use is his death to this country?"

"Lea," answered the young man embarrassedly, "certainly, we have not spoken of it up to now, and I do not believe - you may console yourself - that it will not come to that."

"It will happen, and his fate is in your hands," she whispered. "He told me, I spoke to him: 'If only there were no letter, the letter could ruin me.' Oh, Gustav! Keep him in prison for years, forever, what does it matter to him if he is in chains? Do not die; Gustav, be generous - forget the letter that no one knows about but you - with that weak candle over there you can save a man's life."

"Brother," said Catherine, coming closer and taking his hand, "do it; your conscience cannot be endangered, for it has been rendered harmless forever; burn the letter, it may have been lost."

The young man looked at the weeping girls; an unavoidable feeling fought within him, he wavered for a moment, and Lea, who read this struggle in his expression, took his hand, pressed it passionately to her heart, drew it tenderly to her lips. "He wants to!" she cried delightedly. "Oh, I knew it, he is noble; he does not want to take revenge on the unfortunate man who once offended him, like the others, he does not let him die burdened with sins, he lets him live and become pious and wise. How kind you are, O God, that you have sent one of your angels to this desolate earth, who blesses with the open hand of mercy and does not crush the criminal with the flaming sword of vengeance!"

"No - no - it is not possible!" said Lanbek with deep pain. "Look, Lea, I would give my life to buy your peace, but my honor! My good name! It is not possible! They know about this letter; some have read it and - tomorrow I am to read it. Käthchen! Speak, I beg you, can, may I do it?"

Käthchen wept, and a slight movement of her head seemed to indicate that it seemed impossible to her too. Lea, however, had listened to him with a fixed gaze; the blush of fear spread over her pale cheeks; she leaned forward as if she could not quite hear the terrible denial; when Gustav referred to his sister, she looked at her with a look full of painful confidence, she stretched out her hand convulsively like a drowning man reaching out for a weak branch on the bank - in vain.

"So, he must die," she said quietly after a while, "and you - you break his stick? So that was why I lived and loved? Life is a strange mystery! Would I have thought this when I was still a happy child? Would I have thought that we must perish like this?"

"Poor, unfortunate girl!" said Käthchen, taking her in her arms. "Ah, of course, he cannot act otherwise, I see it myself; and if it can comfort you, come to me as often as you like, you will surely find loyal sympathy -"

"Lea," interrupted her brother, "if there is anything we can do for you; you are accustomed to prosperity—this dress here tells me that you are in need."

"Come, Lea," continued Käthchen, "we are almost the same size, take some of my handkerchiefs, some of my clothes, you will make me happy if you will do it."

"The property your brother possesses abroad," said Gustav, "should and must be saved for you; you have the most immediate claim, and I will certainly do my part."

"Good Gustav," she interrupted, forcing a smile, "let us leave that; people say that he has taken his fortune from the poor of this country. He was wrong, and it would be better if he had never seen this country; but it would be just as wrong of me to make use of this gold, which will bring him death. But from you, dear, beautiful girl, I will accept a handkerchief, because it is now getting so cold. I hear that you are a bride; be very happy! May these be the last tears that now hang in your eyelashes; and if you must weep, let it only be for another's misfortune that your beautiful heart mourns."

"Lea," said the young man with deep pain, "I cannot let you go like this; it is the deceptive calm of despair that speaks from you. Visit my sister, tell me where you live. Oh, if only you were in want! Do not leave me in anger, Lea! God knows that I could not do otherwise!"

"And I know it too, Gustav, and was a foolish girl to put you to this dangerous test; our misfortune is so great that a little help would be too dearly bought with your honour and your peace. Farewell! I need little, perhaps soon nothing at all, and if I should need anything, I am not too proud to come to this friend, the only one who has bought me this misfortune."

"And do you forgive?" said Gustav with tears.

"I have nothing to forgive," she replied, offering him her hand with more composure than the two brothers had received. "Farewell, friend! I am going to water my flowers. May the God of my father's make you as happy as your pure heart deserves!" She said this, cast another loving look at him, and went away, accompanied by Käthchen.

The young man looked after her wistfully; it seemed to him as if this hour had a powerful influence on his life, but he also suspected that he had seen the unfortunate girl for the last time.

15.

It would tire our readers if we were to entertain them any longer with the trial of the Jew Süss. It spread like wildfire through all countries at that time, and is still mentioned here and there today, that on February 4, 1738, the people of Württemberg hanged their finance minister for overly daring financial operations. They hung him on an enormous iron gallows in an iron cage. The decree of the Duke Administrator states: "For him a well-deserved punishment, but for everyone a horrible example." Both the way in which this unfortunate man was able to deal with Württemberg and his punishment are equally striking and incomprehensible at a time when the beginnings of civilization and enlightenment had long been left behind, when the flowering of French literature was sweeping the educated part of Europe upwards with irresistible force.

One would be tempted to accuse the Württemberg of that time of the most shameful barbarism, were it not for a circumstance which men who lived at that time often repeat and which, even if it does not justify the act, seems to demonstrate its necessity. "He had to die on the gallows," they say, "not so much for his own serious crimes as for the outrages and plans of powerful men." Relationships, reputation, secret promises saved the others, the Jew - no one could or wanted to save him, and so, as the old regional consultant Lanbek put it, "what the others had consumed was put on his bill." Ninety years have passed since then and we do not know whether the shameful death of this man calmed and satisfied people's minds more than anything that had previously happened. An edict of the administrator at least does not seem to prove it completely, for he saw himself compelled to decree: "that the subjects should avoid all adverse gossip and unequal judgments about the most blessed lord, under penalty and retribution, and should hold him in the most respectful memory."

Old Lanbek did the latter even without this edict, for whenever the name of Karl Alexander was mentioned, he would lift his cap with a worried expression and say: "God rest his soul!" He also followed the late gentleman under the guardianship of Rudolf von Neustadt. It is said that his son never smiled again, and even brother-in-law Reelzingen could not coax a cheerful face out of him despite the most wonderful jokes. As late as the year 93, he was seen as a tall, thin old man walking across the street with a stick; his expression was serious and gloomy, but his eyes could sometimes be soft and sympathetic. He never married, and the legend at the time was that he had only loved once, and an unfortunate girl who met her own death in the Neckar. Men who knew him assure us that he was usually cold and reserved but was nevertheless very interesting to talk to when he was brought up on certain metaphysical investigations, which he mainly occupied himself with in his old age. He died mourned by many who knew him and his fate and mourned by the poor and unfortunate. My grandfather used to say of him: "He was one of those people who, once they have been very unhappy, can no longer get used to happiness."